Play Your Part

Kathryn Kincaid

Published by Kathryn Kincaid, LLC.

Cover Design by Mary Scarlett LaBerge, M. Scarlett Creative

Edited by Rachel Shipp, Rachel Shipp Editing

Contents

To the readers with a dream, take the big swing.

You won't regret it.

Content warnings

This book explores themes of grief. For content warnings, please visit my website at https://www.authorkathrynkincaid.com/.

1

KENNEDY

NOTHING WOULD GET UNDER my skin today. Not seeing an old classmate announce the purchase of their first home while I scrolled through social media from my childhood bedroom. Not dropping toothpaste on my shirt as I got ready for work. I even kept a smile on my face after being cut off in traffic.

Because tonight, at the Palmer City Wolves' season-opening party, I would arrive on the arm of hockey star Justin Ward.

No, nothing could damper my mood, not even the fight brewing in front of me.

"Mason, give it back!" Izzy flapped her arms in the pool. "Kennedy," she called when Mason didn't comply.

"Mason, give the noodle back to your sister or no hockey practice tomorrow."

Nine months ago, I began working as the McIntyre family nanny to get me out of the house and back into the real world. My father viewed it as a "step in the right direction." He never expected me to settle into it. But I never expected him to compartmentalize his grief over my mom's death to seamlessly transition back into his old life either. So we were even.

I shifted a sleeping Silas to my other arm, shaking out the one that had lost feeling. This kid fought me for this nap, but once he fell asleep, he slept like the dead.

Mason stopped swimming, and with all the confidence of an eight-year-old boy who was growing up in a mansion, hardly ever hearing the word no, he turned his attention to me. "You can't do that."

"Not on purpose," I said. "But I'm very forgetful."

Mason stared me down, waiting for me to blink. I never did. Maybe there were no consequences in life, no justice or general sense of fairness, but when one of these children misbehaved while I was in charge, they didn't get away with it. They lost TV privileges or pizza for lunch—something small in the grand scheme but big enough to keep them in line. I also hoped it would help prevent them from becoming assholes when they were older.

Mason turned to Izzy, about to relent, but Izzy blew a raspberry at him. A six-year-old's declaration of victory. He retaliated by pummeling enough water at her to make her scream. I was swinging my legs over the side of the chaise when the door to the house slid open.

"I'm home!" Connie strolled out of the house, looking like an actress in a sunscreen ad, her long blonde hair fluttering behind her in the wind. She wore a netted white cover-up over a dark bikini, and large sunglasses hid half her face. As soon as she assessed the situation in the pool, she waved me off, kicking off her platform sandals, slipping out of her cover-up, and walking straight into the pool. "I've got this, Kennedy."

Connie gave me this job out of loyalty to my mother. When my father bought the NHL hockey franchise ten years ago and moved it to Palmer

City, my mother started a group for women who loved hockey. Connie was the first person who joined.

"You're home early," I said after Connie quieted the kids. She swam to me and lifted her toned arms onto the concrete, resting her chin on top of them.

"Tonight's a big night. I thought you could use some extra time to get ready. Besides, it's not like work won't be waiting for me bright and early tomorrow morning."

On top of having a hot husband and three adorable kids, Connie ran the HR department at a technology company. She had been well on her way to success by the time she was my age. Surely, no one in her family ever worried whether she was headed in the right direction.

"It's not a big night," I told her.

"Of course it is. Start of another season. Your mom loved the season-opening party." Connie kept right on talking, as if she hadn't brought up the single most important person who was no longer in my life. I preferred this to the people who awkwardly paused, watching my expression to see if it would crumble. But it still hurt—casually dropping her into conversation made it easy to pretend she was still here. "Do you have something to wear tonight?"

I shrugged the shoulder without Silas's adorable head resting on it. "I'll find a dress in my closet."

Connie tilted her head, and a glazed look took over her face. She remained still and silent long enough, I wondered if she'd fallen asleep with her eyes open, but then she snapped her fingers. "Got it. I have a sapphire blue dress that will look divine on you. Trust me."

I opened my mouth to object, but her expectant expression stopped me in my tracks. For whatever reason, this seemed to matter to her, my mom's closest friend. Besides, I would arrive on Justin Ward's arm—finally, after all this time—and dammit if I didn't want to look like I deserved my place there.

I followed Connie upstairs and dropped Silas in his crib before going to her bedroom. She put her other kids in front of the TV to watch their favorite movie, *The Mighty Ducks,* for the hundredth time.

"You look stunning," Connie said behind me, her beaming expression reflected in the mirror. "You will definitely catch the eye of a few players tonight."

I gave her a quick shake of my head. "I'm not looking to meet anyone."

"Why the hell not?"

I hesitated. I didn't want to reveal I was dating someone because Connie would badger *who* out of me. I considered telling her about Justin, knowing she would care, but I promised him I wouldn't share our relationship with anyone. Not until we were both ready to take the next step. These past few months, I'd practically lived at Justin's place, and now he wanted to bring me to a team event in front of my dad. I expected an invitation to officially move in soon.

I could keep this secret for a few more hours. I gave Connie what I hoped would be a plausible excuse. "It's a conflict of interest."

"You're a better person than me. I mean, have you *seen* our team this year? We signed Alexei Volkov." Connie blew out a breath, and her eyes briefly closed so she didn't see the disgust on my face.

Alexei Volkov was the *last* person I would want to get involved with, but I couldn't get into the reasons without revealing my connection to Justin. And if I told her...with the way she liked to gossip, everyone in my mom's Wolves superfan group would know within an hour.

"Oh, to be young again."

I rolled my eyes. "You *are* young."

She flicked her wrist, dismissing my statement. "I'm turning forty this year. And I might still turn heads"—she flashed a dazzling smile and shifted her weight from one hip to the other—"but I've been locked down for a long time. Please don't waste this dress tonight. I need a good story."

Connie dotted a kiss on top of my head as she said goodbye. I closed my eyes, the gesture transporting me to two years ago, the last time I put on a fancy dress. My dad had insisted on hosting the season-opening party that year, even though he'd suffered a heart attack two months earlier. I put college on hold before my senior year because of his heart attack, so instead of being tucked away in a dorm at Prescott College, I was with my mom, setting aside our nerves and blasting music while we dressed for the party.

My mother had slipped her necklace around my neck and kissed the top of my head after securing the clasp. *I'm so proud of you. You know that, don't you, Kennedy?*

I slammed the car door hard, trying to snap myself out of the memory and focus on tonight. I needed to hear Justin's voice, to think about our future rather than my past. I dialed his number, but without a ring, it went to voicemail. We'd agreed to meet at the party and walk in together, but before I knew it, my car headed to his house along the route I knew by heart.

I never doubted my decision to drop out of school to be there for my father. But I never went back—at first because I didn't want to leave and have something else terrible happen while I was far away, then because something terrible *did* happen, and ironically, my presence hadn't made the least bit of difference. After six months of rarely leaving the house or doing anything following my mom's death, Justin made his way back into my life. We picked up where we'd left off, as if nothing had ever separated us. Every day, I felt grateful he'd pulled me out of my self-imposed grief bubble.

My smile at the memory of us slipped as his house came into view. A massive moving truck was parked in his driveway. *What the fuck?* I called Justin again, and again, only his voicemail greeted me.

Screw this. I charged toward the truck. "Where are you going?" I demanded of the first mover I saw standing beside the truck with a clipboard.

The man looked at me, cocking his head to the side. I wasn't sure if his confusion stemmed from my formal outfit or my question. Perhaps both. "Who are you?"

"Justin Ward's girlfriend," I answered before firing the question again. "Where are you going?"

"Aw, hell," he muttered. He cleared his throat, then dropped his gaze to the clipboard. "We're going to Florida."

Florida. My stomach sank as a roar filled my ears, blocking out the noise of the movers loading the truck.

I rummaged around in my purse for my cell phone as I backed away from the truck and moved toward the front door.

Still no answer.

Where the hell was Justin? And why was he moving to Florida without telling me?

I flopped onto the bench in the foyer and dropped my chin into my hands, at a loss for what to do, other than wait for him to come home and explain. When I checked the time, I saw a notification from our local paper. *Wolves captain unloaded in shocking trade.* The article announced Justin had been traded for two first-round picks and a defenseman. The team couldn't come to terms with him on his extension. Rather than lose him next year without a return, they cut their losses and traded him away.

My father traded Justin.

"We taking this chair?" The words pulled me from my thoughts. A young mover stood in the doorway, flashing his toned stomach as he wiped his brow with the bottom of his company shirt.

How the hell would I know? They had seen my shocked face and heard my confusion when I first arrived. Since then, I'd watched them carry away the remnants of my relationship as if I weren't there, ignoring me aside from a few pitying glances. I couldn't imagine what they thought of me, wearing a dress fit for a gala and enormous heels, on the verge of tears.

"It stays." Justin's cool voice hit me before he stepped inside the house. He stopped in his tracks when he spotted me.

Like the first time I met him, those eyes of his—the most unbelievable blue I'd ever seen, just like the song—snagged my attention. Justin had a presence people couldn't ignore, not with the way he took up entirely too much space in any room. It wasn't only his height, which forced me to look up at him, but also his bulk, a bit more than most hockey players. But he always did like to stand out. This was why I imagined he liked to wear those tight shirts, the ones showing exactly how much time he spent in the gym.

"What are you doing here?" he asked, as if he hadn't given me a key to come and go as I pleased, as if I hadn't basically lived here the last six months.

"When did all of this happen?" I motioned around the house with my hand.

Justin's jaw ticked. "When do you *think* it happened, Kennedy?"

"You told me contract negotiations were going well."

His agent and the general manager of the team were quibbling over money and years. Or so I thought. Once Justin knew the contract wasn't getting extended, that they couldn't resolve their differences, he must've known a trade was possible.

I followed him to the kitchen, watching his brown hair bounce in its mesmerizing way.

"Contract negotiations ended two weeks ago," he said.

The words felt like a gut punch. We made plans to go to the season-opening party within the last two weeks. We'd both been busy lately—me staying at the McIntyres' while Connie and Rich took a week-long vacation and Justin with a trip to New York to see his mom—but we *saw* each other. We had dinner and sex and watched a movie with me falling asleep on his shoulder. He'd seemed a little distant, but it didn't feel out of the ordinary. Justin got moody, and I ignored it.

I could practically hear the hinges coming off our relationship, one-by-one, with each word he spoke.

I glared at him. "And you didn't tell me because...?"

Justin glared back. He didn't want this conversation. I came here unannounced. I ruined his chance to sneak away like a thief in the night. I searched the room for a note, my gaze locking on a piece of paper on the countertop. Justin followed my line of sight.

"Justin, what's going on?"

"Your father fucking traded me... after I dedicated myself to his team for five years." He pounded an open palm on the countertop.

I flinched and took a step backward.

"He tossed me aside like I don't matter."

"What does that mean for us?" I asked, my voice barely above a whisper.

Justin looked down at his hands white-knuckling the countertop before finding my gaze again. When he spoke, the anger was gone from his voice. "Kennedy, you know I care about you... but this isn't... you're not... the same person I fell in love with. I thought you'd get back to that..."

My chest constricted, a pain settling in its center. For the first time in a year, I had begun to finally *feel* again, but I couldn't argue with Justin. I wasn't the same person as when we met before my mom died; I didn't know if I could get back to that person. If who I was now wasn't good enough for him...

"I've sold the house," Justin said after a prolonged silence. He looked around the rooms on the first floor, avoiding my gaze. "The movers should have packed your things."

I barely processed the words. This was happening too quickly—my relationship ending, my plans going up in a puff of smoke. Plans I had been sure would include me moving in here. Into this now empty house. I waited for a rush of anger or devastating sadness, but I felt... nothing.

Shock. This must be shock.

"Justin," I whispered, drawing his eyes to mine. I knew him well enough to know that anything I said or did wouldn't get through. His decisiveness was something I'd always admired. But I had to try. "If you give me more time, maybe if I go with you, and we start over away from here—"

"It's been a year, Kennedy. How much longer am I supposed to wait? We want different things. I have dreams, and you... I don't know what you want. It's like you've stalled. How do you expect me to be serious with someone like that?"

A tear slid down my cheek. I thought Justin understood me better than anyone. He knew my history and had seen me at my very worst.

Even so, he couldn't accept me. And how could I blame him? He worked every day toward his future, and all I did was try to keep my head above water.

"Mr. Ward?" The mover with the clipboard stood at the kitchen entrance.

"Just a minute," Justin said before walking to me.

He rested his hand on my shoulder, but I recoiled from his touch. I didn't need a reminder of what I was losing.

"I'm sorry, Kennedy."

"You'll regret this," I said, forcing a fire into my voice I didn't yet feel. I hoped my glower conveyed the fury and hurt that would no doubt hit me later.

Justin walked away from me, his pinched expression remaining unchanged.

I felt outside of myself as I watched him complete the moving paperwork before signing an autograph for the mover's son. As if nothing had happened between us, Justin smiled and asked for the kid's name, handing over a piece of paper that would make that child's day.

I waited until the doors slammed and the house quieted before snatching the envelope Justin left behind. Thinking the goodbye letter would gut me, I wanted to read it alone, to cry in peace. But when I opened it, all that greeted me were instructions for returning my keys to the realtor after I moved my belongings out of the house.

2

ALEXEI

FORTY-EIGHT HOURS AGO, MY hockey career had been dead in the water, so I guess I shouldn't complain about the sweltering heat cooking me alive.

My agent told me I should never complain about anything again, but the heat in Palmer City, North Carolina, carried so much humidity, my filter was on the verge of coming loose. A filter I very much had to keep intact. I loosened my tie and pleaded silently for extreme air-conditioning inside the house.

"Ah, Alexei, I hope you haven't been waiting too long."

Only long enough to consider stripping off my suit in front of my new employer's mansion. "A couple of minutes."

I stuck out my hand to my new coach, Erik Pomroy, who immediately took it in his firm grasp. Erik looked impeccable, as always—perfectly tailored suit and dark, styled hair with a distinguished peppering of gray. He had wide eyes that always made him look wild, and a nose that had clearly been broken several times.

We'd met plenty of times before, but tonight was the first time since I signed a one-year, one million-dollar deal with the Palmer City Wolves. Some called it a redemption deal since the price fell way below the numbers I would produce for them, but given my history, my agent said I should be grateful. Sometimes I wanted to punch my agent in the face.

"Good to see you again, Coach."

He released my hand. "Call me Erik."

I nodded an acknowledgment, still a bit stunned Erik Pomroy was my coach. And I could call him casually by his first name. I grew up watching him play, loving his grit and toughness and how he never hid his true emotions. I remembered seeing him thrust the Stanley Cup in the air as captain of this franchise fifteen years ago when it was still in Maine. Erik coaching me was what I focused on, ignoring all the reasons why I didn't want to be on this mediocre, small-market team.

"Shall we?" He opened the front door to the Wolves owner's house without knocking or ringing the doorbell. Erik had told me to wait outside for him so I wouldn't disturb the big preparations for tonight's season-opening party. I'd played on many teams, but never had I been invited to the owner's home. Behind the open door, people rushed around the enormous space—cleaning, carrying furniture, and decorating anything they could with Wolves' colors, black and forest green. The noise from the activity echoed off the high ceilings. No one looked at us.

"Is it like this every year?" I asked, following Erik down a long hallway.

"More or less."

He stopped in front of a set of black double doors and knocked. A voice called for us to come in, and soon enough, I stood in front of the man who would cut my checks, Cale Cole. He sat behind a large wooden desk in a massive chair, pounding his keyboard. He hadn't acknowledged us, only watched his computer screen from behind thick black frames. I scanned his office as we waited—from the bookcase covering one entire wall to the muted TV tuned to ESPN to the picture of the Wolves' arena, which bore his name.

"Alexei Volkov."

My gaze landed on Cale Cole again. He stood and gestured to two seats in front of his desk. Cale's blonde hair was buzzed close to his head, and his smile didn't reach his eyes. He was about half a foot shorter than Erik, who matched me at six foot four; but in that power suit of his, he was no less intimidating. Maybe it was because, in this situation, he held all the cards.

"It's good to have you in Palmer City."

Not everyone felt that way. Fans bombarded me on social media to let me know how much they *didn't* want me on the Wolves... or in the league. About half the messages came from trolls, telling me to go back to Russia, even though I hadn't lived there in ten years and was a US citizen. The rest ran the gamut from telling me I sucked at hockey to saying I was the greatest player in the league to wanting to fuck me. Your standard array of internet garbage.

"Happy to be here," I said as I took a seat.

If it were only the rivalry between Ward, their captain, and me, the fan base would have gotten over it. Fights in hockey were as much a part of the fabric of the game as the ice, so Ward and I hooking off every time our teams played each other could be forgiven as soon as I wore a Wolves uniform. But there was all the other shit that people objected to—yelling at refs, hard hits bordering on dirty, taunts at the opposing team and its crowd, blunt postgame interviews. I played hard, and I didn't apologize.

Except for the last incident, the one that got me dropped by my former team. Apparently, decking your teammate on the way to the locker room was one step beyond what could be tolerated.

Never mind that the teammate and I had squashed the entire thing within a day. Some asshole in the crowd captured it on video. The collective angry fan reaction plus management's desire for an excuse to let me go landed me without a team for the final two months of last season.

No teams showed interest, not until the Wolves called my agent. Pussies, all of them, for being too scared to sign me over potential bad PR. For the last seven seasons, I'd more than proved my worth on the ice, but none of it meant anything because I was *hotheaded*. The Wolves heard me out, and what I said was good enough, even if the rest of the hockey world wanted to crucify me.

"I trust you're settled?" Cale said, dancing around whatever he wanted to discuss.

"Yeah, Matt helped me find a place." Matt Harris and I played on the same team five years ago, before he was traded to the Wolves. He remained one of the only strong players for this organization, his stellar defensive skills sometimes the only thing preventing embarrassment on the ice. "It's a couple houses down from him."

Cale nodded. "Good, good. We called you here to set ground rules. You know, expectations for how you should behave this season, and we'll go over all that, but—"

"We traded Justin Ward," Erik cut in, clearly exasperated by Cale's slow delivery.

A grin spread across my face before I could stop it.

"You should work on not looking so gleeful before you're around anyone else tonight."

"How he looks is the least of our worries," Cale said. "The news broke this morning before we could get ahead of it, and Justin's already made a statement. Your name came up."

Fucking Christ. Justin Ward was probably the teammate least thrilled about my signing. Our history went back to junior hockey days, but thankfully, we'd only crossed paths as opponents since then. Which meant I could go as hard as I wanted at him without repercussion—at least, without *serious* repercussions. Penalties and a suspension had been worth it. Our intense rivalry generated interest from fans and was deemed "good for hockey" by commentators. By signing with the Wolves, I would have to find a way to coexist with him. I tried not to think too much about it, because again, I wasn't supposed to complain about anything. But with him gone, maybe there was a God.

I leaned forward in my chair. "What did he say?"

Cale picked up the remote. "Better if I show you."

After flipping to a recorded program and unmuting the TV, Justin Ward's nails-on-a-chalkboard voice blared through the quiet office. He sat in front of a white wall, wearing the colors of his new team, talking with the host of a hockey fan video channel. The maroon clashed horribly with his ice-cold blue eyes, something he would hate, but it brought me a petty sense of joy.

"I've been traded, yes. The rumors are true. And I won't lie, I was upset. Hurt, even. I was a Wolf for five years, but what did that get me? No Stanley Cup, no trip to the playoffs. Sure, I've been to the all-star game several times, but that's because of *me*. I was an all-star trapped in a dead-end franchise. You heard the team might have to move again, right? The arena is barely half-full for games, and the crowd is so quiet, it's like playing hockey in a church. And they've signed Alexei fucking Volkov? He's a menace and will be the last injection of poison for that franchise before it collapses."

Holy shit. And people have the balls to criticize my interviews? I'd never come close to that tirade, even after Ward sucker-punched me like a spineless shitbag during the last game we played.

Cale pointed to the screen. "This is a problem we need to fix immediately."

I wanted to ask which problem, but by the pinched look on his face, I figured it would only make things worse. His deathly calm demeanor covered a wave of rage. Game recognizes game.

"Ward was a pain in the ass when he was here and continues to be a pain in the ass after he's gone."

My respect for Cale Cole quadrupled at that statement. He recognized my talent, looked past the media bullshit to sign me, and saw through Justin Ward's choirboy act. Don't get me wrong, Justin's reputation around the league for on-ice antics was as bad as mine—all those after-whistle cheap shots and the near-constant chirping to get under his opponent's skin. If the term *pest* hadn't existed before he joined the league, Ward would have brought it into existence. But he liked to play innocent and could charm the pants off the media.

"The interest will die down," Erik said. "We need to change the story."

"We need to focus on this season," Cale said. "That's where you come in, Alexei."

"This season is my only focus." I trained nonstop all summer, conditioning myself to improve my stamina, working on new skills, and pushing myself harder than ever. It was my only chance to show a team I was ready to step onto the ice and make a difference in the score sheets. I was determined to not make this season a repeat of last year's disappointment.

"Good, because we've chosen to believe in you," Cale said. "Not just in your talent, but in your leadership. I know what they say about you, and I don't care. Show everyone how smart we were for signing you. Step up and lead this team. We need it more than ever with Ward gone. His numbers aren't easy to replace."

Erik fixed his stare on me. "You know I won't tolerate any bullshit, Volkov, but I will have your back every step of the way if you have mine."

I couldn't pretend the words didn't do something to me—the absolute faith these men had in my ability to turn my career around meant more than I could say. "I won't let you down," I said, locking eyes first with Cale, then Erik.

Erik clapped me on the shoulder. He might have seemed like a quiet man, but I'd played against his team for the last four years and watched him as a player before that. When he stepped onto the ice, even as a coach, all bets were off. He would yell when the situation demanded it—to convey an important point when coming out of a timeout, when a ref got a call wrong, when his players didn't execute. If anyone could understand the passion I played with, it would be Erik Pomroy.

I had only one season to turn my hockey career around, and I would not fuck this up.

3

KENNEDY

I SAT IN JUSTIN'S driveway, staring at a piece of paper I'd found while packing my boxes.

The movers apparently hadn't packed everything, leaving me to roam the house to find my stray belongings. Although Justin told me I had three weeks to clear out, I never wanted to come back to this place. While shoving a pile of papers into a box, a list I'd drunkenly wrote one night, months ago after a fight with Justin drifted to the floor. I remembered the night clearly, but not the details of this list in my sloppiest handwriting.

Get Happy

- Move out
- Finish college
- Pick a career??
- Dye hair
- Learn to cook
- Paaaaaaarty
- Risk something

Months had passed, and I had yet to do a single item. Not that I should follow the dreams of my drunk self, but I hadn't done *anything* since then other than bide my time waiting for Justin Ward to invite me to move in with him. To give me something to build on in my life, even though being with him didn't necessarily make me happy. Only less sad.

The realization played on repeat in my mind as I drove to my childhood home. Once there, I beelined to where I knew I would find my father—holding court near a long table of food next to the bar—ready to vent my anger to the only man I could.

"Kenny, I'm glad you made it," my father boomed, placing a hand on my shoulder and turning me toward the men who surrounded him. "I'd like to introduce you all to my daughter, Kennedy."

I stopped listening and waited for the introductions to end. "Dad, we need to talk," I said at the first break in conversation.

A flicker of annoyance passed over his face, brief enough no one else would notice, but I did. Still, he followed me away from his companions to a corner of the room behind the bar.

"What did you want to talk about?"

With his expectant eyes on me, I hesitated. The momentary pause screwed me as someone called to my father from across the room.

"One moment," he shouted before turning to me. "Can this wait until tomorrow?"

No, it can't, I wanted to say. Instead, I nodded, taking the easy out. I grabbed an open bottle of champagne chilling in an ice bucket and curled up in the corner to watch the happy people around me celebrate the upcoming hockey season while I wallowed in what I'd lost. Mercifully, the bartender said nothing.

"Kennedy?"

I let the half-empty bottle drop into my lap, still upright due only to my grip on its neck. My best friend, Gemma, towered over me, her emerald dress brushing my shoes. Even sad and drunk, I marveled at how perfect the color was with her dark skin and how her brown eyes popped against the shimmery fabric.

"Kennedy, what happened?"

"He dumped me." I choked on the last word.

Gemma immediately dropped to the floor and wrapped me tightly in her arms. Her sugary smell from the bakery she owned filled my senses. Until that moment, I didn't know how much I needed a comforting hug.

"Oh, Kennedy," she whispered in my ear. "That tool doesn't deserve you. You hear me, Kens?"

I nodded furiously and swallowed, trying to keep the tears at bay. Gemma and I met two years ago through Justin. At the time, I was dating someone from work, though if I were honest with myself, that relationship started to end as soon as I was pulled into Justin's orbit. At a team function I attended with my parents, Gemma settled into a chair next to me and, without preamble, asked, *You're falling in love with him, huh?* I hadn't yet admitted it to myself, and definitely not to Justin, but this stranger intuitively knew, without me having to say anything at all, like so many other things since. I loved her for it.

I said nothing, continuing to breathe evenly, trying to get myself under control. By the time she pulled back, my emotions were sufficiently tamped down.

"You're in the perfect place for a rebound." Gemma nudged me, smiling devilishly.

"You're joking, right? All I can think about is how my boyfriend was just FedExed to Florida and left me behind, but you think I'll meet a guy. You do realize most men at this party are on the team?"

Gemma raised an eyebrow. “So what?”

“I’m done with dating, but if I weren’t, the last place I would look for a date is the Palmer City Wolves season-opening party.” I muscled my way to my feet, my half-empty champagne bottle dangling at my side. “I only came here to yell at my dad, but—surprise, surprise—he ran from me as well.”

“Kens,” Gemma called, following me as I speedwalked out of the room.

I paused at the hallway entrance and scanned the room for my father, but I didn’t see him in the continually growing crowd.

“I’m worried about you,” she said.

I gulped from the champagne bottle. “I’m fine.”

Gemma’s lips drew into a thin line. She doubted me, as she should. I lost my tolerance when I stopped drinking alcohol in solidarity with Justin—all part of his plan for NHL domination. To say I was feeling it was an understatement.

I wiped the champagne from my mouth with the back of my hand before plastering on a big fake smile.

“Do you want to get out of here?” she asked. Gemma had drunk only carrot juice for the last three days to stun in this dress. No way would I make her leave because I couldn’t hold myself together.

“No, but I’m going to get some air.”

She smiled. “Great idea. I’ll come with you.”

I shook my head. “I’ll be fine. You stay. Enjoy the party.”

"You look like you could use a drink." Matt Harris muttered the words beside my ear as he nodded to the men standing in front of us. Investors in the team, but I committed barely anything they said to memory. Now I wasn't sure that it had been a bad thing that no other coach had ever invited me to their home. After I met with Erik and Cale, I spent most of an hour making boring small talk and sneaking glances at my watch.

"Excuse me," I announced to the men, then followed Matt toward the bar.

"Oh, hello boys," Gemma said as we approached. She held out a beer to Matt, which he accepted and quickly brought to his lips. I declined since I didn't drink much during the season, something I regretted in situations like this. When Matt finished downing his beer, he gripped her waist and pulled her to him. She feigned annoyance, saying something about being in public, but she eventually gave in to a kiss so intense, I had to look away.

Lucky bastard.

"Alexei, I want to introduce you to someone," Gemma said, bringing my attention back to them.

Matt rested his chin on Gemma's head. "Gem, come on, not tonight."

At least I wasn't the only poor unfortunate soul Gemma had taken on as a pet project. She'd already brought me to their home for dinner and sprung one of her friends on me. *Just want you to meet some people in the area.*

Yeah, Gemma, my ass you did. Most people didn't know why my engagement to Cora ended, and they probably thought the worst. I shared the story with Matt and Gemma to explain why I didn't want to be set up. And even though it happened six months ago, Gemma still acted like I was on the verge of a breakdown at any moment, and only a romantic relationship could save me.

"I think they'd get along," she argued.

"*Gemma.*" Matt and Gemma stared at each other for a while; it looked like an entire conversation was taking place. Fucking weird. "Do not meddle in *this* way."

Gemma pouted. "Fine. But it's not like they won't meet eventually."

"I don't want to meet anyone," I said, interrupting the very uncomfortable conversation about me happening in front of me. "Hockey is my priority right now."

"See?" she said to Matt. "He sounds just like her."

"Oh, does she play hockey too?"

Gemma rolled her eyes. "No, but she's sworn off relationships like you."

"She sounds smart."

Gemma nodded enthusiastically, opening her mouth to say something more when my phone interrupted.

"Sorry." I slipped it from the inside of my jacket, relieved by the perfect escape from this conversation. Until I saw the caller ID. I stifled a groan. "My agent. I should take this..."

He wanted to "check in" and make sure I was "following the rules." Cale and Erik made those very clear—arrive on time, work hard, don't talk to the media if it's not prearranged by the team, and keep my head down, avoiding unnecessary attention. *No comment* was my new best friend.

I knew what was at stake. I didn't need another reminder.

I ushered him off the phone as quickly as possible, then called my mom. It took only one ring for her warm voice to fill my phone speaker, instantly lifting my mood. It never mattered how many penalties I took or curse words I said during a press conference... or that I was released from the contract we'd celebrated only three years ago. She remained proud of me and loved me. And when things went to shit, her love was all I could rely on.

"Alyosha," she said as soon as she answered. Even though I learned English seven years ago when I entered the league, hearing my native tongue put me at ease. "I haven't heard from you in a couple of days, and I wanted to call, but I know you're busy..."

"Sorry, Mama. I made it to Palmer City, and I'm all settled in now. How are you? How's Alina?"

Switching the topic to my younger sister always worked to move the heat off me. My mom pitched her voice low. "Fine, fine. You know your sister is always go-go-go. And always with her boyfriend. It's not healthy. But he is better than the last one."

"She always lands on her feet."

"So do you."

These were the words I needed to hear.

"Don't ever forget that."

Mom kept talking, detailing everything she and Alina did that week. I leaned my head back against the deck, letting her words drown out the party behind me along with every single worry. Being alone worked better for me—no one to answer to, no one to let me down. Within moments, my body relaxed, loosening its near-constant tension. I was thinking I might ride out the rest of the party out here by myself when a shout came from the other side of the yard.

"Motherfucker, piece of shit!"

4

KENNEDY

As I MOVED THROUGH the crowd toward the backyard, I tried not to think of Justin.

Not the way we met here two years ago. Or the weekend he spent with me when I was sick and my dad was away on business. He brought me soup, watched movies with me—took care of me.

He should have been beside me when I talked to my father tonight. His hand should have been on my back as we walked through the party to get a drink. He should have been introducing me as his girlfriend. As soon as I stepped into the dimly lit backyard, I had my cell phone in my hand, calling him before I could think twice.

I needed to know how he could leave tonight, as if our relationship hadn't meant anything. Had he always planned to break up with me? And if he had, why did he spend so much time with me the last few months? Why did he let me get attached when he knew what I had lost?

The line immediately went to voicemail. Either he'd turned his phone off, had no service, or... blocked me.

Would he *block* me?

I cursed loudly, the alcohol loosening my filter. At least I was the only person out here to hear my trail of curses. The flash of anger combined with the alcohol made me light-headed all of a sudden. I took a seat at the top of the stairs, leaning my head against the banister, closing my eyes, and hoping to sleep through the rest of this party.

"Everything okay?"

At the sound of a deep, accented voice, my eyes jerked open. After the day I had, my interest in a conversation couldn't be any lower. "I'm fine," I replied stiffly, not even bothering to turn around.

Apparently, my voice didn't effectively convey my feelings, because he stepped closer. On instinct, my head spun like whiplash. A light from inside the house slanted across his face, exposing enough for recognition to hit my alcohol-dulled brain. *Alexei Volkov*. His grin, revealing a dimple on his right cheek, knocked the floor out of my stomach.

"Sure. Cursing alone in the middle of a party is *definitely* the sign of someone who is fine."

The dose of sarcasm was infuriating, but dammit it all to hell if the low tenor of his voice underlined by his coarse accent didn't wash over me. I could easily get lost listening to him.

Alexei's next step put him squarely under the light, the movement reminding me why Connie practically had a stroke talking about him earlier. Alexei Volkov was the kind of hot that made me momentarily forget why I didn't like him. My heart sped up as I took in the way his dark suit molded to his body—the jacket crisp across his broad shoulders and the shirt snug against his abdomen. His rolled sleeves put his strong forearms on display, muscles flexing as he moved his hands to his pockets.

The showstopper? That face of his... universally considered handsome thanks to his strong jawline and sharp brown eyes, but all the more interesting by the way it deviated from blandness. Alexei had a white scar under his left eye and a slight bump in the dip of his nose, no doubt from one of his many fights over the years. The dark scruff covering the lower half of his face, below his chin, and onto his neck had my mouth drying out.

"Of course, it's fucking *you*," I muttered. A maniacal laugh burst out of me.

The universe was clearly screwing with me. I did not like Alexei Volkov. Despised him, actually. Even before I dated Justin. I saw him play against the Wolves every year. I remembered not only because yes, I had eyes and couldn't *not* react to an extremely attractive man, but he had a knack for pissing off the home crowd. He taunted us after scoring and shouted at fans near the penalty box as he waited out his punishment for some dirty play.

"You know me?" Alexei gestured to himself with one hand; the wholesomeness of the action made my chest tight.

What he gained from this humble act, I wasn't sure. He obviously didn't know who I was. And even if he did, he didn't need an "in" with my father. Dad had missed drafting Alexei Volkov by only one spot seven years ago, and every time Alexei's team came to town and beat us, he liked to lament what could have been.

And while Connie hadn't lied about her dress—it did look divine on me—I couldn't imagine Alexei Volkov trying to pick up the unhinged girl in his employer's backyard. He had no lack of other options.

"You can drop the fake modesty." I spread my arms wide. "There's no audience."

Alexei glanced over his shoulder, maybe looking for an out to this conversation.

By all means, I wanted to say. *Leave me the fuck alone.*

"Go ahead, it's a big night for you."

He turned back around, his eyebrows sky-high in confusion.

"The trade. You've got the team all to yourself now."

ALEXEI

When I heard the string of curse words on the other side of the lawn and saw the stunning woman who shouted them, I thought my night had turned around. I might not want a relationship, but my streak of celibacy was getting old. My intense workout schedule the last few months hadn't left much time for women—or much of anything—but I landed the deal I needed. Didn't I deserve a little fun?

And damn, this woman. It wasn't only my dry streak that made me take notice. She looked sexy as hell, that curve-hugging dress dipping low on her chest and flowing to her ankles. There was also something disarmingly adorable about her. Maybe it was the way she wore her dark hair, flowing free to her shoulders. Or how she chewed her bottom lip when she wasn't speaking. It could have been the way her nose scrunched when she realized who I was.

But then she said something that stopped my fantasies from running wild. *The trade. You've got the team all to yourself now.*

"Who *are* you?"

She rose to her feet, swaying enough, I stepped forward to catch her if she fell. The woman death gripped the side of the deck with one hand to keep herself steady. The other held a nearly empty bottle of champagne. "Not a fan of yours."

That didn't narrow things at all. "Join the fucking club. I hear they meet on Thursdays."

I kept studying her. She looked familiar, but I couldn't place her. Her lips slipped for a moment, looking like the beginning of a smile before snapping back into a thin line. Probably better that way—if she hated me, continuing to admire her seemed pointless. My dry spell would remain intact. *Great.*

"The trade," I repeated slowly, fiddling with the dark silver watch on my left wrist. The woman's gaze traced my movements. "You mean Ward, don't you?"

"*Of course* I mean Justin," she said.

Every bit of my attraction to her slipped like sand through my fingers. Ward was Justin to her; that could only mean one thing. The useless prick had landed this woman. Even if the idea of touching anyone Justin Ward previously dated didn't turn my stomach, he'd probably poisoned her mind against me. I should have walked away from this pointless conversation, but I couldn't make myself turn away from her.

"Maybe you're the reason he's gone," she continued, her voice gaining strength. "If my father didn't think you were going to come here and be the answer to all of this team's problems—"

I stopped listening because... what in the *actual* fuck? *Father*? The woman standing in front of me, the one I'd wanted to convince to come home with me tonight before finding out she belonged to Ward, was Cale Cole's daughter?

"Whatever. I'm going to talk to the man who made the decision... give him a piece of my mind."

Those words jolted me back to the moment. Even if she'd dated my enemy and hated my guts, I wouldn't let her walk into the party and embarrass herself or my new boss. I stepped into her path. She stumbled, and I bent down to catch her, momentarily leaving our faces only inches apart, her breath commingling with mine.

Too quickly, she pulled back. I grasped her forearms, keeping her upright and on the deck rather than stumbling off it. Her gaze locked on mine, her dark eyes finding their mark. So damn beautiful.

Wishing was pointless—I knew that—but I wanted nothing more but for her to be someone else, someone not off-limits to me.

"That's a shit idea," I said.

"I think I know what's a good idea," she replied, her voice mockingly distorted.

She wrenched her arms from mine and tucked her hair behind one ear. She remained still, as if she'd given up on storming the party, clearly trying to fake me out. As I expected, she soon tried to scoot past me again. I easily kept her in front of me, and the frustration of being blocked brought a groan to the surface.

"Let. Me. Pass."

"Excuse me if I don't exactly trust your judgment," I told her. "You're dating Ward."

She straightened to her full height, which barely reached my shoulders. "As if you have the right to pass judgment on anyone." She took another swig of her champagne. "He's not that bad—"

I barked out a laugh. Even Justin Ward's girlfriend couldn't find anything good to say about him.

"He's not," she insisted.

I tilted my head to the side, giving her a dubious look.

"And I know him better than you. We dated for a year."

"A year," I repeated, unable to hide my distaste.

The woman threw her hands in the air. "As if I care what *Alexei Volkov* thinks of me."

She said my name like it was a communicable disease. A curse.

"Don't think I haven't heard all about your reputation, the trail of broken hearts you've left in your wake as you skated away."

"You're oddly poetic when you're drunk."

She pointed at me, her finger wildly swaying. "I'm not drunk."

"Drunk *and* stubborn. My favorite combination." I slowly shook my head. "I'm not letting you go back in there like this. So should I get someone?"

"I don't need a babysitter." She ambled back over to the deck steps where I'd found her.

I remained where I stood, not willing to move closer and spook her after she finally settled down. "It's nothing against you," I said, trying to comfort her in the only way I could. When people didn't like me, I didn't like them.

But this woman... she looked haunted, sad in a way I recognized. She looked the way I did last spring when I lost hockey and my fiancée in one week. No one needed to be kicked when they were already down.

"Most people need a babysitter when they're drunk. I've been known to get into a fight or two."

"No surprise there," she mumbled, and I couldn't help but smile.

She tipped back the champagne bottle, gulping down the remaining liquid before tossing it into the grass. I made a mental note to get it before going back inside.

"I don't usually drink. I don't go to parties. I... don't do anything. I'm not... this isn't... things were supposed to be different."

I didn't say a word or move a muscle. She didn't seem to be talking to me any longer. It felt almost intrusive to stand there, listening to her ramble, but I also couldn't leave her to her own devices. That had almost ended in disaster.

"I still live at home, and I never finished college," she continued, slurring her words. "I can't even cook. My mom was supposed to teach me, but I… I never made the time. Why would anyone choose *me* when I can't even take care of myself? Every day is the same… I've never even dyed my hair."

I opened my mouth to say something, my gut churning at the devastation in her voice when Gemma burst through the door from the house.

"Oh, thank God. Kennedy," she said as she walked toward us, "I've been looking all over for you."

Kennedy Cole. That solved one mystery but left me with the other—how she could have tolerated Ward in her life for so long.

Kennedy pushed herself to her feet, spinning to face us. Her eyes grew wide when they landed on me. She forgot I was there.

"I told you I was getting air," Kennedy said.

At the same time, I blurted, "Did you know she was *dating* Justin Ward?"

Gemma looked at Kennedy, one eyebrow raised. "You told *him*? I couldn't even tell Matt!"

"I didn't tell him anything," Kennedy said, nose wrinkled. "I guess he stole it out of me. Like he stole the team."

"I did *not* steal the team."

Gemma placed a hand on my shoulder. "There's no point arguing with her," she whispered.

"Hey…" Kennedy began, hearing the words Gemma meant only for me.

Gemma took a step forward and talked to her in a soothing tone. "Why don't we go home? I can bake cookies, and we can snuggle on the couch and watch that show you're always telling me about."

Kennedy transferred some of her weight to Gemma, then sniffled into her shoulder. "Really?"

Gemma nodded, draping her arm across Kennedy's shoulders. "Alexei, can you tell Matt we're grabbing an Uber home?" Gemma asked over her shoulder as she led Kennedy down the steps. She didn't wait for me to agree before saying, "All right, Kens, hang in there. We'll be home soon."

I headed back into the party after Gemma and Kennedy disappeared. When I found Matt, I didn't tell him about my run-in with Kennedy Cole, too exhausted—and honestly relieved—to be free of the train wreck of a situation. I only relayed Gemma's message before heading to my own home.

I had a sneaking suspicion this was going to be one hell of a season.

5

KENNEDY

The sound of the door swinging open pulled me from a dreamless sleep. The heavy feeling in my skull reminded me of all that had happened yesterday. The breakup. Excessive drinking.

Alexei freaking Volkov invading space that did not belong to him.

My mouth felt like sandpaper, but my head pounded so hard, I couldn't bear the thought of getting out of bed. I sighed deeply, keeping my eyes closed, hoping the originator of the sound would get the hint and leave me alone.

"Kennedy Elizabeth Cole." The bed dipped as Gemma hopped onto it, settling in beside me.

Gemma's expression stopped me cold in my tracks. "What's wrong?"

She thrust her phone into my face. "Did you hook up with Alexei Volkov?"

I seized the phone, analyzing the photo on the screen. In it, I wore the sapphire dress from the party and stood on the deck in my backyard. From the angle of the photo, it looked like Alexei and I were kissing. His hands held me, and our heads dipped toward each other.

"This isn't what it looks like," I said, forcing a laugh, attempting to feel lighter than I actually did.

The photo was uploaded to Instagram with the caption *Volk cleans up at every party* and had already amassed fifty thousand likes. *Crap.*

The silver lining? Alexei mostly hid my face, and only those who knew me well or saw me at the party would realize it was me. In other words, a small circle. *Phew.*

Gemma tapped her bottom lip. "What were you two talking about anyway?"

"Mostly how much I hate him."

"Kennedy!" she hissed.

Against my better judgment, I opened the comments on the photo, unable to contain my curiosity. The first one was from one of his teammates, *Taking Palmer City by storm.* Hilarious.

I rolled my eyes and was about to say something to Gemma when I read the second comment. The words sent ice through my veins. *Enjoy my leftovers.* No wonder this stupid photo went viral. Justin had made it known the woman in the picture was his ex, and she was with Alexei Volkov, his sworn enemy.

Gemma continued to talk, words I entirely blocked out.

I cut in, "Oh my God. Did Justin seriously write *this*? Why would he do that?"

She peered over my shoulder. "Oh, I don't know. He thinks his ex-girlfriend is hooking up with his mortal enemy?"

"Yeah, but my father will see it—"

Our conversation from yesterday came back to me in one startling moment of realization. Justin didn't care what my father thought anymore.

And clearly, he had no love lost for me either.

"Right. I forgot for a second."

"I hate him, Kens. And I know he's my fiancée's friend, but I want to hurt him for what he did to you." Gemma blew out a long breath, shaking her arms as if she had kept those feelings in her limbs. "Oh, it feels so good to tell you how much I never liked him for you."

I threw my arms in the air. "What are you talking about? You told me that all the time."

"Okay, fine. I did. But I'm going to say it again. He was never good enough for you."

I bit my lip. As my friend, Gemma had to say that, but objectively speaking, I offered *nothing* to Justin Ward. He was a famous, award-winning athlete. He had millions of dollars and a legion of fans. I had no career, nothing of substance as I stood by his side. Other women would look better as his arm candy. I couldn't even cook for him.

How had I not expected him to wake up and realize he could do better than me?

"Gem—" I started to speak before abruptly stopping. Those luminous brown eyes never left my face. There was no point in asking her for reassurances I knew weren't true. Instead, I asked, "Do you mind if I stay here for the next few weeks?"

When my dad traveled for business, I usually found somewhere else to stay, not wanting to be alone in the large, empty, quiet house. For the last six months he had been gone more than usual after acquiring a company on the other side of the country. Most of that time, I stayed with Justin, but whenever Justin and Matt hit the road for away games, I crashed here to spend the time gossiping, watching movies, and shopping with Gemma. It never lasted more than a week though.

"Of course," she replied immediately. "Stay as long as you want."

I dipped my head. "Thanks. I just need a little time... to figure out what's next."

Gemma's signature devilish smile returned. "So there's no truth to this?"

"You're joking, right?" I had zero interest in even looking at another man. I couldn't fathom a time when I would, the hurt still too raw for me to think beyond it. And even if I were trying to get back out there, I would not choose Alexei Volkov.

Gemma shrugged. "I would understand. Alexei is *fine.*"

"Not you too. I already got an earful from Connie," I said, rolling my eyes. "Oh shit. What time is it?" I looked around Gemma to the alarm clock on the nightstand. 9:35 a.m. My alarm would have gone off in ten minutes, but since I didn't want to continue this conversation with Gemma, I wrenched the blankets off me and slid out of bed. "I promised Connie breakfast to tell her all about the party."

The McIntyres were committed to spending nearly all their weekends together, which meant most of my weekends belonged to me. Every so often, I babysat for them to go to an event or helped if either were going through a particularly stressful week of work. And sometimes, like today, I saw Connie because of how close we had grown this past year.

Gemma laughed softly. "Well, that conversation will certainly be entertaining."

I paused rifling through the closet to turn back to her. "You think she saw the picture?"

"Oh, Kens. That whole *we're obsessed with the Wolves* group probably already knows it's you."

I wore Connie's dress; if anyone could identify me in the picture, it was her. But even if she did tell that group, did it matter if people assumed Alexei and I kissed in the backyard? Justin's comment made it clear we'd broken up, so I wasn't cheating on him. Alexei had a reputation for hooking up with many different women. It wasn't like we did anything wrong. It was a funny story, and people would move on in an hour, after something else interesting happened.

"Aren't you *in* that group?"

Gemma hopped off the bed and headed to the hall. "I was. To get the lowdown on Matt. They have the best dirt." She paused in the doorway, a gleam in her eye. "Have fun at your lunch."

ALEXEI

THE FIRST PRESS QUESTION about that fucking photo didn't happen until two days after the party.

I'd seen the photo the next morning thanks to countless messages on social media. Ward couldn't help but comment, bringing massive attention to something that would have otherwise disappeared without fanfare. In the photo, Kennedy's face was hidden behind me, but someone must have recognized her. When I sat down to do my scheduled press conference—a.k.a. the bane of my existence—the Sunday morning before our first preseason game, it was the main topic the media wanted to discuss.

"There's speculation around the internet that Kennedy Cole, daughter of Wolves owner, Cale Cole, is the woman in the photo from the season-opening party. Can you confirm that's true?"

My mind went blank. No one prepared me for this question. This was a standard press conference to talk about *hockey,* not internet gossip. If I confirmed it was her, it would unleash more questions about what happened between us. Denying it was her, though, would make me a liar, and it wouldn't be long until someone could definitively prove it.

After an extended silence, I finally mustered a response. "I'm not here to talk about that."

"So you're saying there is something to talk about?" another reporter pressed.

I sat stone-faced, unwilling to acknowledge the questions. Ignoring them didn't stop the onslaught though. *What happened between you and Kennedy Cole at that party? Did you know she was Justin Ward's ex? Did you go after her to get back at him for that cheap shot last season? Have you heard from Cale Cole?* After a minute of nonstop questions, I shoved out of my seat and stormed out of the room without a word.

Erik stood against the opposite wall when I exited, arms crossed, with the same expression he wore when he disagreed with a call during a game. "Volkov," he said coolly, tilting his head down the hall. "My office."

I followed him two doors down, then closed the door behind us.

He took a seat at his neatly ordered desk. "I'm going to make this quick because I have a million things to do to get ready for this season. Did we not make ourselves clear about our expectations?" Erik didn't wait for an answer before plowing forward, his voice building in volume. "You're here to play hockey. Your focus should be on hockey. Not... whatever the hell you're doing with *your boss's* daughter."

"Nothing happened," I said resolutely, stepping toward him. "We talked at the party. That's it. It's the camera—"

Erik put up a hand. "Is this going to be a problem?"

"No, sir. My focus is entirely on the season. Playing well for you, for this team. If they ask again, I'll answer the questions, and it'll blow over."

Seemingly satisfied, Erik nodded. "Good. Go get on the ice."

Except the attention didn't blow over by the next time I sat down with the media. In the three days between press conferences, Ward had given a statement saying his focus was on hockey rather than banging the owner's daughter. *SportsCenter* picked up the story and ran Justin's tailor-made sound bite. It wasn't long before social media did what it did best—stir shit up and make it bigger than it should be.

And all the hate was directed at me.

"Got a minute?" A woman with pin-straight black hair, heavy eye makeup, and wearing a power suit waited for me outside the locker room after practice.

"Who are you?"

"Deandra Collins, lead for media advertising." She held out her hand, giving one strong shake once we connected. "Also the person who can get you out of this mess."

The next day after practice, I stood in front of a mansion beside Deandra Collins and Peter Travis, director of marketing for the Wolves. It took some convincing to get me on board with this batshit idea to fix my media problem, but after the beating I'd taken in the press these past few days, I would try anything to stop the bleeding.

Even if it felt like a waste of time... time I could have spent at the arena, improving my game. A game I could lose if I didn't fix this PR nightmare.

I swallowed my rage as the door opened to reveal two children—a girl with bright blonde hair in pigtails and a boy about double her height with light brown hair, wearing a Wolves jersey. As soon as they saw me, they started screaming and bouncing on their feet.

"Izzy! Mason!" a familiar voice called from inside the house above the sound of a wailing baby. "What did I tell you about opening the door to strangers?"

Moments later, Kennedy came into view, carrying a baby whose diaper she held secure with one hand. Upon seeing us, she stopped abruptly, as if she'd slammed into an invisible wall. No elegant dress or jewelry today, but disappointingly distracting in black leggings and a loose tank top, her hair pulled into a messy bun. It got worse for me when she wrinkled her nose.

"Kennedy," Mason said, his voice defiant as he pointed to us. "This isn't a stranger. It's *Volk*."

I gave the kid an approving nod before directing my attention to her. "Are you going to invite us in?"

Kennedy's gaze quickly bounced around, falling on each of us before she answered. "Um, sure. I just need to text Connie to let her know we have visitors."

Mason grabbed my arm. "Can I show you my room?"

I looked at Kennedy, resisting the tug on my arm until I had her answer. "I need to clean Silas up."

"Yes!" Mason shouted, taking her vague response as permission. When he pulled my arm this time, I trailed behind him as he told me about his last hockey game. Izzy shouted for us to wait for her.

When I glanced behind me, I found Kennedy's assessing gaze following me up the stairs, as if she didn't even trust me with these children.

7

KENNEDY

My gaze remained on Alexei as he climbed the steps to the second floor. He looked entirely different this morning, but unfortunately, my heart rate responded in much the same way as at the party, a mix of appreciation and anger. He wore what looked to be workout clothes, a gray T-shirt with *Wolves* written across the chest in forest green along with the logo—the scowling face of a Wolf—and black shorts over black leggings. His sweat-soaked brown hair clung to his forehead and neck. A backward baseball cap sat on top of his head. A pink flush covered his cheeks.

His aggravating, self-satisfied smirk also made an appearance.

"Hey, Kens," Deandra greeted me as she walked past me to the kitchen. The reservation in her voice, her uncertainty about how to talk to me, felt like a punch to the gut.

"You cut your hair," I said. Apparently, I had no idea what to say to her either.

She grasped the dark tips of her black hair. The formidable blunt cut barely grazed her shoulders, such a contrast to the beach waves that had flowed down her back the last time I saw her. "You know how it is... long hair is such a drag in the summer."

Like me, Deandra didn't grow up here; like anyone who wasn't born to withstand brutal summers, we whined about being soaked in sweat, then blasted with air-conditioning for three months every year.

"Always good to see you, kid." Peter lightly squeezed my shoulder as he passed. He was half a decade younger than my dad but no longer looked it with a full head of gray hair.

I instructed them to wait in the kitchen while I changed Silas in the bathroom before settling him into his favorite bouncer. When I returned, I asked Deandra, "So, um, how have you been?"

Peter had yet to look up from his phone, leaving Deandra and me to stare at each other. Once friends, now strangers.

"Good," she said, nodding vigorously. "You'll be happy to hear I dumped Brian six months ago."

I allowed a small smile, my chest tightening at the thought of how much I'd missed.

"I also got promoted—lead for media advertising at your service."

"Wow. Congratulations, D, that's amazing."

Deandra and I had talked about running the Wolves organization one day—her in charge of communications and me leading operations. Technically, the team would become mine one day, I supposed, but that was far in the future. Besides, I was less interested in the hockey side of operations and more in the financial, logistic, and general management of running a business.

Silence descended for a beat, but before I could ask her why they were here, Alexei strode into the room and took a seat across from me. He let me know the kids were back at their video games.

Peter dropped his phone onto the table. "Ready to get down to business?"

"Business?" I repeated. "What kind of business could I have with *him*?"

Alexei glared. "I see someone still has her panties in a twist over being dumped."

Peter let out a high-pitched whistle. "Oh, this is starting off swimmingly."

"Kennedy, we have a proposal for you," Deandra said.

Peter chuckled. "Let's be clear. *Deandra* has a proposal. I'm chaperoning to make sure this doesn't go off the rails."

"What are you talking about?" I asked.

Deandra folded her hands on top of the table. "There's been a lot of interest in that photo. I don't know if you've heard, but *SportsCenter* covered it this morning." Alexei's jaw tightened as Deandra continued. "And we've been getting a lot of requests for comment, including at player press conferences."

Three days since the party, and the interest hadn't slowed. Matt and Gemma had called me in to watch a *SportsCenter* segment this morning. It included a clip of Alexei storming out of a press conference when he was first asked about it. It also showed him the next day, answering questions with as much joy as someone getting their fingernails ripped out one-by-one. This time, he told them we met at the party, had a pleasant conversation—ha!—and did absolutely nothing wrong. His defensive answers made people believe something did, in fact, happen.

"I fail to see how him screwing up answers to media questions has anything to do with me."

Alexei opened his mouth, no doubt to snap at me, but Deandra swooped in.

"We have people's attention, which means we have an opportunity."

"Stop beating around the bush," Peter said. "We don't have all day."

Their dynamic hadn't changed at all since I last worked with them.

She sighed dramatically. "We need to wrest back control of the narrative. This rivalry between Alexei and Justin can draw much-needed attention to the team, but we need the public to root for us. Right now... well, let's just say they aren't. But we can use this to our advantage."

I'd seen that too, thanks to Gemma's near-obsessive watch of social media. The fan base assumed Alexei preyed on me—the poor wayward girl who lost her mother and was dumped by her boyfriend before he left town. The outrage over his signing hadn't even dropped to a simmer before this scandal started. I wondered if my father regretted signing Alexei Volkov yet. I supposed I might find out at our next video call—he'd moved it up from our usual Sunday time to tomorrow night after work.

"This?" I asked. "This what?"

Deandra gestured between Alexei and me with one hand. "The two of you."

"There is no 'two of us,'" I answered immediately. My gaze flicked to Alexei to find him watching me, but he didn't turn away. My stomach did a somersault.

"But there *could* be."

Wait... *what*? "What the hell does that mean?"

"She wants us to pretend to date," Alexei said calmly, as if those words were entirely normal. He couldn't possibly think this was a good idea.

"How would that help anything?" I asked. "If you want good press, then the team needs to win. That's all the strategy you need."

"Winning won't be a problem," Alexei said, unable to resist the bait I tossed his way. His *win* sounded like *vin,* the charming nature of which I had to ignore.

I locked my gaze on him before exaggerating an eye roll. "Okay, hot-shot, you just lost your captain, one of your highest scorers. You might want to temper expectations."

"This team is better with him gone."

Deandra clapped her hands to halt our argument. "We need people to care about this team again. We also need to fix Alexei's... likability problem."

"And your best idea is for me to date him? Deandra, this is absurd."

"That's what I told her," Peter said, fidgeting with his shirtsleeve cuffs. "And if your father ever found out we went behind his back like this... let's just say he wouldn't like it."

The room went silent, all of us imagining exactly what my dad would think about this arrangement. Based on the stiff expressions around the table, we all knew it wouldn't be good.

Finally, Deandra broke the silence. "Nothing else is working. Everyone is convinced Alexei used you to get back at Justin, the captain they are still pissed we traded right before the season started. If they see it's more than that, it lets the air out of this angry balloon."

Angry balloon. Where did Deandra even come up with these phrases? Though it did sound better than the truth—an assault backed by pure hatred.

"I understand what *he* gets out of this," I said, nodding in Alexei's direction. "But what about me?"

Deandra fought a smile. She thought she'd already won, but I was far from convinced. "You know the team is struggling, right? We might need to move again."

Some of the articles I'd read online about Justin's trade mentioned this, but hearing it from someone inside the organization felt different. My dad hadn't said anything to me about issues with the team, though

I couldn't remember the last time we talked about it. After my mother's death, I avoided the team like an allergen. "I don't care about that."

"We would pay you," Deandra said. "I can't imagine working as a nanny has you flush with cash."

I ignored the insult from my former friend, that I would date someone for money. I also didn't appreciate the reminder of what people thought of my choices. Instead, I said, "We don't even like each other."

"You don't have to like each other," Deandra said. "You just have to pretend. Make a few appearances, let the gossip mill take care of the rest."

Alexei blew out a breath. "This is a waste of time. She's not going to say yes... which might be for the best. I doubt she could pull it off."

"Oh, Kennedy is a great actress." Deandra's voice had an edge to it.

Before my mom died, we were friends who told each other everything, but I hadn't said a word to her about Justin. "I couldn't tell you," I said, my face heating. "I agreed not to tell anyone."

Earning my ire, Alexei chipped in, "You told Gemma."

I spoke directly to him. "You really are an asshole, you know that?"

"I would've kept the secret for you," Deandra added, ratcheting up my feelings of guilt.

I placed a hand on her arm. "I was going to tell you at the start of last season, and then..."

She nodded, her eyes downcast to the table. "Right. I know."

"What happened at the beginning of last season?" Alexei asked.

Shit. No way was I getting into this with him. "This conversation doesn't involve you, *Volkov*. We'll let you know when we need you."

The air in the room shifted. Deandra stared at me, open-mouthed, at a loss for words for the first time in her life. I could feel the weight of Alexei's stare and braced myself for his scathing words. They never came, which made me feel like even more of a jerk. He didn't deserve me snapping at him, even if I didn't like him. But I didn't want to talk about what happened to my mom... especially not with someone who couldn't care less about me.

Peter cleared his throat. "If anyone found out this wasn't real, it would be a clusterfuck."

"It's a win-win-win," Deandra said, pushing past Peter's warning. Turning to me, she continued, "The team needs attention. You want to get back at Justin. Alexei needs people to like him so they want to watch him play."

"People will want to watch him play because he's good, not because of who he dates," I said. A beat later, I realized my mistake after seeing the smirk on Alexei's face. "Or so I've heard."

"Kens," Deandra said. "Some people will want to see him because he's good, but no one will *care* about him because he's good. He's a player in a helmet who can do tricks. You can tell them his story—what makes him human, what makes him just like them. You show them a person, and they will *want* to root for him. Even against their old captain."

Dammit if Deandra wasn't convincing.

"Ward will hate it," Alexei added, not even trying to conceal the relish in his tone at the idea of making Justin angry. "And I don't care if you want to get back with that asshole or get revenge on him—either way, you and I dating will get his attention. It will get you what you want."

It unnerved me how he knew I wanted Justin's attention, something I hadn't even admitted to myself until that moment. I thought about the text from Justin after the photo went viral, *So that's how you want to play it.*

He hadn't questioned whether it was me in the photo, or if it really was what people assumed. Justin didn't wonder how I'd held up after being dumped in one of the worst ways imaginable. He didn't care about anything other than his image, his success, himself. Maybe I missed him and the life I imagined we'd have, but I also hated him. Hated that he could leave me behind.

Alexei wasn't wrong; Justin would pay attention if I dated his nemesis.

But it was more than that. I thought about the list I found while packing my stuff at Justin's place. The list born of my dissatisfaction with my life, something I tried to ignore, but it sometimes pushed its way to the surface despite my best efforts.

Six months since I wrote it and nothing had changed.

I needed *something* to change.

But was this really that change? The risk I wanted to take?

"I want to talk to Alexei first."

For too long, I'd taken a back seat in my own life, content to mold myself around what others wanted.

I stood from my chair and looked at Alexei. "Alone."

I didn't wait for a response before walking to the McIntyres' backyard.

8

ALEXEI

THE DOOR BARELY CLICKED shut before Kennedy hurled a question my way. "You *seriously* want to do this?"

She caught a glimpse of her reflection in the sliding glass door and hurriedly smoothed wild stray hairs. I resisted my instinct to grin. I knew the concern with her appearance had nothing to do with me. Kennedy Cole didn't care what I thought of her; she showed no embarrassment after she'd stumbled around drunk in front of me, and rambled about everything wrong with her life.

Maybe she didn't remember.

"I wouldn't be wasting my time here if I weren't serious," I said.

She took a seat on one of the chairs surrounding an unlit firepit. "Why do you want to do this?"

"You mean besides the stellar impression you made the other night?"

"Watch it or—"

I didn't need her to voice the threat. I opted for the truth, knowing it was my only chance to win her over. "I can't get them off my back. The media, my agent, the fans. Everyone is waiting for me to fail, except Erik and... your dad, who told me I needed to stay out of trouble only hours before shit hit the fan."

I risked a glance at Kennedy to see if my admission made any difference or if I should throw in the towel. Showing her how much I needed her made my skin crawl; I wouldn't beg if I had no shot. She watched me closely, her head inclined to the side. Engaged, considering.

I kept going. "They're going to shine a light on me, there's no way around it. This way, I can give them something people might want to root for."

"You think people want to root for us?" she asked, gesturing between us.

"Not yet, but they will. We can make them."

She raised her eyebrows.

"People like redemption and love and all that crap. It won't be hard to convince them."

"All that crap?"

"I've sworn off relationships," I told her. "And I don't believe in redemption, because whose fucking standard are we supposed to live up to anyway? People can hate me and what I've done all they want, but it only matters if *I* can live with it."

Kennedy rolled her eyes as she leaned back in her seat. "God, you're an insufferable ass." She huffed a laugh. "You know there is such a thing as being a good person?"

"'Good' people end up alone, drunk, and sad in the backyard at a party."

"And the 'bad' people are there because no one wants to be around them." Kennedy possessed more bark than I expected. This would be so much easier if I didn't find her attractive. "At least *I* tried."

"Is this why you brought me out here, to insult me?" I would put up with insults if I helped my hockey career, but only then.

"Do you..." She hesitated, uncrossing then recrossing her legs. Helplessly, I watched the movement. "Do *you* want to do this to get back at Justin?"

My attention snapped back to the conversation. *That* was her hesitation? I didn't expect her to say yes. It was a small miracle she hadn't laughed us out of the house. But to know she was considering it, and that Justin fucking Ward could get in the way.... "It's an added bonus."

She nodded, pausing briefly before saying, "We need to decide on terms. If we don't go back in there with our own plan, Deandra will take over completely. You don't want that. Trust me."

Deandra told me she knew Kennedy, and that meant she could get her to consider this ridiculous idea, but the level of familiarity between them went beyond what I'd expected. "How do you know each other?"

"We used to work together," she answered before hastily moving on. "What would you want from me?"

I strolled slowly toward her, then took a seat across the firepit. "Some dates—coffee or dinner, whatever. We need to be seen together, having a good time. I told the media we met at the party, so we can say we hit it off and we're seeing where it goes."

"Sounds simple enough."

"But they need to believe it's real."

She looked toward the house, avoiding my gaze. "And making it seem real means what, exactly?"

"We'd have to keep it going for at least three months."

Kennedy's head swiveled toward me, like whiplash. "Three months?"

"Anything shorter, and the rumors will start again. Speculation that will make me look bad."

She crossed her arms over her chest. "Isn't this going to cramp your style... or whatever?"

"Cramp my style?"

She blew out a breath. "Yes. You know... with all your... *female* fans."

I couldn't stop the smirk overtaking my face. "We're not even together yet, and you're already so territorial."

She tossed a pillow at me, which I easily swatted away. "So if it's just coffee and dinner, then we're keeping this casual?"

"At first," I said. "But I doubt that'll be enough to... improve my reputation."

She smiled. "Being Kennedy Cole's boyfriend will?"

"This fan base loves you."

"Don't sound so surprised. Your lack of affinity for me speaks more about you than me."

I laughed, loud and genuine. She probably wasn't wrong. More than anything, I resented what running into her that night meant for my life, my career. If she'd held it together, none of this would have happened. It felt like one more way for Justin Ward to get at me, even when he wasn't trying.

"You'll need to go to some of my games. I can get you one of my jerseys to wear."

Her nose wrinkled. All traces of ease from the last few minutes fell away, her limbs locking up and becoming stiff. "I'm not going to any games. And I will eat dirt before wearing your jersey."

I scoffed. Was she serious? All of my girlfriends had gone to every game they could. "People will expect you to attend."

"It's nonnegotiable."

We stared each other down, seeing who would blink first. Giving in to her made me seem vulnerable, and I hated that. Her saying no screwed me. I didn't doubt she could get Ward's attention another way—hell, she already *had* his attention—but I didn't have any other options.

"Then what are you willing to do?" I finally asked through gritted teeth.

"I'll go out with you no more than three times each month—you can choose what we do. I'll go to one team function. We can post pictures on social media and hold hands and—"

"Let me guess, you have a maximum number of times I can kiss you."

Kennedy's cheeks turned pink. She tried to hide it by turning away from me and futzing with her hair. "You can kiss me once," she said as she locked eyes with me. "So choose wisely when to do it."

There was so much I wanted to retort back at her, but here was her agreement. That was all I needed.

"Fine," I relented with an exhale. "But you need to sell the hell out of this relationship. Always assume people are watching us. Make them believe I'm someone you like."

She laughed quietly. "That's going to take effort, but I'll manage." She rose from her seat, walking away without warning. Over her shoulder, she muttered, "Just don't forget I'm pretending."

I caught up to her before she opened the sliding glass door and thrust my hand out to her. Kennedy stared at it a moment before taking it.

"There's no danger of that," I taunted. "For me."

KENNEDY

ALL DAY, I COULD focus on nothing other than this moment. This moment of truth with my dad.

His business trips kept him working long hours, though it wasn't *that* different from how he spent his days at home. Still, we were steadfast and saw each other at least once per week during Sunday brunch at the same restaurant if he was in town. For those weeks he wasn't, we opted for a video call. Always on Sunday, his least busy day of the week.

Asking to move our Sunday brunch to Friday sent a message.

He wasn't the yelling type, at least not with me, but from the calls I sometimes overheard, I knew he had it in him. I wasn't sure how he'd take the news of all that had happened in the last week. I was an adult. I didn't need his permission to do anything, but dammit if I didn't want his approval.

He was the only parent I had left.

My father waited for me to join the video call, his expression unreadable. When he glanced up from his phone and saw me, his face broke into a smile. Never had I been more grateful for a father who could simultaneously be disappointed in me and love the shit out of me. Not hearing from him this last week had set me on edge. We didn't talk or text every day, especially with his near-constant travel, but after something this high profile, I didn't understand why he hadn't said *anything*.

Maybe he was too disappointed for words.

Or maybe he needed us to see each other to talk.

"Hey, Dad," I said as I leaned against the wall. I wished we were together in person so I could lean into him and rest my head on his shoulder, the one I leaned on in the immediate aftermath of Mom's death. It was him and me in a self-imposed grief bubble only we could understand.

His eyes narrowed, assessing my face, looking for signs I wasn't okay. "How's my girl?"

"Okay..." I said, unsure how to answer that question. Before that stupid photo, my dad had no idea about my relationship with Justin. And now, I would have to tell him I was dating his newly acquired black sheep of the NHL. The thought made my stomach sink to the floor. Having only each other, we tended not to beat around the bush. "I'm sorry, Dad. About the party. And the news. I didn't —"

My father held up a hand. "What were you thinking?"

The question didn't seem rhetorical, but I didn't know what, exactly, he referred to, so I remained quiet.

"Justin Ward, Kennedy? Of all the men in the world, of all the men on *my team,* you pick *him*?"

Maybe this was the real reason I'd waited so long to tell my dad about Justin. Justin wanted to wait, and I never pushed it. Partially because I didn't think I could convince Justin, and I didn't want the disappointment. But... maybe I knew my dad wouldn't approve, and I couldn't stand to have that confirmed. Justin had been my tether to a life; I didn't want that broken, even if some part of me knew I wasn't truly happy.

"He made you hide your relationship," Dad went on. "That tells me everything I need to know."

I blinked. Who told him Justin made me keep this secret?

As if reading my mind, he added, "You think I don't know why you didn't tell me?"

"Dad—"

He frowned. "I hate that you didn't think you could talk to me."

"I agreed not to." An agreement I quickly regretted, but I didn't want to rock the boat between Justin and me. Waiting to tell people until the time was right felt like a small sacrifice.

In a voice barely above a whisper, Dad asked, "You hear how problematic that is, right?"

"Dad—"

"Kennedy, I don't care who he is," he continued, undeterred, voice still low but growing in conviction. "All I'm going to say is, he's lucky he's multiple states away."

I huffed a sigh of relief that his disappointment stemmed from concern rather than disapproval. "Thanks, Dad."

"Where have you been staying?" He sipped from his water bottle.

"Gemma's."

He nodded a quick bob of approval. "Good. I don't want you shacking up with a guy you just met because you think you can't come home."

"I-I'm not..." Even with a lifetime of his directness, I shrunk beneath it and fumbled my way through a response.

"Because you can come home," he said, looking at me pointedly. "Any time."

His words brought a sting of heat to my eyes. The words weren't new, but I hadn't ever embarrassed him this way before. Disappointed him, sure. He made it clear he disapproved of how I'd never re-enrolled into college and quit working for the Wolves. It wasn't that he expected me to work for the team, but he expected *more.* Leeching child of a billionaire was a played-out cliché, one he never thought he would have to deal with. Since I was young, I'd had a plan, one of academic success before following his footsteps into business.

But after a heart attack nearly took him down and my mother died, I found it hard to care. What was the point of a plan when it could be demolished by something out of our control?

"I know," I said with a swift nod. "Thank you."

The gratitude was real, but this level of support had been my crutch. I thought about the list I found—the list with items I thought might make me happy. And one of them was moving out. Not to get away from my father, but to stand on my own.

Living with Justin wouldn't have counted. Crashing with Gemma certainly didn't.

Maybe it was time for me to change things.

"Now what's this business with Alexei Volkov?"

I stilled at the abrupt question. I was prepared to talk about Alexei, practiced potential questions and answers so I wouldn't look or sound like a complete idiot. I needed to convince my dad, the person who knew me better than anyone, I had feelings for Alexei.

But he would see through all my practiced answers.

"Honestly?" I said, opting for some kernel of truth. "I'm not sure. It... took me by surprise."

Dad pinched the bridge of his nose. "What I've been hearing is true, then?"

"What have you been hearing?"

His forehead scrunched at my evasive answer, but I recognized the technique a mile away. He hoped I would supply him details. "My daughter is caught between one of the biggest rivalries in the league."

"Not true," I said with a tight smile. The next words out of my mouth felt unnatural, and I had to fight the instinct to say nothing. "Justin and I are done, and Alexei and I are... going to see what happens."

Alexei's words rang in my ears, *Making him think we're dating will get his attention. It'll get you what you want.* Right now, I wanted to hurt Justin. Hurt him the way he hurt me. Saying we were done wasn't quite right; this arrangement with Alexei guaranteed he would loom over my life a bit longer.

"See what happens," Dad repeated.

I reached for the beer on my nightstand and downed half of it. My dad raised an eyebrow at me.

"Is this where you warn me away from him?"

"Would it matter if I did?"

"Come on, Dad. What are you worried about?"

"I am always worried about you. You, Kennedy Elizabeth, are too good for this world," he said with unrelenting eye contact.

That was it? All he wanted was to make sure I was safe from being hurt. Justin convinced me my dad would be an obstacle between us, which was why we couldn't tell him until our relationship was strong enough to withstand it. Our strength would gain my dad's approval. Why didn't I listen to the voice in the back of my mind telling me it was bullshit?

"And this season is crucial for us," my dad continued. "I can't have my new star distracted."

Without a strong season, my father might have to sell the team or move it to a new location. My mom's team—the thing she most enjoyed in life outside our family—would no longer exist. Before she died, I'd had every intention of coming home after college and becoming a part of this organization. Some part of me wasn't ready to let go of that yet.

"Who knows what will happen? Maybe we'll hate each other."

Dad let out a big-bellied laugh. "Not likely, Kenny."

If he only knew the truth.

For the next ten minutes, Dad caught me up on his week. We talked about holiday plans, even though it wasn't even October until tomorrow. I told him about the near disasters at my job this week until he had to sign off for a client dinner.

"I love you, sweetheart."

These words, I never took for granted. I almost lost him once. From then on, I promised myself *no regrets* when it came to my parents. Life was too unpredictable.

"You come to me if that boy does anything you don't like. You hear me?"

"Sure, Dad." I failed to sound anything but sarcastic. Three months with Alexei meant I would deal with a lot I didn't like, far too much to bother my dad with. Besides, I had to pretend I *liked* Alexei. The day Deandra and Alexei pitched the idea, I proclaimed to everyone I could pull this off. My stubbornness sometimes made me overconfident.

But too much rode on the success of this arrangement for me not to rise to the occasion.

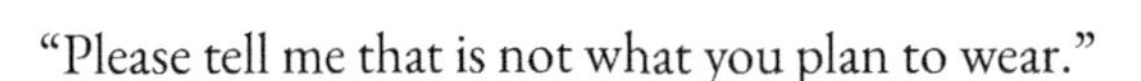

"Please tell me that is not what you plan to wear."

I looked down at my clothes—black leggings and an oversized tank from my high school track team. "To eat at home tonight? Yes."

"I think you might want to change." Gemma pushed past me into my room.

"Why." The word came out as an accusation rather than a question. When Gemma looked away from me, I knew my worry had been warranted. She'd meddled. "You didn't?"

I should've known better than to tell Gemma about the deal between Alexei and me, but keeping the truth from her didn't seem likely. When I called her right after Alexei, Deandra, and Peter left the McIntyres, Gemma was so excited, she accidentally dropped her phone into cake batter. Within minutes, she called back and ordered me to tell her everything. It took an extremely long time because she kept interrupting, demanding details like *the look in his eye* when Alexei said certain things. No matter how much I grumbled, her requests did not stop.

Gemma took a couple of steps back. "We made these plans with Alexei last week. It's not a big deal, just told him to drop by. You know, he's probably lonely living by himself in a new city."

I sighed deeply, sinking onto my bed and nestling under my blankets, my limbs suddenly heavy. When I learned Alexei lived only a few houses down from Gemma and Matt, I dreaded nights when he *dropped by*. Even if being neighbors was temporary.

The guilt hit me all over again for imposing on Gemma and Matt, even though they said it was fine. But I wanted the comfort of my friends as I came to terms with all the change in my life, as I figured out my next steps.

"I thought I had more time before seeing him again."

Alexei and I agreed we'd have lunch on his next game-free day—Sunday, two days from now, a week after the photo was released and all hell broke loose. Enough time to make it seem natural we might see each other again. After the date, he would share the explanation we decided on—we hit it off and were going to spend some time together.

Plans for this fake relationship made me anxious and calm in equal measure. We had clear rules and a set end date, which I liked. But we would put on this act for three months, and anything that went on that long may no longer be an act. It could become your life.

Gemma pulled back my blanket in one swift motion, removing the only barrier between me and the frigid air in the apartment. I had no right to complain, but keeping an apartment at sixty-five degrees was not normal.

"Honestly, Kennedy, Alexei Volkov will be here in minutes—a sentence many women would dream to hear—and you're what... sulking?"

"Women are pathetic," I said as I tried to wrest the blanket out of her grip.

"Says the one hiding from a hot, rich dude who could break most men in half."

"Does Matt know about your freakish crush on his new neighbor?"

Gemma huffed out a breath. "Matt Harris knows he has *nothing* to worry about. Trust." She swatted my arm, then wrapped both hands around one of my biceps, pulling me to my feet. "Is this going to be a problem?"

"No," I grumbled. "I mean, it's not like he's here a lot..."

"Oh, he'll end up being here a lot." Gemma laughed. "You know, since *his girlfriend* lives here."

"I'm not his girlfriend."

Gemma pointed to the ceiling as she sing-songed a response. "Ye-et." She walked over and took a seat on the bed opposite me. "Kennedy, this is a good thing. You'll get to spend time with him with other people around. You know, *practice* with a friendly audience. Maybe you'll find you like him?"

"I seriously doubt it." Though her point about practicing our relationship in a safer space did make sense. I needed to hide my true feelings about Alexei Volkov, and it would take practice. We had to fool Matt, but Gemma could give feedback.

"Is this still about Justin?" Gemma asked, judgment clear as day in her tone. For the last six months, she hadn't hidden how much she wanted me to move on from him. She didn't like that I couldn't tell anyone about our relationship. I didn't like it, either, but I knew it would change soon. Or so I thought. "Because he doesn't deserve your loyalty, Kens."

"It has nothing to do with Justin," I said. "I don't like Alexei, all thanks to him."

"Uh-huh. Can't wait to hear this. Lay it on me."

I pulled my legs into a pretzel. "He's a prick, Gem. He fights with his own teammates, yells at the refs, antagonizes the visiting team's fans. And do you remember that video a couple years ago of him leaving a club with several women when he had a girlfriend?"

"For someone who claims hatred, you remember an awful lot about him."

I fixed her with a glare.

"Maybe you should get to know him instead of assuming you have the facts based on the media. I think you've seen by now, it can be deceptive."

Her words gave me pause, but then I remembered every interaction we had so far. I witnessed his assholery up close and personal. And now everything between us would be fake. I couldn't trust I would know what was real and what was an act.

When the silence stretched too long, Gemma said, "All right, come on, girl. You don't want to keep your *boyfriend* waiting."

I sneered at her. "You're enjoying this too much."

Gemma winked. "Oh, you haven't seen anything yet."

"I'm wearing this," I said defiantly. Though once the words were out, I felt childish.

Gemma paused in the doorway, her eyes roaming from my toes to the top of my head. "Suit yourself."

I looked at my outfit again, then groaned. Of course I needed to look better than this to convince Matt of my interest in Alexei. That was the *only* reason I changed my clothes into something that demonstrated effort.

10

ALEXEI

I THOUGHT ABOUT LAST night's game as I walked over to Gemma and Matt's place. It had only been a few days since I told Kennedy, *Winning won't be a problem.* Part of that came from her putting my back against the wall, but I was also impressed with the players assembled during the offseason. Our team was better than I—and the rest of the hockey world—had thought. They had also gotten rid of the poison that was Justin Ward, who held this team back with his bullshit.

But we barely squeaked out a win last night against one of the worst teams in the league—in a preseason game and our first as this newly assembled team, but still. We looked shaky across the board—a couple leaky goals, some shit passes, and inconsistent puck control. And then there was an injury in the third period. Clark was hit hard while going for the puck in the o-zone and had to leave the ice, unable to put pressure on his right leg. We didn't know how long he would be out of commission yet, but any time out of the lineup would hurt us.

Winning might be a problem.

I shook my head, trying to clear the thought as I knocked on the door. The overwhelming smell of baking cookies hit me as soon as Gemma opened it.

"Come on in," she said, stepping aside to let me go through the foyer and into the kitchen.

Gemma and Matt's house had the same layout as mine, but walking in felt like coming home. My house was quiet. Painstakingly quiet. Quiet had been my constant companion for months. Even before Cora and I broke up, our conversations had become stilted. Road trips illuminated a problem that was easy to ignore when we were both home, attending events and spending time with other people. When we removed everything else from the equation, we had very little to say to each other.

"Kennedy is in her room."

"Her room?" I repeated. "Does she *live* here?"

Shit. I was not prepared to see Kennedy tonight. To *pretend* with Kennedy tonight.

"Temporarily." Gemma nodded down the hall. "Second door on the left."

I glanced in that direction, weighing my next move. "Do you... want me to get her?"

Gemma sighed. "Seriously, Alexei. You two are hopeless. How are you going to convince anyone?"

"She told you?" Half relief, part fury filled me. One less person to convince, but I hoped Kennedy understood the importance of discretion.

Gemma opened the oven, peeking at the cookies. A delicious wave wafted my way, and I nearly groaned.

"Step up your game, Volk. Now, go get your girl."

Kennedy opened the door to her room after one knock, as if she were about to exit. Her appearance surprised me enough, I took a small step back. For dinner at home, I expected her to be more casual. But her full face of makeup—dark eyes, pink cheeks, red lips—and curve-hugging emerald sweater dress signaled a night out.

"Why are you looking at me like that?"

All sharp edges. As if she knew how to speak to me any other way.

"I didn't expect—"

"That I would try to impress you?" She tried to finish my sentence, though my ending veered from her conclusion. "Yeah, well, don't let the effort go to your head. We have a job to do."

A job. Right. I swallowed every last word about how she looked and focused on the practical matters at hand. I held out my arm to her. "Shall we get to work then?"

She used a wrist to flip her brown hair over her right shoulder. "Why not?"

She hooked her arm around mine, but it only lasted until we hit the kitchen, where Kennedy spotted Gemma's cookies sitting on the counter. She dropped my arm as if it were on fire and snatched two cookies from the plate. "Gem, please tell me you made buttercream icing?"

"What kind of friend would I be if I didn't?" Gemma hoisted a container bigger than any found in grocery stores and gave it to Kennedy, who took it as if it were made of glass.

"I thought we were having dinner," I said.

"We are." Gemma looked over her shoulder from where she was moving cookies from the baking sheet to a plate.

Kennedy didn't spare me a look, too focused on the task in front of her. "I like dessert first."

I stood idly to the side of the kitchen, watching Kennedy sandwich an enormous amount of icing between two cookies. When she'd packed the cookie sandwich to her satisfaction, she bit into it and let out a satisfied sigh that had blood flowing to parts of me with no business reacting to Kennedy. Her tongue darted out to catch a smudge of icing on the side of her lips.

Fuck.

I cleared my throat. "Matt around?"

Gemma smiled knowingly at me, as if she could hear every unsavory thought. "He's picking up pizza. He should be back soon."

"You won't tell Matt," I said to Gemma. A statement, not a question.

Gemma and Matt seemed like the kind of couple who shared everything, but she sure as hell should not mention a word about this. Matt wouldn't say anything on purpose, but the risk was too high. He could slip during the countless hours we would spend with the team.

Gemma moved her fingers across her mouth, miming a zipper. "I think we should be more worried about *you* telling Matt."

"I know what's at stake."

"You can stop being all growly," Kennedy said. "She won't say anything." She took the last bite of her cookie sandwich, then ran a finger across her lower lip to catch excess icing.

"How long have you lived here?" I asked Kennedy, eager to paper over my reaction to her.

Her shoulders tensed. "Since Gemma brought me home from the party."

She hadn't been home in days? It couldn't have been a coincidence—Kennedy moving in with Gemma and Matt the same day Justin was traded to another team. Was she living with that prick? A strange feeling of defensiveness on her behalf flooded me. Maybe it was the fake boyfriend title. Or the sadness in her big brown eyes, enough it was difficult to look too long into them.

Kennedy quickly added, "It's temporary."

The front door swung open, and Matt breezed in carrying about five bags in one hand, as if they were filled with cotton rather than a week of groceries. In the other, he balanced two pizza boxes. No surprise—he hated making more than one trip to carry anything anywhere. I once saw him carry the equivalent of one hundred pounds of hockey equipment because he refused to walk fifty extra yards for a second trip.

His whistling stopped at the sight of his wife with the two people at the center of the biggest hockey drama this year. Clearly, Gemma was the only person aware all four of us would be here tonight. He plunked the grocery bags on the counter, then carefully slid the pizza boxes down beside them.

"You're home," Gemma said as she strode to him, straight into his arms.

"Hey, baby," Matt murmured into her hair, the words audible in the silent room.

"Y'all are so cute, it's disgusting," Kennedy said, smiling. "But save it for the honeymoon."

I pitched my voice low. "When's the wedding?"

"In December," she said slowly as if I should have known that. Maybe she was right, even if I had plenty of valid excuses for not knowing. "Before Christmas. The whole team is invited, so clear your calendar."

"Maybe if I play my cards right, it won't be the only reason I'm invited," I said, trying out a line on her for the first time.

Kennedy's eyebrows shot up, pure alarm entering her features at the idea I might be flirting with her. But then, realization dawned on her face that I'd slipped into my role. "We'll see," she said.

This would be a long three months if that was all she gave me to work with.

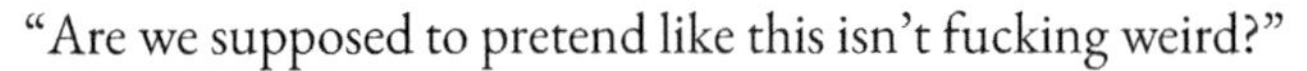

"Are we supposed to pretend like this isn't fucking weird?"

"Matt!" Gemma hissed as Kennedy raised pizza to her mouth to avoid having to say anything.

He held up his hands. "A week ago, Kennedy was dating my old teammate, and now she's with my new teammate?"

Gemma stared firmly at Matt's profile. He kept his eyes on Kennedy and me, but there was no way he didn't feel the weight of her attention.

"It's fine," I jumped in, wanting to save my friend from the wrath of his fiancée. "He's not wrong."

Matt pointed at me, triumphantly exclaiming, "Thank you. I thought I was the only one feeling this. But it's freaking weird, right? You two were on *SportsCenter*. You're still trending on Twitter."

"That's because Ward won't stop talking about it."

Kennedy's eyes snapped to me. "He won't? What has he said?"

I found it interesting Kennedy didn't already know. She agreed to this charade to get his attention, probably to get back with him, and yet, she wasn't monitoring everything he said about it.

"It's a lot of the same. It's better you don't look."

She nodded, though I didn't doubt she would read all his comments later tonight.

"Anyone want to watch a movie?" Gemma asked, breaking the awkward moment. She rose from her seat, taking her plate into the kitchen. "Don't worry, we can keep eating pizza."

I took the seat on the couch furthest from the kitchen, giving myself a beat before I needed to turn my attention to Kennedy again. My physical reaction to Kennedy Cole should have helped me pull off this fake relationship, but instead, my thoughts were running wild. I had to get them under control. Thinking back to my first interactions with her, I hadn't had this problem. The difference? We argued and weren't pretending we were into each other.

I needed to get back to getting under her skin to keep her from getting under mine.

"Any preferences?" Gemma asked, pulling me from my thoughts.

She settled on the opposite end of the couch, leaving Kennedy with the choice to either sit next to me or take what should be Matt's spot beside Gemma. With Matt's skepticism about us, it wasn't much of a choice. Kennedy sat next to me but left the kind of room kids leave between them and their first crush.

"Something with action?"

Gemma wiggled her eyebrows. "What kind of action, Volk?"

Kennedy sighed. "Just don't make it a western."

"What do you have against westerns?" I asked.

She shrugged. "Not my thing."

"What is your thing?"

She paused a moment, likely determining whether to answer truthfully or not. "I like true crime. I'll watch a documentary, a fictional retelling of the crime, interviews, any of it."

Gemma blew out a breath. "We're not watching one of your freaky documentaries, Kens. I'm sorry."

Matt plopped down on the couch, shifting Kennedy in my direction. "Why not, babe? You know I'll tell you when to open your eyes."

"I've got a compromise," Gemma said as she continued to flip through options. She landed on a movie about a woman on a crusade to avenge her friend, targeting skeezy guys.

As the movie went on, with Gemma's words in my mind, I stepped up my game with Kennedy. First, I scooted closer until our legs touched from thigh to ankle. She sucked in a small breath at the contact and moved in her seat to free up some space for herself.

But I didn't let her off the hook, only pushed into her space every time she moved away. Eventually, I slid one arm along the back of the sofa, close enough to play with her hair, my fingers brushing the skin on the back of her neck, leaving goosebumps in their wake.

Knowing this small bit of contact could unsettle her made me feel back in control.

Halfway through the movie, we stopped for a bathroom and snack break. Matt and Gemma headed upstairs, leaving me alone with Kennedy. She followed me to the kitchen, where I started to make one of those cookie sandwiches I saw her enjoy earlier.

"What are you doing?" Kennedy asked as she sidled up beside me at the kitchen counter. Her heavier-than-normal breathing pulled me from my task. When I turned to her, I noticed her cheeks were flushed.

"Getting something to ea—"

"No, I mean back there. With the..." She made a grabbing motion with both hands, implying I honked her breasts or ass, which I didn't appreciate.

I dropped the knife. "Okay, hold on. There was none of that."

"You know what I mean," she said with an eye roll. She watched me resume her cookie sandwich routine for a moment before motioning for the knife. "I can't watch this anymore. Hand it over."

I fixed her with a look, but she did not relent, only continued to hold her hand out for the knife and cookies.

"I'm playing my part—"

"Of what, a horny teenager?"

"Of a man falling in love," I said a little louder than intended. Both of us quickly looked toward the stairs, but thankfully, neither Gemma nor Matt had returned yet. "At least I don't look like someone has a gun to my back. Do you recoil at everyone's touch?"

Kennedy offered a snide, half smile. "Only from those I can't stand." She finished icing the cookie sandwich and handed it to me, placing the knife on a paper towel on the counter. "Stop trying so hard. Gemma already knows this isn't real."

"We need to convince Matt. If *he* believes, the rest of the team will. So play your part, all right?"

"Play my part," she repeated with a sharp nod. She placed one hand on my shoulder, then trailed it across my back as she walked out of the kitchen, my skin tingling at her touch. "Okay. Sure, *babe*, no problem."

Back in the living room, Kennedy wasted no time before showing me what those words meant. She inched closer, much closer than we were before, and draped her legs over mine. The position made her sweater dress slide up her thighs, revealing creamy skin that had me thoroughly distracted. This move of Kennedy's sent Gemma's eyebrows sky-high when she saw us while descending the steps. Gemma opened her mouth to speak but stopped when she heard Matt lumbering behind her, lamenting a twist in the movie. His eyes fell on us, and he cleared his throat and took his seat beside Gemma.

Kennedy snaked an arm around one of my shoulders, her fingers dancing across the base of my skull as she tugged lightly at the hair there. "What do you think, Alexei?"

"Of what?" I croaked a terribly embarrassing sound I hadn't made since I was an inexperienced teenager. What was it about this woman that made me act like this?

She nodded toward the TV. "This movie."

My breathing increased. "It's... fine."

Kennedy smirked. "So what's your thing?" she asked, borrowing my words from earlier.

Gemma stopped watching the screen, her too-wide eyes rapt on Kennedy. Maybe she'd never seen her best friend behave like this. I wondered what her dynamic with Ward had been. The thought pissed me off, but before I could fixate too closely, Kennedy tugged my hand toward her ass. The action caught me off guard, and I didn't resist the movement. So there I sat, with my hand cupping one of Kennedy's ass cheeks, trying to think of anything other than how amazing she felt beneath my touch and how I wanted to bunch up the fabric of her dress—

Shit. I needed to put some distance between us.

But when I pulled my hand away from her, Kennedy upped the ante by pushing herself into my lap. I sucked in a breath as she adjusted her position, back and forth, then back again, each movement grinding against my crotch.

"Kennedy," I hissed. I blew out a breath, directing my stare to the ceiling and my thoughts to anything but the feel of her on top of me.

"Something wrong?" she whispered, her breath hot against my ear. Her teasing voice, full of false innocence, pulled my gaze to her. I cursed my mistake; meeting those eyes of hers—those soft brown eyes, the dark freckle underneath her right eye, the way she captured her bottom lip in her teeth—caused me to lose the last bit of control.

Kennedy went stock-still when she felt me harden beneath her.

"Stay still," I said directly into her ear. My hands rested on either side of her hips, keeping her in place. "I need a minute."

The combination of violence on screen and taking deep breaths resolved the situation. Kennedy hopped off my lap as soon as the movie ended and walked quickly into the kitchen. I couldn't help but watch as she snagged a beer from the fridge and launched her head backward to chug half of it. The action was the most relatable thing I'd ever seen her do. Except I needed something stronger to erase what happened. Maybe we managed to convince Matt about our relationship tonight, but things were infinitely more awkward between us.

Kennedy plastered her back against the counter as she saw me approach. I would have stopped in my tracks, but I couldn't say what I needed to say from this distance, not without risking Gemma or Matt overhearing. "Kennedy, I'm sorry, I didn't—"

She put up one hand, placing the beer bottle on the counter with the other. "Don't—"

"I didn't mean for that to happen—"

"It's fine," she cut me off again. "Let's forget about it, okay?"

She didn't wait for a response before brushing past me, bidding goodnight to Matt and Gemma before heading to her room without even a glance in my direction.

11

KENNEDY

My brain refused to forget about what happened with Alexei two nights ago. And last night's dream felt more realistic than that of the night before, as if forcing these thoughts down deep made them explode to the forefront as soon as I closed my eyes.

I felt Alexei's strong hands locked on each hip, keeping me still as he took deep breaths that hit the back of my neck on his exhale. The idea of him working so hard to calm himself down made my heart race faster. In my dream, I did what I'd wanted to do in real life—I turned, swinging one leg over him until I straddled him, until *he* was between my legs. My skin felt on fire as he gripped my hips tighter. As I leaned toward his lips, I pushed myself harder against him, and—

My eyes bolted open.

The temptation to reach into the drawer next to my bed so I could finish what the dream started hit me so strongly, I forced myself out of bed and into workout clothes.

Today was Sunday, the day of the dreaded first "date" between Alexei and me.

I would run until I could only think about why I disliked him and nothing else. Only then, could I face him again.

I wished I'd never found that stupid list. I thought this over and over as I scanned the menu at *Carter's on the Corner*, a bar and restaurant near the arena and a favorite of the Wolves players. Fans often came here, hoping to run into them, asking for a selfie or an autograph, walking away with a story about how they met their hero. Eyes tracked us as soon as we entered, something Alexei counted on.

I shouldn't have told him he could choose all of our dates. I was being a brat. I also didn't want to put any more effort into this arrangement than required. And now I sat in arguably the most pro-Wolves place in Palmer City—aside from the arena—with their brand new star.

I huffed as I scanned the menu.

"Something wrong?"

"Other than everyone in this bar watching us? No." I didn't look at him—seeing his long, long stroll from his car to the restaurant was enough. I'd wished for him to be late so I could start this date by complaining, but no, he arrived on time. And looked hot in dark-wash jeans that reminded me exactly why Connie always went on and on about hockey players' thighs. A backward baseball cap sat on his head, my reaction to which should be commissioned for scientific study. *It's just a hat.*

When I finally looked up from the menu, I plastered a false smile on my face. "But you know, you're right. I'm here with *the* Alexei Volkov. I should be grateful."

"Are you always going to call me by both names?"

I closed my menu, hoping to hurry the waitress, then shrugged, trying to project nonchalance. Inside, though, my emotions swirled—anger at Justin for leaving me behind, annoyance at Deandra for dreaming this up, and exasperation at myself for agreeing to it.

And then there was the feeling I didn't want to name when I looked too long in Alexei's direction. He'd bothered me for as long as I could remember because he was the ass who played for a rival team, the person at the center of Justin's worst fights. He didn't seem real. He'd been my boyfriend's terrible coworker, a looming figure in stories about his day. Until now, I didn't have to sit across a table and stare into his absurdly handsome face. At least that dimple hadn't made a reappearance.

"Maybe. Alexei Volkov."

He nodded, one quick bob of his head, and curled his lip, seeming to imply he found my answer real mature. But I didn't care what he thought. Alexei's place in my life was temporary and only because he needed me to redeem him.

"Have you always lived here?"

"What?" I asked, thrown by the question.

"When Deandra mentioned the team might move, I could tell it bothered you."

My heart rate ticked higher, but I rolled my eyes, hoping my outward act of calm would still my internal reaction. "The team could move to Timbuktu for all I care."

Alexei narrowed his eyes at me. "You don't like the hockey," he stated, much like he would have accused me of not liking chocolate or hating the Beatles.

With waning attendance numbers, he should have realized this was a common phenomenon, but the guy probably lived in a bubble, with nearly every person in his life connected to hockey. It explained why the idea of another person having interests beyond slapping a puck into a net astounded him.

"I don't think much of hockey," I corrected.

"Your father owns a professional hockey team."

"I'm fully aware of that, thanks. Still doesn't change my opinion."

Alexei shook his head slowly. "That would have been a dream come true for me."

I leaned back in my seat and gestured to him vertically. "Well, you play on a professional hockey team, so I'm sure you feel just fine now."

He watched me, his brows furrowing, exaggerating the crease between his eyes. Alexei kept searching for some answer, and it deeply unsettled me, this unrelenting study of my features.

The waitress, who finally graced us with her presence, pulled his attention away from me. She took one look at him and melted into a puddle. "Volk," she said with a gasp. She fumbled in her smock pocket for her notepad and pen. "What can I get you?"

"Cheeseburger, medium well, sweet potato fries, and a Pepsi."

Alexei's attention turned to me, his head tilting in surprise, which was my first clue I was gaping at him. I couldn't help it. Justin *never* ate like that. He ate nothing fun during the season, just boring salads and grilled chicken and veggies. I once saw him eat a dessert, which resulted in two hours in his personal gym afterward. The worst part was I'd followed his lead in solidarity. It sucked.

But now I could eat whatever I wanted. And I wouldn't have to hide the evidence of my straying diet while he was out of town either.

Our waitress's derisive voice cut into my thoughts. "You're the girl from the internet." She said the next words slowly, trying to piece together what she saw before her. "And you're here... with Volk."

"It appears that way, doesn't it?" I replied, my voice filled with fake honey.

"So you two…" She trailed off but motioned between us with one hand.

Alexei leaned toward her to whisper, "She doesn't like to label things."

This girl's eyes nearly rolled into the back of her head. "She doesn't like to label things… with you."

And this was where our innocent lunch took a turn south, the moment Alexei turned his grin on this girl and then on me. It illuminated his entire face and surfaced that treacherous dimple I wished to never see again.

Okay, he looked cute when he smiled… so what? Lots of people did. And what was a dimple anyway, just a divot in your face? If anything, people should consider it an imperfection. There was no reason to feel any type of way about it.

"I need to make sure he can handle me." I winked at her.

Under the table, I felt Alexei's leg brush mine in warning. If that was his goal, mission accomplished because alarm bells sounded in my head. Every one of my instincts yelled to put distance between us, but I couldn't leave, so I endured his leg pressing mine.

I hoped the flush I felt didn't reach my face.

I refused to look at him, instead focusing on the waitress as I recited my order. "Chicken tenders and sweet potato fries. Oh, and a shot of rum and a soda. Please."

As soon as she scampered away, Alexei said, "Another thing we have in common."

"We both like fries," I marveled. "Groundbreaking."

Wait, what is the first thing we have in common? Maybe he meant being involved in this stupid photo debacle. I was about to ask when the pressure from Alexei's leg abated, offering much-needed relief. When I could no longer feign interest in the bar, I looked across from me, at Alexei, who wore a smirk on his face.

"No need to look so smug," I said. "Everyone here hated you last week, in case you've forgotten."

He ran his finger along the rim of his water glass. "She still would have gone home with me."

"You're disgusting."

"Don't play innocent with me, *Kens*. You were with Justin Ward."

"First, don't call me that ever again," I said, holding up a finger. "And second, Justin was my friend before he was anything else. I wouldn't sleep with someone just because they were famous."

"Why would Ward want to be just friends with you?"

I opened my mouth to match his repulsed tone with ire of my own.

But then, he added, "He obviously wanted more. You didn't?"

"I wasn't single at the time."

The waitress returned at that moment. She placed our drinks in front of us, poised to say something before taking in the scene in front of her—Alexei and I staring each other down. I broke eye contact with him to pick up my shot and down it, loving the hot sensation running through my throat. The waitress left again without saying a word.

"How long did you make him wait?"

"I didn't *make* him do anything."

Alexei held my gaze, waiting for my answer.

"We started dating six months after we met."

He whistled. "He must have had quite a thing for you, waiting that long."

"Not everyone plows their way through local restaurants."

Alexei barked out a laugh. "You think you know me."

"I know your type."

"My type?" Alexei repeated.

"You like people being in awe of you. I saw your face when that woman stumbled over her words. You thrive on it."

Alexei gestured around the restaurant with one hand. "Don't try to pretend you don't love the attention."

"I hate the attention."

"So what... you were with Ward for his dazzling personality?"

"His huge penis, actually."

Alexei spat his drink back into his glass. Catching him off guard like that brought me sick satisfaction.

"Just because the women you date only want you for attention doesn't mean I'm like that."

Alexei's face fell but only for a moment. I looked away, not wanting to see the hurt, and pretended to search for something around the bar again. I clocked our waitress huddled with several colleagues, no doubt retelling the story of perfect Volk and the terrible shrew he deigned to date. Alexei belonged to the Wolves fan base now; even if they considered him an asshole, he was *their* asshole.

That stupid curious stare of his immediately met my gaze when I turned back. "What?" I snapped.

"I was wondering whether Ward started dating you because of this attitude or whether you developed it because he rubbed off on you."

"Excuse me?"

Alexei barreled on as if I hadn't said a word. "You're acting just like him. Too good to give me the time of day. Thinking you're so much better than everyone around you. When you told me you were dating him—"

"I didn't tell you anything," I muttered.

"—I didn't get it. His grouchy, overbearing ass and you?" He paused, likely expecting me to steamroll him, but his words had stunned me silent. "But I get it now."

"I hate you," I said, staring daggers in his direction. I felt so called out, dissected by someone who didn't know me, and who was arrogant, presuming he did.

Alexei barked out another laugh, and that's when I noticed he had *two* freaking dimples, one in each cheek. Good lord. Someone please make this stop.

"Same maturity level as him too."

"Screw you."

"You sounded like you were planning to," he replied, one side of his lips tugging up. "First date is a little early for me, if I'm being honest."

Anger was never a comfortable emotion. I hated the unpredictability of it. Sometimes it slowly took over my body at the speed of an object falling through quicksand; other times, like now, it shot through me like a heat-seeking missile. I never knew how to process it, only how to spit it out at someone as quickly as possible to purge it from my body.

"You will have me in your fucking dreams," I said in a low voice, not wanting to cause a scene. My hands shook beneath the table where they sat in my lap. "And nowhere else. Not now, not ever."

"Do you want to bet?"

My pulse hummed faster, adrenaline coursing through me. "That I won't sleep with you? It's a losing proposition, buddy. And deeply stupid, because you're giving me a bigger incentive not to. Trust me, the odds were already stacked against you."

He leaned forward, elbows resting on the table. "I never back down. Maybe you missed that when you were sticking your nose up at hockey."

This man.

"Oh, I've seen you play," I said, locking eyes with him, projecting what I hoped he would see as confidence. "And I've seen better. In fact, I've *dated* better."

I kept my eyes on him while I sipped my drink. Alexei's nostrils flared, and his hand on the table spasmed nearly into a fist before reopening.

For the rest of lunch, we remained silent.

12

ALEXEI

KENNEDY OPENED THE PASSENGER door of my car as soon as I parked. "Seriously?" she said as she sunk into the passenger seat. "Is this your big first-date move?"

"Oh, she speaks," I muttered as I leaned forward to slip my wallet into the glove box.

Kennedy scoffed. "I could say the same to you. Don't change the subject."

The silence had started after I cracked that joke about betting on whether Kennedy would sleep with me. I hadn't planned on saying it, but something about her insistence that I would never have sex with her got under my skin. My entire career was about making the impossible possible. The odds of me making it to the NHL were shit. Getting drafted late in the second round hadn't made anyone believe I would become one of the best players in the league.

But I didn't let any commentary get to me. I kept my head down, worked hard, and proved everyone wrong.

It wasn't like that with Kennedy though. I didn't *want* to sleep with her. Okay, that was a damn lie. I *wouldn't* sleep with her. I didn't need the complication. But I hated the way she looked around the restaurant, ignoring me, as if she would rather be anywhere else.

And she made it too damn fun to get under her skin.

"You think I would waste a big move on you? You're a sure thing."

Kennedy opened her mouth, no doubt to say something scathing, but I finished my thought before she could.

"Metaphorically speaking."

The tension in her shoulders deflated when she realized I didn't mean it. "It's a wasted opportunity," she said. "You could show me your best, and I could give you feedback."

"Show you my best and make you want me?" I flashed her my most charming smile. "I don't think so. This situation is awkward enough without adding letting you down easily to the list."

"I will never want you." Kennedy echoed her words from earlier—"*You will have me in your fucking dreams. And nowhere else. Not now, not ever.*"—in case they hadn't been clear. "Hope that doesn't bruise too hard."

"No, but if it did, it wouldn't be difficult to find someone to kiss it and make it better," I said, opening my door. "Not everyone finds me as repulsive as you do."

A fact that bothered me to no end and that I tried not to dwell on.

I wished it were only an ego thing. I told myself it was... but it was *her*. Those brown eyes that always seemed to snag my attention looked especially big tonight. She wore her hair down in curls around her shoulders. Her shirt hadn't left much to the imagination with the way it hugged her curves and exposed a hint of cleavage, and she'd paired it with simple dark-wash jeans that got anything but a simple reaction from me when she turned around.

"We're not playing hockey," I said after Kennedy caught up to me as I approached the rink where our team practiced. This venue was public, which was the genius of choosing it. People—youth hockey players and their parents—would see Kennedy and me together, and the odds of someone taking a photo and sharing it online were high.

"Then, what are we doing?"

The commotion created by my entrance drowned out my answer. Players and parents leaving practice rushed toward me. She hung back as I signed autographs and took pictures. The smiles I offered were nothing but genuine. After being dropped by my last team, I didn't know if I would have this again—fans clamoring for my attention, a community happy to have me as part of their team. Even if I had no interest in relocating to Palmer City permanently, this support would never get old; I'd experienced how quickly it could disappear.

When I looked up from my last autograph, I saw Kennedy chatting with a couple of women. I was familiar with her scowl, one she would hate to hear I found cute. But this smile—not directed at me, of course—full of unabashed joy, it decimated me.

This is fake. This is fake. This is fake.

Kennedy Cole wanted nothing to do with me. Hell, I shouldn't want anything to do with her either—the ex-girlfriend of my enemy, the daughter of the man who paid my salary. But I couldn't wrench my gaze off her face.

She said her goodbyes as soon as I caught her eye and motioned for her to follow me. We waved to the remaining crowd and headed toward the rink. I didn't need to look behind me to know many of them would hang around to watch us.

"What did they want?" I asked as we walked through the door toward the ice, out of earshot of everyone.

"Your adoring female fans?" Kennedy rolled her eyes as she settled onto one of the benches. "I'm sure you can guess."

I could've told her it didn't mean anything—if I didn't play professional hockey or make millions of dollars, most of them would give me an appraising look and move on. Their interest had nothing to do with *me* as a person, only with my occupation. But I didn't clarify this with her; I wanted her to be reminded that people *wanted* to date me.

"We're being watched." Kennedy peered at me from where she sat lacing up her skates.

I turned away quickly, after catching an eyeful of her chest. Maybe she wore that shirt to throw me off my game. Thanks to her antics the other night, she knew exactly how my body could react to her.

"Ignore them," I said, reaching for her hand.

Kennedy looked around for anything else to support her getting to her feet. Finding nothing, she took my hand. Her eyes remained on our joined hands when she said, "Some of us aren't used to this kind of attention."

"You not getting attention is hard to believe," I said, sporting my most obnoxious smirk. "This isn't a real first date. You don't have to pretend with me."

She pulled her hand out of mine. "I hate being the center of attention."

"Right." Every woman I ever dated liked the attention dating me brought her. Most of them drew eyes all on their own—sometimes because of their career, but other times because they put in the kind of effort that made people look. Kennedy didn't fit into either of those buckets. Especially not now that she had thrown her hair in a messy bun. She tucked loose, shorter strands of hair behind her right ear.

I couldn't take my eyes off her. I cleared my throat. "You know how to skate?"

She glared at me. "As you like to remind me, my father owns a professional hockey team. Yes, I know how to skate, Alexei."

I held out my arms toward the ice, *Have at it.*

Kennedy stared out onto the ice before she took a step forward. She skated better than I expected for someone who didn't like hockey. There were other ice sports though. Maybe one of those was her thing. I followed her out, allowing the rush of skating to drown out my thoughts.

Like always, it did the trick.

13

ALEXEI

KENNEDY AND I SKATED silently for a long while, and as predicted, we had an audience. Behind the glass, several kids and their parents watched us, and at least two phones followed us.

I moved closer to Kennedy until I could hook my arm in hers. Close like this, I could smell vanilla and orange, the same scent that had filled my car. She looked up at me in confusion, but I didn't say anything, only waved to our audience. Kennedy didn't miss a beat, following my lead and flashing a big smile at them. For someone who hated attention, she handled it well.

"I imagine you're usually a big hero, teaching your dates to skate."

She sounded pleased with herself, as if she had ruined a move of mine. I hadn't ever taken a date ice-skating, but I wasn't about to share that with her in case she read into it. Not that I should worry she would. Kennedy's body language almost always shouted to leave her alone. Even arm-in-arm with me, she felt stiff.

"You seem awfully interested in my dating life."

She scowled, bringing me the satisfaction of knowing I ruined her plan to throw me off-kilter. "I want to know what else I'm in for during these few months."

"Oh, Kennedy, you know I wouldn't treat you like anyone else. I'd have to be trying to impress you to do that."

"You won't be getting the usual Kennedy Cole dating experience either."

Despite myself, I wondered what she meant. How would she behave differently if she wanted to impress me? Did she have this degree of sassiness with everyone? Or did her dislike of me bring it out of her? Part of me hoped it was the latter, that I got to see a side of her other people didn't.

"So you don't usually insult your dates?"

Kennedy ignored me and continued her needling. "I know all about your reputation."

"My reputation?"

She'd raised this before, and her comments hadn't been too far off... if she believed rumors. Several years ago, a video of me leaving a club with women who weren't my girlfriend got posted online. Many people took it as ironclad proof I wasn't a dick only on the ice. Never mind that the Uber dropped me at home before the party train rolled on to my teammate's place.

For the most part, I kept my life private, not posting photos with women on my social media accounts or answering questions about my love life. People taking pictures was out of my control, but I never commented on it. That's why no one knew I had been engaged, ready to commit myself to one woman for the rest of my life. I wouldn't even share that information to knock the judgmental look off Kennedy's face. My business was my own.

Or at least, it had been my own.

"Do tell how you heard all about that in your no-hockey bubble. Been asking around about me?"

Kennedy's smug smile fell into something resembling sadness, but it was gone in a blink, making me wonder if I'd imagined it. "You wish, hotshot."

My jaw ticked at the nickname and the impeccably insulting way Kennedy delivered it.

"So what's next in your playbook?" she asked. "Are we supposed to hold hands and skate in circles? Or should I stand to the side as you zip and zag across the rink?"

"You think I lead with the hockey because that's all I have?"

Kennedy unhooked her arm from mine and skated away from me. "I imagine some women are into this whole strong, cocky man thing you have going on." She waved her hand around, encompassing my entire body.

I scoffed. "Some women."

"I'm sure they're out there." Kennedy grinned, the first genuine one she'd deigned to toss my way. And it had been in service of mocking me. "Don't give up hope."

I couldn't keep up with her changing tactics from *I'm a fuckboy* to *I'll never find someone to tolerate me.* Although they weren't far from the same insult. There was no shortage of women who would bang Alexei Volkov, winger for the Palmer City Wolves, but there were few who would stick around if I were only Alexei. Cora hadn't. Kennedy had no way of knowing how dead-on her insult was to the most insecure part of me. Would it bring her joy to know how much those words stung? Or would she see our similarities—two people left behind by the people who knew us best, who supposedly loved us?

"Finding someone is the furthest thing from my mind," I told her.

"Me too."

"So..." I said, moving away from this topic. "What was it like growing up with the owner of a professional hockey team?"

"It was fine, as you would expect."

"Did you ever go to any games?"

This question brought her assessing eyes back to mine, full of wariness. "I went to some."

"And?" I prompted.

"And what?"

"What turned you against it?" I asked, desperate to understand how Kennedy could hate this sport I loved more than anything else in the world. "Bad game? Food made you sick? You resented moving here?"

She closed her eyes so all I could see was her dark eye shadow. "I stopped liking it." She affected a casual shrug as her eyes opened. "I got bored, I guess."

"Bored," I repeated. For all the complaints about my sport, feeling bored while watching a game was the one I heard the least. Hockey games flew by, thanks to near-constant action and very few breaks.

"Yes, bored," she said as her skating speed dropped to a crawl. It was a strategy to lose me, going so slow I couldn't stand it. Too bad my stubbornness trumped my impatience. "Like I counted the minutes until I could leave. Satisfied?"

"I bet Ward loved hearing that."

"I don't want to talk to you about Justin."

"You don't want to talk to me about anything."

"Ding, ding, ding," Kennedy said, punctuating each word with a jab of her finger in the air. She stopped skating altogether and plastered herself against the boards.

I glanced toward the glass separating the rink from the lobby. The crowd had waned, but we still weren't alone. "This is no picnic for me either," I said in a low voice. No one could hear us from so far away; I knew it, but my paranoia over someone finding out about our arrangement had me barely whispering the words. If people found out, Kennedy could hide away for a few weeks, but I would be screwed.

"Glad we're finally on the same page about something," she said.

"But you agreed to do this. For whatever reason." I gave her a pointed glare, conveying I knew full well why she agreed. I let her see my judgment. The fact that what I needed to fix this whole media mess would also bring her back to that prick filled me with resentment. Even when Ward lost, he won. "So we need to know enough about each other to pass at this whole dating thing."

Kennedy crossed her arms over her chest. "Then why don't you tell me three things about your life, hotshot? I'll do the same, then we can call it a night."

The nickname prickled at my skin. Still, I wouldn't back down from the challenge she'd thrown my way. The smugness in her voice made it clear she assumed I wouldn't share a damn thing with her. She underestimated how much I wanted to prove her wrong and needed to make this work. "What do you want to know?"

Kennedy drummed her fingertips on the side of her jaw. "When was your last relationship?"

The longer I held her gaze, the more she flushed.

"Keep asking about my dating life, Cole, and I might think you care."

"It's something people would expect me to know. Who you were with before me." She diverted her gaze to the crowd watching us. Only two people remained. "You know all about *my* last relationship."

"Her name was Cora. She ended things around the time I was released from my last team, six months ago."

"She ended things before or after you got released?"

I gritted my teeth. "After."

Kennedy nodded sympathetically, which almost felt worse than her holier-than-thou judgment. "I see."

She paused for a long moment, writing and rewriting a question in her mind. I knew what she wanted to know before she asked it, but no way would I give her an out from saying it out loud.

"And no one since then?"

I huffed out a laugh, my hot breath visible in the air. "Are you asking for my list, Kennedy?"

Her cheeks turned scarlet. The look suited her. It was the only explanation for why I offered her what I did.

"It would be empty. Hence, my *reaction* the other night..."

Her eyes snapped to mine, surprised. Either she hadn't expected me to ever bring that night up—and honestly, join the fucking club—or her shock stemmed from me being celibate for so long.

"I could see why you wouldn't want to date, but—"

"Why wasn't I—how did you put it?—plowing my way through local restaurants?" I asked with a smirk. She shuffled uncomfortably on her skates but kept her eyes on me as I answered. "I was focused on getting my career back on track. It didn't leave time for dating. And... I wanted to be alone."

After my relationship with Cora ended, I'd thrown myself into training to avoid focusing on what I lost. Opportunities to break my drought were present, but I couldn't stand the idea of playing that game. What I enjoyed five years ago wasn't at all what I wanted now. I wanted the plans Cora and I made. I wanted someone waiting at home for me when I came back from a road trip. I wanted someone to give a shit about *me*—beyond my money, fame, and stats.

But even though I wanted what came with a committed relationship, I couldn't imagine putting myself through the pain required to find one. And there was no guarantee I ever would find one. Some people lived happy lives alone; maybe that was in the cards for me. The drought grew, and I told myself I was fine with it. Except apparently, it wasn't true for one part of me in particular.

"Last question."

Kennedy's usually sharp stare went soft as her eyes roamed my face. This, more than any insult from her, made me itch to take off around the rink and leave her in the dust. Our back-and-forth, filled with sharp retorts and open dislike, felt more comfortable than the direction I imagined she would try to take us now. Before the softball question came out of her mouth, I knew it would piss me off more than anything she'd said to me to date.

"What's your favorite movie?"

She thought she'd given me a gift by not forcing me to answer a tough question, but it only drove the knife deeper. Her pity over how pathetic my life had become over the last six months knotted my stomach. Barely hanging-on career. Dumped by the woman I planned to marry, even though Kennedy didn't know *that*. No home. No sex. Things were starting to turn around, but damn if these last few months weren't hard to shake. Could I even get back to what my life looked like six months ago?

"Don't do that," I said.

"What?"

"Ask me a real fucking question."

Kennedy recoiled, but I couldn't find it in me to smooth it over. She saw too much of what existed beneath my confident act. I would take every ounce of hatred over ever seeing that look of pity again.

"Fine," she said, her voice all sharp edges again. She pushed off the wall, gliding forward one stride, so close vanilla and orange hit my senses again. I towered over Kennedy enough to see her chest perfectly from this angle, but I stopped my treasonous eyes from lingering there. "Did you get hard the other night because you haven't had sex for six months? Or because it was *me* in your lap?"

Her words might have been quiet, but they packed a punch. Pushing Kennedy's back against the wall brought out a different side to her. She kept her gaze fixed on me, not a trace of shyness on her face.

I refused to drop my own stare. "You jumped into my lap, Kennedy. What did you think was going to happen?"

"Oh, I don't know... you could have exercised restraint."

"What? Like you did?" I skated toward her, slowly easing her back against the boards, her accelerated breathing audible in the silent rink. I reached down, placing one hand on each of her hips as I had that night, and whispered into her ear, "Don't think I didn't notice how my hands on you affected your breathing."

Her lips parted, all brazenness melting off. A shift to the left, and my lips would land on hers. Lips I watched now, considering.

Our agreement included only one kiss. Doing it now, like this, would be a waste.

"My turn now, huh?" I said, pulling back from her, bit by bit, until enough space existed between us, someone could skate through without issue. For the first time in six months, the distance bothered me. I wanted to close it again. With Kennedy, the woman I was fake-dating, who wouldn't be here if not for the agreement between us. These next three months would be slow torture, an unending punishment. Unless I could keep us at odds and remind myself of the reason I shouldn't feel any kind of attraction toward her. "How could you stand dating that prick for as long as you did?"

I assumed she would refuse to answer and end the game because it took a turn she didn't like. Surprisingly, she only hesitated for a few moments before answering.

Her expression turned blank, unreadable. "Justin understood me and my choices. I didn't have to explain anything to him. He's the only person I could be myself around. He accepted me as I am. Or at least, I thought he did."

"You'd get back with him if you could?"

Kennedy hesitated, clearly not expecting the question. "I-I don't know."

I shook my head in disgust. I'd suspected her intentions from the start, so I shouldn't have been surprised. And yet... I expected more from her. Ridiculous, I knew, but I had a hard time reconciling the woman who had no problem calling me out with the woman who would accept shit from Justin Ward. "The guy calls you leftovers, and you'd still take him back?"

The words hit her with the force of a puck slapped against the boards. "That's enough for tonight. I'm going home."

Her sharp-edged tone made me wish I could rewind the last five minutes. I did this. I pushed us in this uncomfortable direction, all because she tried to be *nice* to me. It wasn't her fault I was someone to pity. That landed only on my shoulders.

People had warned me about my temper for as long as I could remember. How if I let it control me, I would never get what I wanted. When my name was called on draft day, I felt vindicated for ignoring them. After signing my first big contract, I laughed when I thought about every single person who wanted to change me. But then my antics caught up with me, and a narrative was built, one that grew a life of its own.

Kennedy knew the narrative of Alexei Volkov—the aggressive hockey player who would take on anyone in his way. Even the heartbroken, closed-off woman who stood before him.

She took off toward the opposite side of the rink.

"Kennedy!" I called, but she didn't answer.

She held all the cards in our situation. She could find another way to get Ward back. But without her, how the hell would I convince anyone I hadn't arrived in Palmer City and banged the owner's daughter to get at my rival?

Needing *her* like this was the worst punishment anyone could have designed for me.

Despite my assholery, Kennedy waited for me behind the bench. We still had an audience of one. I met her with a warm smile, painfully clenching my teeth to keep my lips from falling into a grimace. After peeling off our skates, I placed a hand on the small of her back as we left the rink, side by side. Neither of us broke from our act as we walked to our cars, just in case anyone saw us.

I tried to catch her eye before she climbed into her car, but Kennedy slipped on sunglasses and slammed her door closed. I didn't blame her.

But I didn't expect it to bother me as much as it did.

14

KENNEDY

FOUR DAYS AFTER OUR date, I opened the door to a half-asleep Alexei Volkov cradling a box from Gemma's bakery in his arms.

"What are you doing here?" I asked, eyebrow raised.

Since the disastrous end to our date, I hadn't heard from Alexei. Not that I'd reached out to him either. I wasn't sure if he was waiting for me to contact him after I worked through my anger. Or maybe he was ending this little experiment because we couldn't make it through even one public outing without wanting to tear each other down.

It was also entirely possible we were both just terrible communicators.

"Can we talk?" Alexei propped open the box, revealing an impressive spread of baked goods—chocolate chip cookie sandwiches, brownies with icing, chocolate-covered pretzels, and a cupcake decorated with a Wolf (Gemma called it "a pack cupcake"). "I brought a peace offering."

I blew out a breath as I snatched a brownie from the box, then took a bite. I covered my mouth with my free hand. "Damn, you might apologize better than you hockey." I swallowed the remainder of my bite. "Wait... this is an apology, right?"

"Yes, this is an apology," he replied, but from the way his jaw twitched, I didn't know how much of it he meant. Armed as he was with the box of baked goods, it was easy to overlook any reluctance I detected.

"I'm on my way to work," I said, stepping onto the porch beside him and pulling the door shut behind me. Barely six thirty in the morning and the sun already felt oppressive, making me regret slipping on a sweater. I couldn't wait for actual fall weather.

"I know." Alexei ran a hand through his unruly hair. His accent sounded thick this morning, maybe because he wasn't fully awake. "Can I drive with you? I'll Uber back."

As if I could say no to *this* Alexei Volkov with mussed hair, carrying my favorite baked goods, sounding unfairly hot with his accent.

"Um, sure," I said, hiking my bag onto my shoulder as I headed to the car parked in front of the house. Alexei followed wordlessly, giving me time to brace myself for our conversation.

When I started the car, Alexei turned to me. "We've got twelve weeks together."

"Someone's got a countdown going," I muttered, pulling away from the curb.

Alexei laughed. "As if you don't, Cole. And maybe you could let me get this out before you come at me." His tone offset his words, more joking than serious, though he meant what he said. I motioned a circle with one hand, urging him to continue. "These last two weeks have been exhausting. A month ago, I didn't know if I would even be playing this season. And now I'm here, and management has made it clear I can't screw up. This year is my shot, Kennedy. I've worked harder than I ever have, and it might mean nothing because of some stupid photo."

I glanced over at him as I came to a stop at a light. He looked more serious than I had ever seen him, and it felt different from all those times when he'd fixed me with a stare I couldn't read. Because, for once, I could read every single emotion on his face—in the visible circles under his eyes, the tightness in his jaw, the downturn of his lips. He projected his worry as an aura, something I couldn't *not* pick up on. Was it because he wanted me to? Or had his stress caused him to drop the mask, allowing me to see *him* for the first time?

"I have enough to worry about with the hockey." He ran his hand through his hair again. "I can't worry about this too."

"I've gotta say, I'm not exactly feeling like our relationship is a priority for you." I cracked a smile, hoping to lighten the mood, but Alexei's expression didn't change. "Not in a joking mood. Got it. Well, I don't know why you're worried about this. I'm going to see it through, even if you were a gigantic prick the other night."

"And you were a perfect angel?"

"I only responded to what you put down."

"What about all your little barbs? You never miss."

I winced, but then I remembered what he said at lunch. "You tried to bet me about whether we'd have sex."

Alexei threw his hands in the air before smacking them against his thighs. "It was a joke."

"Kind of a fucked-up thing to joke about, don't you think?"

"You... this"—Alexei gestured between us—"throws me off my game."

I paused a moment, gliding to another stop at a stop sign. "You don't seem off your game," I said after analyzing his expression to determine the sincerity of his words.

"Well, I am." He looked like he wanted to snatch back the words, which, ironically, was what I needed to know I could trust him.

"You pressed on something I don't want to talk about. Maybe I lashed out a little," I said.

I pulled onto the McIntyres' street but eased the car to a stop several houses away so we could finish this conversation. If the kids saw my car in the driveway, they would sprint outside and lose their minds over finding Alexei with me. As much as I wanted to end this conversation, something tugged at my chest at seeing him so disheveled.

I put the car in park and turned toward him.

Alexei sighed, tension deflating from his posture like a popped balloon. "You did too."

"Easy solution then," I said. "We stop asking each other questions."

"We have to talk to each other, Kennedy. We're... dating."

"What if we develop a list of safe topics and others that are off-limits?"

"Safe topics?" he prompted before running his fingers over his chin, covered in dark stubble, as always.

"You know, like conversation starters. That way, we don't accidentally step on landmines." *Or on purpose now we know each other's weak spots.*

He nodded several times as he said, "I think that could work."

Fink instead of *think.* Why, oh why did his accent have to charm me?

"You send me your list, and I'll send you mine." He held his phone out to me. "Add your number, and I'll text you later."

His agreement felt too easy, but then again, I found something we both wanted—a way to manufacture a relationship without actually having one.

"Wouldn't actual dating be easier if everyone did this?" I typed my number into his phone. It was freeing not to worry about what Alexei thought of me. I could say whatever I wanted, without it becoming something that signified more about the relationship.

Alexei took the phone back from me, his fingers brushing mine, leaving an inconvenient tingle in the wake of his touch. He smiled, a lopsided half grin. "I couldn't agree more."

If only I could outline allowable emotions for my body to feel. I needed to stop the zap to the pit of my stomach every time our eye contact held too long or we touched or he flashed me a two-dimple smile. Every moment of it felt devastating; this strong physical reaction to someone wasn't something I'd experienced since my earliest crushes years ago. I found plenty of guys hot, and I felt hot for plenty of guys, but nothing immediate like this. No feelings over simple glances and brushes of skin. What a waste to feel something so rare for someone I couldn't wait to push out of my life.

"I think we should end on this positive note before one of us says something to screw it up," I said.

Alexei chuckled. "Good call." He opened the door, placing one foot outside of the car, then paused before sticking a hand out to me. Clearly, he had no reaction to our contact like I did. "Nice doing business with you."

I huffed a laugh, taking his hand and releasing it as quickly as possible. "Likewise, you dork."

His smile grew genuine, crinkling the corners of his eyes. He looked like he might say something more, but then he turned away from me, ducking his head as he exited the car. He tapped once on the roof giving me the all-clear to drive away, something I did without a second glance at him. Part of me loved the idea of navigating our conversations away from fraught topics. I wouldn't have to entertain questions about hockey or Justin or anything that seemed innocuous to him but carried too much weight for me.

But there was another part of me... the part that *felt* too much in his presence, that needed us to butt heads and talk about the topics he wanted to avoid, to see all of his warts and blemishes. I needed our arguments and silences to keep that small part from growing into something I couldn't contain. He had a reputation for a reason. The more I knew him, the more my opinion of him would cement and stop my basic human instincts from running wild.

I hoped.

The next night, Gemma came to my room to see if I wanted to go out to dinner with her. She nestled into my bed and beneath my covers. There was no way either of us was getting dressed to leave the house, despite Gemma's best intentions.

"Matt's not home?" I asked.

"No, he's at Volk's. They have a whole postgame ritual."

I muscled my way to a proper sitting position. "Oh, do tell."

Gemma waved a hand. "It's not a big deal. They sit in the hot tub and order pizza. They claim it helps with recovery."

I laughed. "Pizza helps with recovery?"

"How would I know?" she asked. "Do you know what I like most about hockey, Kennedy? It's after someone scores, and the men all hug each other. Besides that, I've got nothing."

I leaned into her and sank back into the bed. "I like that too, you know."

"Volk is under the impression you hate hockey."

I looked up to find her gaze on me, but I struggled to read the expression on her face. "I grew out of it. Besides, I like annoying him."

"You have an interesting way of annoying him," Gemma said as she ran her fingers through a section of my hair, smoothing it behind my ear. "*I* don't often sit in the laps of my enemies."

My face flushed at the memory I wished Matt and Gemma would forget. Alexei and I agreed to pretend it never happened; it seemed rude it wasn't automatically plucked from the minds of others. "I was proving a point to him."

"That he wants to have sex with you?" Gemma asked, her voice shaking with laughter. "Because—"

I pushed away from her. "No—"

I tried to interrupt but Gemma kept talking, fighting to get the words out through her laughter.

"I thought you already established that when he tried to make a bet with you."

I rolled my eyes. "That was a joke."

"If that's also how you describe his reaction to you the other night, I'd keep it to yourself." Gemma rose from the bed, then flicked her hair out of her face. "I've found men can be very self-conscious when it comes to their penises."

"Gemma!" I shouted, bringing my hands up to cover my face.

She grinned at me. "Kens, he's hot. If I were you, I would've dragged him out of the house and—"

I plugged my ears and sang *la-la-la-la*. When her lips stopped moving, I removed my hands from my ears. "Again, I have to ask. Is Matt okay with the unhinged affection you have for Alexei?"

Gemma smirked. "Please. I've told him my hotness ranking of all his teammates."

"Oh my God."

"What? He needs to know I have options. It helps him stay on his game."

"As if he needs a reminder. He's obsessed with you."

Gemma shrugged, pinning me with an expression that said it all. *It can't be helped.* "Did Alexei tell you about the newest Wolf?"

"Alexei and I are not actually dating, Gem. So no." Although Alexei and I did have a coffee date this morning, and he hadn't mentioned anything to me.

Gemma slipped her phone out of the back pocket of her jeans, unlocked it, then held it out to me. "Emil Clark got hurt, so they had to call up—"

"I know who Zach Briggs is," I said, looking at the baby-faced kid on Gemma's phone. Light freckles across his cheeks, brownish-blonde hair, not a trace of facial hair.

The Wolves picked Zach Briggs first in the draft last year. I sat with my mom at the arena, watching it on the jumbotron with season ticket members. The crowd cheered when the announcement was made—this fan base thought he would save the team. When he walked onto the stage with an enormous grin on his face, I couldn't help but think how it was an awful lot of pressure to put on a gangly, eighteen-year-old kid who'd sat in a high school math class a week before being handed a million-dollar contract.

But then I saw him play. He skated with such ease, faster than many players, and he had this uncanny ability to find weak spots on the ice at the right time. Even though other players had the height advantage, he charged his way fearlessly toward the goal, positioning himself to chip in pucks, bumping elbows with guys who weighed fifty pounds more than him. Often, he won those battles.

Zach Briggs was the real deal. The fan base didn't love that he hadn't made the roster right away, but management hadn't wanted to rush his development. He was their future.

"Right," she said with a nod. "Of course you do. Well, because Emil's injury turned out to be worse than they thought, Zach is staying with the team. Living with none other than your man."

I laughed, loud and obnoxious. "What wonderful human can I thank for this development?"

"Alexei volunteered to take Zach in," Gemma said, tilting her head from side to side. "Zach could be sent back to the AHL at any time, and Alexei offered his house so Zach wouldn't have to live at a hotel when they were in Palmer City."

"I will need to see this to believe it," I told Gemma.

Alexei volunteering to help the future star of this franchise shocked me. From everything I knew, Zach receiving any bit of the spotlight would land him on Alexei's shit list rather than as his roommate. Although hitching his ride to a future star of the team could endear him to the fan base and show all those other teams—the ones he would prefer to play for—he could be a good teammate. Alexei was nothing if not strategic.

"Better catch them before Sunday when they take off for a week."

"Sunday. Right." I sent myself a reminder by email.

Gemma laughed and shoved against my shoulder. "You're a terrible girlfriend." When my face fell, she added, "Come on, it was a joke, Kens."

Except now, I realized, Alexei housed a teammate who might notice just how terrible I was. I groaned internally at the thought of stepping up my game to convince him our relationship was real.

15

ALEXEI

ZACHARY BRIGGS CLOMPED DOWN the steps, sneakers untied as he dragged his suitcase behind him. It had been three days since I came home to find him sprawled on my couch, clutching a game controller and shouting obscenities. I considered dragging him out by his ear, but I didn't think anyone would approve of that. Deandra texted *You keep making my job easier* after finding out I asked Zach to move in. I hadn't made the offer to gain brownie points with the organization, team, or fans. The lad looked sad waiting alone for an Uber to drive him back to the hotel, and I had an extra room in my house. After finding out that the fans wanted to hear about our living situation, I had to find a way to make it work.

So instead of tossing Zach out on his ass that day, I walked upstairs without saying a word.

Ignoring the problem lasted less than a day.

Zach took up residence in front of the TV, playing video games every moment he wasn't at the rink or sleeping. One night, his yelling forced me awake. Downstairs in his usual spot, his eyes remained glued to the screen in a dazed kind of way. The room around him was in total chaos—a half-eaten pizza in an open box, two empty beer bottles on their sides beside an open bag of chips, crumbs in front, as if he'd pulled chips from the bag without looking. A singular sock was beneath his naked feet.

I wasn't proud about what I screamed at him, but it, along with new guidelines I established the following day, improved the situation to a livable level. Zach didn't need to know my threat to kick him out wasn't real.

"You have everything?" I asked, leaning against the counter. My bags had been packed since last night for our three-game, week-long trip—the first of the season.

"Think so," he said, plopping the bag at my feet. He unzipped it and riffled inside as he announced everything in there. Unnecessary, but at least Zach wouldn't get to the airport and remember he left something at the house.

Training him felt like housebreaking an animal. Whenever we needed to leave the house together, I told him to be at the door fifteen minutes before the time we needed to leave. So far, he hadn't been late.

"You know, I have been on road trips before," Zach said indignantly after we confirmed he had everything.

I opened the front door, what I planned to say dying behind my lips when I saw Kennedy standing there, about to ring the bell.

"Oh. Hey." She took a step back, retracting her outstretched hand to steady the carton carrier with four coffee cups. She looked as if she came from the gym, wearing stretchy blank pants and an oversized T-shirt. Her hair was twisted on top of her head in a loose bun. "On your way out already?"

"He has a thing about being late," Zach chimed in behind me. Glancing over my shoulder, I glimpsed his shit-eating grin. We usually arrived at practice thirty minutes before everyone else. It gave the lad and me more time on the ice, which he loved as much as I did. But still, he enjoyed giving me shit.

Zach nudged me to the side as he approached Kennedy, who knowingly stared at me. She'd learned about my pet peeve when she showed up ten minutes late to our coffee date earlier this week.

"Is one of those coffees for me?"

I tapped him lightly on the back of the head. "Manners."

Kennedy thrust the carton toward him as she said to me, "It's fine. I brought them for both of you. Matt said you usually grab coffee before jumping on the plane."

"Thank you," I said, taking the coffee with my name on it. She took the time to collect our orders from Matt. If this had been a real relationship, this gesture would have meant a lot. I took the small win anyway, remembering how every interaction between us used to be a shitshow.

Since that day we decided to create our list of safe and no-go topics, everything had become surprisingly easy.

This is a ridiculous list, I texted Kennedy immediately after she sent hers. My no-go list contained what I considered normal items—past relationships and every interaction between Kennedy and me before that day—while she listed hockey first. I expected to see Justin Ward listed—he was second—but didn't expect a moratorium on my entire sport.

I play hockey, I texted, then without waiting for her answer added, People will expect you to know about my job.

In my head, I could hear her response, Fine, hockey only as it pertains to you, with an exhale of breath in that bored, annoyed voice of hers. She wanted to make sure I couldn't ask her about her outright refusal to come to a single game. Before the list, I considered it, even though I stood no chance of getting a real answer.

Her list of safe topics was arguably strange, filled with weird hypothetical questions, some oddly specific. She also added topics she liked to discuss, like true crime and mystery novels. Our safe topics lists didn't overlap much, not as much as our no-go topics, so the hypotheticals came through on our coffee date. We debated the existence of ghosts, designed our own national holidays, and talked about how we would handle a zombie apocalypse.

Kennedy cleared her throat, bringing me back into the present. "Kennedy, this is Zach Briggs. Briggsy, this is Kennedy."

Zach swallowed a large gulp of coffee. "Good to put a face to my emergency contact."

The McIntyres had kept Kennedy late all week, so Zach hadn't met her, but I programmed her number into his phone in case he needed someone and I wasn't there. He'd met Gemma and Matt, but Kennedy, as my girlfriend, was on the hook to coparent this adult child until he knew whether he was staying or going back to the AHL.

Kennedy flashed him one of her genuine smiles, the kind that didn't tense her face. The kind so rarely offered to me, at least in a nonmocking manner. "It's always nice to meet anyone who can get under this guy's skin."

"Then, you must be happy meeting most people."

"O-kay, note to self to keep you two apart," I said, rummaging in my suit pocket to find my keys. I unlocked the car doors. "Zach, go to the car. I'll be there in a second."

Zach rolled his eyes but followed my direction. "Thanks for the coffee, Kennedy," he said over his shoulder as he walked toward the driveway.

I watched him place his suitcase in the trunk before climbing into the passenger seat. Once he was out of earshot, I said, "Nice touch with the coffee."

She lifted her hand, palm up, as if to say it wasn't a big deal. "My gym is next to a coffee shop, and I needed to refuel after my kickboxing class."

"Did you go overboard because you imagined my face?"

A weird expression passed over hers. "Not exactly." She paused like she wanted to say something more but went another way. "I don't want to make you *late*. Just wanted to meet Zach and wish you luck."

"We don't need luck," I told her. "If we play our game, the rest will take care of itself. We're that good."

"I meant on the flight." Her words sounded serious, but a smile poked through her blank expression.

"Ha ha." I stepped closer to her, mindful of Zach watching us. Kennedy's eyebrows rose, but I didn't give her time to react, closing the distance and wrapping my arms around her. She inhaled sharply at our first contact, but slowly exhaled after a beat. She smelled of vanilla and orange even after a workout. She also looked good, which defied the laws of nature. "I'll see you when I'm back, all right?"

She stepped back. "Yep, for the Wolves annual Halloween party. I'm still surprised you're wasting your one team-sanctioned event with me for this. It's not even public."

"Exactly," I said, grasping onto this explanation and pushing aside the one lingering in the back of my mind. The words she said the first night we met. "It seems more natural."

"I guess the one-month mark seems as good as any," she said with a shrug.

Right. Sometimes I forgot that next week would be four weeks since her father's party. *Four weeks.* The me from a month ago would barely recognize this life—hamming it up with a girlfriend for the cameras, taking in a kid, playing the best hockey I had in years. Relaxed.

Maybe things would work out as I hoped, even if it looked different than I thought.

16

KENNEDY

Each morning of my Alexei-free week followed the same routine—snooze my alarm three times, force myself out of bed, run outside until I couldn't breathe, shower, dress for work, and shovel down a bowl of cereal before shuffling out the door.

It wasn't unlike my routine before Alexei entered my life. It took only two days for that thought to drive me a bit mad. Agreeing to fake-date Alexei meant I could cross off the last item on my list—*Take a risk*—but disappointingly, I stared at the remainder of the list, realizing that after a month, I'd accomplish nothing else.

Get Happy

- Move out
- Finish college
- Pick a career??
- Dye hair
- Learn to cook
- Paaaaaaarty
- Risk something

I supposed next week's Halloween party meant I could cross off another item, but as much as going to a party with my fake boyfriend *technically* made progress, it wouldn't change my life. It certainly wouldn't—and hadn't—make me happy.

And yet, when I chose another item to complete to make myself feel like I had done *something*, I chose the easiest one.

On the day the Wolves returned from their road trip, I stood under the hot shower, watching blue hair dye circle the drain.

It had taken four hours to add midnight blue to my hair—a commitment by itself, but while I sat in the chair, I promised myself I would tackle something substantive next time. I would start easy by making a call to the admissions office for the University of Palmer City, UPC, and see what I would need to do to finish my degree. Knowing the information didn't mean I had to act on it. And just because this list existed, it didn't mean I had to finish it quickly… or at all.

That was one benefit of being left behind. I no longer had anyone to answer to.

At the insistent ringing of the doorbell, I picked up the pace and dried myself as quickly as possible. My damp legs strained as I hopped around, trying to slide into jeans. More effort than my actual workout.

The doorbell rang again. "Coming!" I shouted, though I had no idea if they could hear me. I tossed on a T-shirt, forgoing a bra in my haste. It wasn't like I was going to leave the house—let's be real, though, sometimes that didn't stop me—and my boobs weren't so large they'd be distracting in this baggy shirt anyway. When I finally reached the front door, I glanced into the peephole to see Zach Briggs, jabbing at his phone screen and frantically talking to himself.

"Oh thank God! Where have you been? I've been calling you!" Zach's breath came out in pants. He dropped the phone to his side and focused on me with wild eyes. "Do you have a fire extinguisher?"

"What?"

"A fire extinguisher." He motioned with his hands the action of taking down flames. "There's a fire... I didn't mean to but... Volk said if he wasn't around, I could call you, and then you didn't answer, so I sprinted over—"

I moved quickly to the kitchen and grabbed the extinguisher, not wanting to waste another second if there was, in fact, a raging fire in Alexei's house. Zach sprinted back to the house as soon as I reappeared in the doorway. Despite my aching legs, I followed, running through the door Zach held open for me and directly into the kitchen. No fire alarms blared, but flames leaped out of something on the stovetop that was impossible to see thanks to an impressive amount of smoke. I didn't waste more than a second before stepping toward the flames and pulling back the pin, raining foam until all that remained was the smoke of a dead fire.

Zach moved tentatively toward the oven. "Whoa, that was—"

"What were you thinking leaving the house with a full-ass fire raging?"

His eyes grew wide in surprise because I yelled at him. Or, I hoped, from the realization of how stupid it was to leave a fire brewing on the stovetop without doing a thing.

"I didn't know where the extinguisher was, and you didn't answer your phone—"

"Ever think of calling the fire department?" I asked. I was surprised Alexei didn't have a sophisticated security system like Gemma and Matt, one that called the fire department automatically after the fire alarm beeped for longer than a minute. Over the top of us, I spotted the smoke detector hanging from the ceiling and pointed. "Did you do that?"

Zach's ears turned full-on red. "Volk can't find out. He'll kick me out, and I'll have to go back to the hotel, and I *hated* living all alone there. Plus, he has so many video games. I don't want to leave the video games."

I continued to glare at him, taking a moment to absorb the word vomit hurled my way.

"Please don't tell. Please."

"You think he won't find out with this mess?" I waved my arm around the kitchen. Alexei's house looked otherwise pristine, and I had zero faith Zach could hide what happened. "Good luck with that."

Zach followed me to the front door, but instead of closing it, he trailed me straight through it. I continued walking past the three houses separating our temporary residences. Once we reached the door, I spun to face him, causing us to collide. He was considered on the shorter side for hockey but still had several inches on me.

"What are you doing?" I asked, narrowing my eyes. Did he think he could torch Alexei's place, then move his destruction someplace new?

"I... can I stay here for a few minutes?" Zach asked. His expression screamed lost puppy, and dammit if it didn't pull at my heartstrings. "Please."

I blew out a breath. "Fine."

Zach quickly moved inside once the door opened, as if he didn't want to risk getting shut out. Almost immediately, I wished I'd shut the door in his deceptively innocent face.

"What were you looking at?" he asked.

He snatched the laptop off the counter where I left it before my show-er. Deandra had emailed a link to a tweet gaining considerable attention, thanking Alexei and me for keeping up the good work. It looked to contain a postgame interview Alexei gave while on the road. My curiosity had niggled at me since I saw the email, but I didn't care so much I couldn't shower the sweat off first.

I'd planned to watch it as I air-dried and snacked as a means of emotional support for whatever awaited me in that interview. So much for that.

"Zach, no, give it back."

Zach held the computer away from me as I tried to seize it from him. "Ooh, watching Volk's interview, I see."

I rolled my eyes at his childish tone. "I'm dating Alexei," I said, surprised at how easily the words rolled off my tongue. "It's hardly breaking news I would watch his interviews."

He placed the laptop back where he found it, the joke losing its luster when the object of it didn't react. "Soo... you're really the owner's daughter?"

I leaned against the counter. "Yes."

"Cool, cool," Zach said with two quick bobs of his head. "Can you put in a good word for me?" His question surprised me so much I could only stare. Zach Briggs, a first-round draft pick and predicted future savior of this franchise, wanted me to... what? Tell my father he was a nice guy who absolutely did not almost burn his teammate's house to the ground? After I took too long to answer, Zach hurriedly added, "That'd be, like, obvious, wouldn't it? Forget it."

"It's cool if I stay?" he asked almost immediately, before turning from me and rummaging through the cabinets. "Oh shit, there's cookies!"

"If you eat all my cookies, I will kick you out."

He took a bite of one, then pouted with the half-eaten cookie hanging from his mouth. After he finished it, he said, "Fine. Let's order pizza. You like pizza?"

Zach's ping-ponging thoughts brought a smile to my lips. I knew he probably drove Alexei up a wall. "Yes, of course I like pizza."

I didn't love the idea of eating pizza after I suffered through a grueling workout, but Zach seemed to need the win after his disastrous afternoon. He held steadfast to his preference for an everything pizza, which I could not handle, so we ordered two pies. The good thing about living with and in the vicinity of hockey players was that we were never at risk of wasting food.

"You going to play the interview?" Zach asked once we stopped quibbling over our pizza order and had thirty minutes to burn before it arrived. "The suspense is killing me."

"You haven't watched it?"

"None of the guys watch that stuff. Why are you watching?"

"A friend sent it to me. I assume I'm mentioned."

Before I could stop him, Zach pressed play. "Then we have to watch."

On screen, Alexei sat in front of a black background covered in Wolves logos and team sponsors. Strands of sweat-soaked hair matted to the top of his forehead. His dark eyes looked the size of saucers, but after a win, that kind of adrenaline and euphoria was expected. That smile of his—the one I couldn't take—slipped off his face as soon as he heard the question.

"Volk, since Justin Ward's trade, he's been taking shots at you online. Yesterday he posted about being focused on winning hockey games and not nailing someone's leftovers."

Alexei ground his jaw, his mouth forming one thin unhappy line. I wanted to know what thoughts were flashing through his mind at that precise moment. Was it his hatred of Justin, frustration at the media for asking the question, or anger at me for causing this entire situation?

"What would you say to him?"

Alexei leaned forward to the mic. "Some of us can win the hockey games while also keeping our women satisfied. Might be how his girlfriend ended up with me."

My mouth fell open. What. The. Fuck?

Zach laughed, one hand smacking the counter in his merriment. "Sick burn, dude."

A chorus of *Oohs* ran through the reporters. Alexei Volkov had delivered them a sound bite that would make all of their stories. The tweet had over 150 comments, 1,000 retweets, and 8,000 likes. No wonder Deandra jumped for joy. Scrolling through the comments revealed most people sided with Alexei, but a small, strong minority thought Justin Ward had been done dirty by both the team and me.

"Um, no. Not sick burn, dude," I said, clicking pause on the video. "What the hell is he doing saying shit like that?"

Zach's laughing ebbed. "Was he wrong?"

I leveled him with a look. "Don't make me kick you out."

His laughter resumed, and I did think about kicking him out. In my deal to fake-date Alexei, nobody said anything about babysitting his kid roommate after preventing him from burning Alexei's property. But then Zach grinned, and he looked like such a kid, giving me a glimpse of what it would have been like to have a petulant younger brother.

"I'd love to see you try. I might not be as tall as your boyfriend, but good luck getting me to leave. Especially when pizzas are about to get here." *Aboot.* Canadian accents were so cute.

I didn't think I'd get used to people describing Alexei Volkov as my boyfriend, which, I guess, wasn't a problem since I only had to pretend for three months. Although, after he told the press about *keeping me satisfied*, he might not live that long.

Zach played the clip again, laughing gleefully, as if he hadn't heard the joke before. Meanwhile, I texted the link to Alexei followed by What the hell, Volkov?

We hadn't seen each other since he got back, but we already had plans for our next engagement—the team Halloween party in three days.

Alexei's response came almost immediately. I didn't post that.

But you said it, I fired back. I don't want the world (and my DAD) to think I'm sleeping with you.

This man seriously had the balls to respond. Why not? It's a step up.

I sent him a GIF of a girl clicking a button on her remote with the word MUTE flashing on the screen. The rational part of me knew Alexei had only done what we agreed, but I hated people knowing this much about my personal life. Even if it was fake. And couldn't he have put it another way? Sure, his snappy response made for a perfect sound bite, but he should have considered how it characterized me. Not that it mattered if people thought I jumped from one hockey player's bed to another. I could do whatever I wanted, and it was no one's business.

Except we'd made it everyone's business.

Which was the real source of my problem, though I preferred taking it out on Alexei.

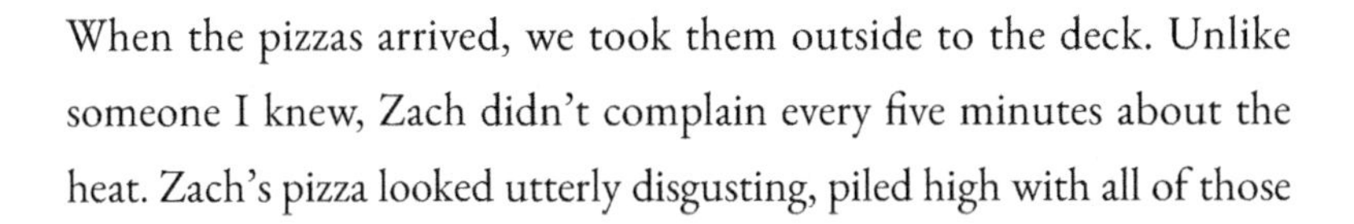

When the pizzas arrived, we took them outside to the deck. Unlike someone I knew, Zach didn't complain every five minutes about the heat. Zach's pizza looked utterly disgusting, piled high with all of those toppings, but at least it kept him distracted enough to not cause more destruction.

"How'd you end up living with Alexei?" I asked, pretending I didn't know to verify what Gemma told me.

"He offered, and I'm new to the team. And living in hotels gets old fast."

"In other words, you didn't have another option?"

Zach placed his pizza back on his plate, giving me his full attention. "I wouldn't want another option. Two years ago, I watched him play on TV and now we share the same ice. I live with him. It's wild."

Great, another Alexei Volkov fan. "It's not one of those *don't meet your hero* situations?"

Zach's eyebrows squished together in confusion. "You're dating the dude. You know what he's like."

I shrugged, trying to make light of my accusation since, you know, I was supposed to be feigning that I, too, was a megafan of Alexei. "We only just started dating. We don't know each other very well yet."

"I think what you see is what you get with Volk. He leads by example. He shows up early and leaves late. He pushes us without being a dick. People like him better."

I picked up my pizza slice, trying to ignore the way my heart pounded a little harder. "What do you mean?"

"Justin Ward wasn't everyone's favorite."

"Oh?" I asked around my bite of pizza, one hand covering my mouth.

Zach seemed oblivious to the way this subject had my haunches up. "Yeah, dude liked to give everyone shit. He worked hard, and he made sure you knew it. And he made you feel like shit for not keeping up. That's with his own team. You already know how the rest of the league feels about him."

I'd worried about Justin's reputation from the start, but only because he dated through the Wolves' staff. Sure, people thought he played dirty, but he was one of the best players in the league. I chalked the talk of Justin up to a mixture of testosterone and jealousy.

"No, I don't watch much hockey."

"Okay, we'll come back to that later," Zach said, pointing his slice of pizza at me. "Our fans liked him, but he's a rat and the rest of the league knows it."

The familiar instinct to defend Justin bubbled inside me, but he was no longer mine to defend. And why should I *want* to defend him after everything he put me through? He left me behind because he couldn't love me as I was. Sometimes, memories of the good moments snuck in between the cold hard facts. Like the first time I saw him six months after my mom died. He took me to a rage room to break shit, then held me as I cried. It was the least alone I'd felt since she passed.

"What's—" Zach stopped short, realization dawning on him. He fidgeted uncomfortably in his seat. "Oh shit, I forgot for a second."

Zach had serious skills of blocking out his surroundings and focusing on what was at hand. The fire at Alexei's house had become a thing of the past as soon as he saw the press conference clip. Maybe that was one of the reasons he succeeded in hockey.

"The team is better off without him?" I asked, remembering Alexei's claims. I initially dismissed them. Justin put up good numbers year after year, but the team failed to reach the playoffs each of the last five years. With someone so talented in their ranks, it raised the question of *why* they couldn't win when it mattered.

Zach hesitated a moment, but I held his gaze, silently communicating I wanted the truth. "I've only been here for a week, but from the stories I've heard... I'd say you traded up."

I shook my head. "It's not like that. We met by accident."

"I didn't… I didn't mean *that*. Just that Volk's the real deal. You've chosen well."

Goosebumps sprouted on my forearms. I needed to change the subject. Fast. "You seeing anyone?"

Zach's shoulders sagged, tension leaking out of them at the subject change. Funny, I would have thought pushing the conversation back to him would have caused the opposite reaction. "Nah. It's hockey season. I'm trying to keep up with this team. I don't have time for distractions."

If only my life could be that simple.

17

KENNEDY

My phone vibrated loudly on the kitchen table as I heard the garage door open. Come over. Your boy needs you tonight.

"Kennedy, we won!" Connie's voice followed by Rich's hushing reached me a second before I saw them. Rich shouldered much of Connie's weight as they walked through the house in matching forest green Wolves jerseys. "Volk got a hat trick, and we shut the other team out. It was amaaaazing."

Rich shifted Connie to his other arm and covered his wife's ears. He motioned with his head to the stairs. "I'm going to get my lovely, drunk wife to bed. Thanks for watching the kids tonight, Kennedy."

I waved a hand. "Of course. I'm glad you both had fun."

"Oh, and tell Volk to keep that winning streak going," he said, flashing me a smile.

I knew about the winning streak because I started to pay attention to Wolves hockey again after Deandra sent the clip from Alexei's press conference a couple of days ago. I wouldn't be blindsided by something like that again. Every morning after I snoozed my alarm, instead of catching an extra ten minutes of sleep, I read a recap of the Wolves' game, watched new interviews with Alexei, and scanned comments on the Wolves' social media accounts. I tried not to think too closely about it.

This new practice of mine revealed the Wolves started the season strong after a shaky preseason. And their attendance numbers reflected it. Everyone loved a winner.

By the time I grabbed my phone, I already had another text from Zach.

Stop ignoring me.

Following the near house-burning situation, Zach and I slipped into what felt like the beginning of a friendship. Mostly, it revolved around food, but many friendships had started with less. He stopped by after practice sometimes to eat from my stash of chocolate chip cookie sandwiches and to watch online videos, usually of people doing stupid things.

What's wrong? I asked, immediately regretting it. Because if I were dating Alexei, I should have known. Hopefully, Zach would believe Alexei's pride kept him from telling me. He might lack a bit of common sense when it came to practical matters, but Zach was more perceptive than he seemed.

Come over and ask him yourself.

I responded by sending him a GIF of a person giving the middle finger, then followed up with On my way. If I didn't go, Zach would doubt my commitment to Alexei. Before jumping in my car, I quickly brushed my hair and changed into a backup T-shirt, one that didn't smell like spit-up. It wasn't as if I cared what Alexei thought about my appearance, but I did need to impress upon Zach that I did. My rational brain wholeheartedly accepted this explanation, and yet, as I got closer to his house, my heart rate steadily rose.

Zach opened the door before I knocked. "Took you long enough," he said, pushing the door open wider so I could enter.

"I was at work when you texted," I grumbled. "It's only been, like, fifteen minutes."

"Well, it felt longer." We both fell silent, still in the foyer. "Do you need me to show you to his room?"

I cocked my head to the side, tossing him an annoyed look. "I think I can manage to find it."

Zach nodded, satisfied enough to head back to his video game as I made my way upstairs. Alexei's room didn't take long to find since all the others were open. I knocked lightly on the closed door at the end of the hall.

"Zach, I told you I'm not in the mood for video games!" Alexei shouted.

By the time he finished his answer, I had opened the door so he could see I wasn't Zach. Before he could get a word out, I blurted out, "Oh my God, what happened to you?"

Alexei lay shirtless against the headboard, a fact which would have been distracting in and of itself, but the dark bruise forming over his ribs and the red slash across his cheek captured my attention. He jerked into a sitting position and muted the TV. "Kennedy, what are you doing here?"

"I heard you needed your girlfriend tonight," I told him as I shut the door behind me.

"Briggsy needs to mind his own damn business."

The annoyance in his voice made me hesitate. Maybe he didn't want me here at all. "Should I go?"

He shook his head slightly, his dark brown hair swaying with the motion. "No."

I shouldn't have felt relieved he wanted me to stay, but it was there, right alongside anxiety. Staying with him felt like a risk I couldn't afford, but I wouldn't leave, not unless he asked.

"Well, if you need help or to talk or whatever, you could've called me," I said, still standing in front of the closed door.

"The hockey is off-limits." *The* hockey. I loved when he tossed in that *the*.

"Maybe we can set that aside for tonight? You look sad and bruised. You deserve a win."

He grinned at me, both dimples popping. "Already got one."

"Right, the hat trick. Congratulations."

He raised his eyebrows.

"My employers told me when they got home from the game tonight. So are you going to tell me what happened?"

I moved toward him, the compulsion to comfort him an instinct I didn't anticipate.

"Hockey."

"Ha ha," I said, hovering at the end of his bed, not allowing myself to move any closer.

At this distance, I saw a pretty array of bruises blossoming along the ribs on the other side of his body as well. I quickly looked away, not wanting to give Alexei the satisfaction of knowing how closely I had looked. But I already saw more than enough; I wouldn't be able to forget any time soon how much I wanted to run my hands down his lean chest and sculpted abdomen.

I swallowed, reminding myself that however good he looked, I did not need him or his arrogance in my life. Our proximity was temporary. I only needed to get through another two months, then I wouldn't have to ever see him again. At least not like this.

"Seriously, what happened?" I pressed.

Alexei told me how he and one of the opposing players ended up dropping the gloves and punching each other senseless tonight. The fight broke out when the opposing player cross-checked Alexei after he went for a loose puck near the goal.

"I'll be fine," he said, but the grimace he tried to hide as he shifted told me he was in more pain than he would let on.

That was when I realized my gaze had drifted to his body again. *Shit.* I quickly looked up to meet his eyes, and the little gleam there told me he knew exactly what I'd been doing. Thankfully, he didn't call me out on it. Maybe he didn't have the energy.

"Just need to rest up before our game tomorrow."

"Don't you need more time than that?" I asked, walking as close to him as I could without getting into the bed. "What if you get more injured?"

Alexei grinned at me. "I didn't know you cared."

"I don't... I'm only here to keep up appearances."

"With Briggsy?"

"Yeah. And Matt. He knows I'm a very caring person."

"Funny, I haven't seen that side of you."

I swatted his arm, and Alexei raised his eyebrows as if to say, *I rest my case.*

"So if this were real, what would you do?"

For the second time tonight, my mouth went so dry I involuntarily swallowed. The question felt intimate with only the two of us in Alexei's bedroom. My gaze roamed over his taut, tanned chest before lowering to his abdomen, appreciating the definition in each muscled ridge.

If this were real and Alexei hadn't been mocking me, I would have climbed into his lap and made him forget all about the fight.

The way he was jutting out his chin at me, it felt like he could hear every unsavory thought. I had to put him on the defensive. I kneeled one leg on the mattress, making sure my leg grazed his, then leaned toward him to do what I'd fantasized about earlier. My hand traveled from his scruffy jaw, down his neck, over his torso, feeling the hard muscles in his chest and abdomen, liking the way they clenched in response to my touch.

Alexei's breathing hitched, the sound so sexy, I realized too late this game I was playing with him wasn't good for me either. Because I liked the feel of him under my fingertips. I relished the power I had, the way I could affect his breathing with such simple action.

I hated the weak part of me that wanted him to touch me back.

"Too bad you'll never know," I whispered, my mouth mere inches from his.

Before I could pull back, Alexei grabbed my wrist. "We never did make that bet, did we?"

I rolled my eyes and tried to get myself under control, but when I spoke, my voice came out breathless. "You wish, hotshot."

Alexei dropped my hand, then cleared his throat. I pulled back from the bed, and turned to walk out the door.

He called out, "I don't think you should leave yet."

I felt the surprise of those words plunge into the pit of my stomach. I turned back around, waiting for his explanation.

"You're my girlfriend. He called you because he thought I needed you. It would look weird for you to leave right away."

I shrugged, suddenly itching to put distance between us. "Maybe you don't need me."

"In any way?" Alexei stared at me meaningfully.

I scoffed. "I'm not pretending to have sex with you for the benefit of your roommate."

"No— I wasn't—" Alexei cut himself off with a sigh. He roughly thrust a hand through his hair. "Just don't leave. Hang out here awhile. That's all I meant."

"Oh. Right. I guess I can do that." I looked around the room for somewhere to sit, but the options were limited. He didn't have any chairs, so it meant the floor or on the bed next to him. I ducked to settle against the foot of his bed when Alexei barked out a laugh.

"You're not sitting on the floor." He gestured to the space beside him.

"Only if you put a shirt on." The words flew out of my mouth before I could stop them.

"Whatever will make you comfortable." His haughty grin and teasing voice made me want to fall through the floor. After kicking him in the nuts, of course.

I slipped out of my shoes, then walked to the opposite side of the bed. Thankfully, Alexei was wearing a shirt by the time I settled on the edge, as far from him as I could be without falling onto the floor. Alexei laughed quietly at the massive distance I left between us.

But all I could focus on was getting through this time together.

I would do whatever was necessary, even if it revealed more of my weakness than I would have liked.

18

ALEXEI

"I'M NOT GOING TO jump you, if that's what you're worried about."

Kennedy parked herself on the edge of the bed, one shuffle away from falling on her ass. After her little show, I didn't expect this display of modesty, as if she needed to make it any clearer nothing would ever happen between us. Her message had landed each of the hundred times she said it, including no less than five minutes ago.

She crossed her arms over her chest as her cheeks turned a bit pink. "I'm not worried about that."

"Is there another reason you're hovering on the edge of the bed then?"

"I'm not." She made a show of looking over and discovering she might fall off the bed with the slightest movement. She shifted toward me, still leaving significant space between us. "I didn't realize."

I nodded, pretending to agree, but only because if I pushed more, the tenuous peace between us might snap. Pushing Kennedy's back against the wall had backfired more than once. Doing it figuratively or literally—something I couldn't stop thinking about now that I had her in my room—would send us back to each other's throats.

I grabbed a strand of her hair. "I like the new color. Even if it isn't one of ours." She'd dyed it darker than her natural brown and added blue, which changed shades as her hair moved in the light. Not everyone could pull off a color this bold, but it suited her fair skin so well, she might as well have been born with it. "Something you've wanted to do for a while or spur of the moment?"

Her gaze remained on my hand holding a lock of her hair. "It was time for change." She definitely didn't remember what she said in the backyard at the season-opening party then.

I released the strand of hair. "So what would you be doing if the wunderkind hadn't texted you?"

She blinked. "That doesn't bother you?"

"What? Briggsy texting you?"

I knew that Briggsy contacting her saved my house and our new rookie from burning up in a grease fire. Like most people who travel, I had installed cameras. When I got home from a massage appointment and found my house smelling like smoke and my pan burnt to an unrecognizable crisp and buried under trash, I watched the security footage. On it, Zach left bacon cooking on the stovetop unattended, only coming back when the smoke alarm sounded and flames were sky high.

"No. That Zach is getting all this attention," she clarified.

I leaned back against the headboard, tilting my head her way and studying her expression. "Oh, you're serious? No, I don't give a shit. I had the attention before, and it's nice, but I've been on the opposite side of it. I'd rather stay clear."

"Except now you can't."

"No, not exactly."

"You blame me for that?" Kennedy fiddled with the hem of her shirt.

At one point, I might have blamed Kennedy, but that was because she was here and the real culprit wasn't. Besides, she'd fallen victim to Hurricane Ward as much as I had. It didn't seem fair to hold anything against her, even if it did keep my other feelings about her at bay. More than anything, though, I could tell she needed someone to be on her side.

"No, I blame your asshole ex."

Kennedy nodded once, then fell back against the headboard as well. "If I were home, I'd be watching TV."

"True crime?"

Her eyebrows shot up. "Yeah. How did you—" Kennedy stopped abruptly, a slow smile appearing on her face before she covered it with one of her hands. I learned about her true crime obsession that first night at Gemma and Matt's. The night my attraction to her became clear... to both of us. It wasn't as if finding Kennedy beautiful was new, but wanting her was something I hadn't let myself feel until she forced it on me when she landed in my lap.

"Pitch it to me."

"What?"

"Your best true crime story. We have to do something." I gestured around the room. What I would prefer to do was off the table. "Whoever pitches best, wins."

"And who will be the judge? It's just us here."

Trust me, I thought, *I don't need that reminder*.

"I think we can be adults about it and come to an agreement."

She batted her eyelashes at me. "And what will you be pitching me on? Backward baseball caps? The value of public insinuations about our relationship?"

"You're still harping on that?" I teased with a smirk.

She made a show of huffing loudly, but I could tell it was in good fun rather than actual annoyance.

"I'm going to pitch you hockey."

Kennedy stilled. "You don't need to pitch me hockey, Alexei."

"Why? You've made up your mind for all eternity?" I asked, not sure why I was pressing her. "I can't believe you find my sport boring. Brutal or hard to follow—"

"Alexei—"

"I bet I can make you change your mind." I grinned at her, bringing out both my dimples—something that never seemed to fail me with women in the past.

"You don't have to pitch me hockey because I used to love it," Kennedy said, fixing her gaze anywhere but on my face. "I never found it boring. I only said that to annoy you." She swallowed. "I actually used to work for the team. That's how Deandra and I know each other."

The heaviness of her confession eclipsed the victory of getting her to admit the truth. She shrugged as if it didn't matter, but I knew this went beyond trying to annoy me. I watched her intently, willing myself quiet, hoping she would tell me more.

Kennedy took a long inhale before continuing. "My dad bought the team for my mom because hockey was her favorite thing in the world... besides us. I remember when I was about eight, we went to a game for the first time, the three of us, and her eyes lit up the moment she saw the ice. My dad liked hockey, but I think he bought the team because he loved seeing her eyes light up like that.

"When we moved here, my mom and I watched every game together. The same seats, ten rows behind the Wolves bench. It was our thing, you know?" Her voice snagged on the last words, and she paused again before taking a deep breath. "She died last year."

The words landed like a punch to my gut. So much about Kennedy suddenly made sense, including my instinct that she was fucking sad, but not because of her breakup with Ward.

"Hey," I said, gently touching her shoulder. She turned toward me, eyes brimming with unshed tears. "I'm sorry. I didn't know. This is why you don't work for the team anymore?"

"It doesn't feel right... without her."

It meaning working for the Wolves, or watching games, or talking about the sport. She reached for her water bottle beside the bed. My hand dropped from her shoulder with the movement. The position felt so natural I'd forgotten it still lingered.

"I think... I stayed with Justin because he knew my history. Never questioned me until..."

I nodded my understanding. She didn't have to have this conversation to explain it... or any of her other life choices. Suffocating, uncomfortable silence filled the room. Kennedy stared blankly ahead. She hadn't wanted to talk about this—not tonight, not ever—so the least I could do was move the fuck on, try to get back the energy we had before I brought up a topic from our no-go list.

"Well, your pitch can't be any worse than that," I said, mentally crossing my fingers she wouldn't see it as insensitive.

Kennedy let out a snort-laugh. I looked over to find her shoulders no longer bunched up to her ears. She wiped a stray tear from her cheek, then turned her head against the headboard to meet my gaze. She held eye contact, for one beat and then another, extending far longer than usual.

Maybe it made me an asshole, but all I could think about was leaning forward and capturing her bottom lip in mine. My stomach clenched in anticipation, the feeling strong enough, I had to look away before I acted on it. The last thing she wanted after a confession like that was a guy coming on to her.

And from me, she never wanted that.

I tapped her knee. "Come on. I'll let you pitch while we get food."

"You can cook?" Kennedy asked, sitting on one of the counter stools, watching as I collected ingredients and cooking utensils.

I glanced over my shoulder, suppressing a wince with the movement. "When the occasion calls for it."

"And what's the occasion?"

I could hear the smile in her voice, half the reason I brought us down here.

"Your big pitch. What else?"

She laughed. "What are you making?"

"Blinis," I told her as I moved over to her counter so she could watch. "Or what you would consider small pancakes. One of my favorite foods and perfect for this time of night."

"I love pancakes."

"Great," I said. "You can help me."

She remained where she sat, cocking her head to the side. "You know this counts, right?"

"What?"

"If we cook together, this becomes a date. Your final date of the month. Aside from the Halloween party, since that's a team event."

I shrugged, trying to snuff out my disappointment at the reminder that we were only here together because of our deal. This counted toward an allotment of time I could spend with her. I hadn't forgotten, but for a second, while we joked and laughed together, it didn't feel like pretending. "It's cute you think that'll affect me more than you."

She glared at me, but I continued as if I hadn't seen it.

"You can use it as an anecdote at the party tomorrow to show how I'm the greatest boyfriend to ever exist."

"Don't get ahead of yourself. I know nothing about cooking, so this is going to test your patience."

"I had to show Briggsy how to make pasta," I said, pushing the bowl toward her. "You can't be worse than him."

Together, we walked through the recipe, which was perfect for a beginner. It involved throwing a bunch of ingredients into a bowl and mixing or whisking at each step until the batter was ready to be cooked on the stovetop. I let her watch me add the first round of batter to the skillet.

"Have you ever heard of *The Nightstand*?" she asked as I flipped the first round of blinis. I shook my head. "Gregory Berk ring any bells?"

I smiled. "I don't watch true crime."

"Okay. Well, ten years ago, a woman died a couple of towns from here. Her husband was the only one there with her and he called 9-1-1."

"He killed her?" I surmised.

"That's the thing, it's unclear." Kennedy gestured animatedly with her hands. Her eyes tracked my movements, though, as I carefully moved the blinis to a plate. "He was charged with murder, but there were chain-of-custody issues with the evidence, so his conviction was thrown out. He was having an affair and she was the breadwinner, so a lot of people think he killed her for life insurance. Other people think she tripped and fell in the middle of the night because her sleeping pills disoriented her. Or someone broke in, maybe a person she knew or the husband's mistress, since there were no signs of forced entry."

"Wasn't he sleeping beside her?"

"They slept in separate bedrooms, and he wore a sleep apnea mask at night. It's *possible* he wouldn't have heard an intruder."

"What do you think?"

"I can't tell you that. Half the fun is hearing what other people think happened. Comparing notes." Kennedy stared at me expectantly. "Do you want to watch it?"

I wasn't a fan of the genre, but I did like the way it lit Kennedy's eyes. "You don't mind watching again?"

"Absolutely not."

I laughed at the immediacy of her answer. "All right. I'll give it a shot, but only if you can successfully make this last round of blinis."

She didn't hesitate and rose to the challenge. I leaned against the counter and slipped my hands into the pockets of my sweatpants. Even if she burned the shit out of these blinis, I would eat them without complaint.

19

ALEXEI

OPENING MY EYES THE next morning to Kennedy settled snugly against me did funny things to my chest.

Her eyes remained closed, her breath steady and slow. I allowed myself to watch her in this rare, unguarded moment. Kennedy's black-blue hair spread over my arm and onto the white pillow behind us, now covered in residual blue. She still wore the clothes from last night, a loose T-shirt over denim shorts that revealed toned legs. She fell asleep before she could remove her makeup, leaving a dark line beneath each eyelid. I smiled at the mismatched socks on her feet, one with blue and red stripes, the other gray with black stars. Not even close.

Last night, we let episode one continue into episode two, and before we knew it, we finished three episodes of the show. Kennedy hadn't oversold the mystery unraveling in front of us. I didn't know if I would have enjoyed it as much without her commentary or reactions, but now I needed to know how it ended. Especially after the twist that caused me to grab the remote to pause the show. "You're shitting me, right? He knew someone else who died in his bedroom?"

Kennedy grinned wide like a Cheshire cat. "Quite the twist, huh?"

I took a long drink of my soda, letting the bubbles soothe my parched mouth. "There's no way this guy didn't kill his wife."

She shrugged as she mimed that her lips were sealed.

"You think he's innocent then? Death by nightstand?"

Kennedy laughed, loud and unrestrained. No covering her mouth to hide the emotion this time. It complicated things, loving that sound as much as I did. "You'll have to wait and see."

"Want to keep watching? I don't have a media interview until ten, and it'll be better if I look wrecked for that anyway."

She rolled her eyes, but her smile remained. "You won't even have to imply we're banging then."

I swallowed hard, fixing a neutral expression to hide what those words did to me. *Christ*. I needed to get a grip.

Kennedy wasn't having the same dilemma as me. She easily drew the line between what was real and what was for show. She also continued to remind me she wasn't interested in me, despite our clear chemistry. Maybe all I could hope for was a temporary friendship, moments like last night when we could have fun together as we finished out this charade. I was in no shape for a relationship anyway, and I had a sneaking suspicion Kennedy had trouble with casual.

Kennedy's long eyelashes fluttered, pulling me out of my memories of last night. I forced my eyes shut.

"Oh shit," she muttered as she stirred against my chest and pushed herself off me.

I pretended to wake up for the first time. "What's wrong?"

"I… didn't mean to fall asleep here."

"It's fine," I said as I stretched. The arm Kennedy had lain on was asleep, but I refused to shift, liking the feel of her on me too damn much.

She didn't move quickly enough to disguise her watching of me. She sat frozen, mouth parted, eyes focused on a small, visible sliver of skin on my stomach that had been revealed by the movement. Dammit if it didn't feel good knowing Kennedy liked what she saw of me, even if she wouldn't admit it. She didn't hide it last night, either, when she barged into my room and saw me without a shirt for the first time.

The reminder would never get old.

"It helps our story anyway, right?" I added. "People expect us to stay the night with each other."

Kennedy cleared her throat, shifting her eyes to the wall. "Uh, yeah. I guess."

"I've got to get to the arena. You can hide up here until Zach and I leave."

She scoffed. "I don't need to hide."

I raised an eyebrow and challenged her. "You sure?"

Kennedy hopped out of bed. "Yes. I'll go make coffee while you get ready."

Warmth filled my chest. It took only one night with Kennedy to remind me of what I'd always wanted and never found. A simple relationship. Someone to share my life with. To wake up to in the morning, with a feeling of gratitude that they existed and chose me. Someone to do normal life stuff with, like eat breakfast and tell stories about our days.

"What? Do you not want me to touch your coffee machine or something?" she asked, watching me, her eyebrows pulled together in concern.

I shook my head. *This is fake.* I was starting to conflate my feelings of loneliness with desire for her. I barely knew her, and we were *pretending* to date, for fuck's sake. What was wrong with me? "No, it's fine. I'll... see you downstairs."

Kennedy stared in concern for a beat before leaving the room. I watched as she went because I was only human after all. She left the door ajar, so I could hear Zach's long strand of *oohs* as she descended the stairs. That kid had zero chill. Curiosity launched me out of bed. I wanted to hear Zach and Kennedy's conversation. I threw on a sweatshirt before following her.

Apparently, I also had zero chill.

"Look who's making a walk of shame this morning," Zach said.

"Shut up," Kennedy answered. I perched on the top step like a goddamn creep. "He's my boyfriend, you know."

Boyfriend. The word gripped my heart like a vise. This ten-day road trip couldn't come soon enough. I needed a break from Kennedy before I lost my mind.

Even if I could win her over, she deserved better than what I could offer. And it wasn't like she would be the person I needed either. We couldn't hide in true crime documentaries and barbs forever. A relationship meant sharing, and she didn't want to share. Hell, I didn't want to share either. We had a no-go topic list for a reason. Violating those terms last night led directly to this morning's conundrum. Never again.

A clanging sound rang out from the kitchen. "Yeah, but you never stay here."

"We just started dating." Kennedy sighed loudly. "Ugh, this isn't your business."

"A *you're welcome* wouldn't hurt, you know? I'm the reason you came over last night."

"If you don't shut up, I'm going to be the reason *you* have a black eye."

I walked down the stairs, stomping my feet louder than usual to signal my presence. "So violent," I said. "Should I expect this every morning?"

Kennedy froze, her empty hand midway to the coffee cup on the counter. She resumed movement after a second, but when she turned to me, I saw the question in her eyes. *What the hell are you saying, and why are you saying it?*

I'd tell you if I had any fucking clue. It was as if sleeping beside her, consuming her vanilla and orange scent all night had irreparably altered my brain chemistry.

"You're awfully confident I'll be back," she said as she strode toward me, a steaming coffee cup in each hand.

I flashed her a grin. "You mean you didn't have a good time last night?"

Zach put his hands flat over his ears. "*La-la-la*. I do not want to hear this."

Kennedy rolled her eyes at him. "Grow up, Briggsy." She stuck a to-go cup of coffee out to me.

Fucking hell. Why did she have to be considerate? I needed the Kennedy from the night at her father's house. Okay, not stupidly drunk, but the version of her who blamed me for Ward being traded. The version of her who cast immovable judgment on me. The version of her who didn't know me. I wished I could go back to the version of her I didn't know either.

"Thank you," I said, then I took a step forward, closing the distance between us, and placing my lips on hers before she could register the movement. Her soft lips tasted like cinnamon from the coffee she'd made. I kissed her because I needed to sell this relationship to Zach, but I also wanted to know what it felt like, hoped it would shatter the fantasy.

The kiss lasted only a few seconds, but in that time, the power of it coursed through me. I wanted to do it again and again and again. Enough times to get this stupid infatuation out of my system. She didn't want me, which made me want her. That had to be it. We all wanted what we couldn't have.

"I'll see you later for the party."

Kennedy bobbled her head. "Later... yeah."

"Zach, be ready in ten, all right?"

Zach saluted me, and we both ascended the steps. When I got back to my room, a text waited for me. What in the actual fuck was that?

Just playing my part, I texted back.

Being Kennedy's boyfriend was a role I'd slipped too far into. Nothing distance couldn't fix.

20

KENNEDY

MATT LET OUT A deep-bellied laugh when I entered the kitchen in my Halloween costume.

"Just how every woman wants to be greeted," I said as I approached the fridge to grab a bottle of water. "Really helps the self-esteem."

"I'm... s-sorry... Kennedy," he said, pushing out the words between his laughs. "It's... not... you."

I sipped my water, waiting for him to knock off his antics. Matt wore the bottom half of his Batman costume, the mask resting on the countertop in front of him. Gemma chose their costumes, opting for this one so she could don a skintight Catwoman bodysuit that made her look so good, it was honestly unfair.

"I take it Alexei didn't tell you what costumes he chose," I said. Due to our initial agreement, Alexei chose all of our dates, which meant he picked our couple's costume without input from me. The arrogant ass chose Little Red Riding Hood and the Big Bad Wolf as a *fuck you* to everyone who thought he'd preyed on me while I was in a vulnerable state, to all those people who caused us to embark on this fake relationship. "I told him it was a bit on the nose."

At least I looked good. The costume was sexy without showing too much skin. I wore boots over fishnet stockings. The red dress hit midthigh and showed no cleavage, but it perfectly hugged my curves. The finishing touches—long black gloves, a black bow for my neck, and the red hood that was not yet covering my wavy hair—would tie it all together.

Matt shook his head. "Why did you let him choose?"

I shrugged. "It's his party. I'm a plus-one. And I was feeling generous. He bought me baked goods."

"He already knows your weakness," Matt said with a teasing smile.

My stomach dropped at those words. I pushed away all that happened yesterday, as I had been doing since I left Alexei's house.

"I know his biggest weakness too." Alexei cared about hockey more than anything else; if I wanted to hurt him, all I needed to do was leave him to deal with his reputation problem and the media on his own.

Matt held up his hands in mock innocence. "Go easy on him, all right?"

"Wait—you're worried about *him*?" I asked.

Matt knew Alexei long before he ever knew me, but I thought he would take my side if it came down to it. Because I was his fiancée's best friend, but also because we had become friends this past year.

He folded his arms across his chest, some seriously impressive muscles bulging through the tight sleeves of his costume. "I've talked to him. He knows what's at stake if he hurts you."

"Oh," I said, fumbling with the fabric of my skirt. "Well... thank you."

He shrugged one shoulder as if it were nothing. "Of course I'll have your back until the end of time." Then he dropped his voice to a whisper. "I hope I never have to intervene. You seem good for each other."

I smothered my scoff. What did he base that on? The night Alexei and I tortured each other in their living room as we all watched a movie? A big part of me wanted an answer, but I let the cowardly part take the reins. "He's deadly to me," I said, pointing to my outfit.

Matt winked. "Right."

"Y'all ready?" Gemma called from the second floor. Matt and I turned toward the stairs to watch Gemma make her grand entrance, knowing her question was about that rather than our readiness to leave the house.

As if on cue, the doorbell rang a moment before Zach, dressed as a pirate, burst through without waiting for anyone to answer it. "Aye, mateys!" he shouted as he thrust a sword into the air. The maroon sleeve of his jacket slipped up his arm with the movement.

"Whoever gave him a sword was an idiot," I muttered.

"Watch what you say."

The deep, accented voice skittered down my spine. This morning, the reverberations of that voice had played against my skin before I could shove myself off his chest. The ungodly strong chest I'd slept against, warm and peaceful.

"You don't want to anger a wolf."

I refused to turn around. I knew I needed to, was expected to, and yet… I couldn't force myself to face those eyes that had stared at me with such tenderness when I told him about my mom. Alexei didn't hesitate to position himself behind me, his arms around my waist as he rested his head on top of mine.

"Everything okay?" he whispered in my ear, his scruff scratching against my skin. The warmth of his apple cinnamon scent enveloped me, bringing back every memory of yesterday that had played on repeat all day long.

I nodded vigorously, almost immediately, but… no. Those lips inches from my ear had been on mine.

Alexei Volkov *kissed* me.

The one kiss our agreement allowed him. A chaste kiss in front of one teammate without a camera in sight. I still had no idea what his angle was.

Waking up that morning felt good, a feeling that quickly changed to panic as my sleep-induced haze cleared, and I realized the chest I rested on belonged to Alexei. He seemed unaffected by my presence in his bed, while my internal organs were on the verge of combustion. And then in the kitchen, Alexei didn't do anything more than press his lips softly to mine, and it set my blood on fire. He tasted like mint and something undefinably him. I would never forget it.

When he'd pulled back, my instinct had been to surge forward to continue kissing him. When his eyes opened, and he met my stunned expression with a smirk, I had never been more thankful for keeping those base instincts at bay.

"You're breathing hard," he said into my ear. I could hear the teasing smile in his voice. "Nervous for tonight?"

Distantly, I heard other voices in the room, but I could only focus on Alexei's hand moving slowly against my stomach. It tightened as warmth pooled low in my gut. Not being able to step out of his encompassing embrace because of our audience meant I had to endure this agonizing torture.

Turning in his arms, I finally took in his costume. A patch of fur coated his chest in the gap left by his sleek dark suit jacket, which attached to a headpiece of fur topped by two wolf ears.

"You're dangerous," I said, locking eyes with him. "I'm supposed to be nervous."

That double-dimpled grin brought back the memory of him flashing one last night before he pitched me hockey. It had made me feel as I did now, like my stomach had been put through a blender. I'd desperately wanted to distract him enough that I talked about my mother, a topic I didn't discuss with *anyone*. I wondered if there was anything Alexei couldn't convince me to do with that grin.

His hand dropped to my hip while a finger from his other hand traced a path from my cheek, to my neck, down my arm. "You do look good enough to eat."

"You'd have to catch me first," I said, smirking. "Not likely, hotshot."

He laughed, picking up a strand of my hair and twirling it around his finger. "Oh, Kennedy, don't you know that's the beauty of a trap? By the time you realize you're in it, it's too late."

A joke, I knew, but something in those words made me uncomfortable. I took a step back and lifted my hood over my hair. "Oh, how cute. Someone doesn't know how this fairy tale ends." I cupped my hand around my mouth and pitched my voice lower. "Spoiler alert, I'd watch your back."

He grinned without a care. A wolf with two dimples; was there anything more deadly?

21

KENNEDY

Alexei led me through the party with his hand on my lower back. We walked in behind Zach, who carelessly waved his sword through the air while speaking in an overly exaggerated pirate voice. Gemma danced her way through the room, lapping up the attention and catcalls from a group of women who stood in the corner, sipping champagne. Her friends, I assumed, called her over and she obliged.

"Welcome to your first Wolves Halloween party," Matt said, turning toward us. "Is it all you imagined?"

The house where this year's Halloween party took place looked like it belonged in an interior design magazine with every piece of furniture, art, and decoration blending perfectly together to create an atmosphere that shouted cozy yet sleek. The room had been decked out in Halloween decorations—balloons spelled out Happy Halloween, decorated pumpkins lined the countertop, spiderwebs hung in the corners of the room, and a large talking witch stood next to the snack table. Every person wore a costume and clustered in groups around the room. Pop music blasted from somewhere, but not so loud it was difficult to have a conversation.

Did it look like a Halloween party fit for the Palmer City Wolves? Absolutely.

"Yes," I said, winking. "But you know the real party will start later."

Matt groaned. "Come on, Kennedy, you're like a sister to me." He pointed two fingers at his own eyes before turning them around to Alexei. *I'm watching you.* "You better take care of her, man."

"I always *take care* of her," Alexei said with a haughty grin.

Matt groaned again. "You two are the worst," he said before trailing after Gemma.

"He makes it too easy," I said, laughing.

Alexei slipped his hand into mine, threading our fingers together. "It's good you got that out of your system before you talk to anyone else here."

I looked up at him, noticing the hard crease between his eyes. "You're nervous," I said, surprised. It was such a rare thing to catch him like this, maybe the only other time had been in my car when he apologized for our poor first date, when he worried I might quit on him and he'd have to handle the media on his own.

He bent over and whispered into my ear. "My hockey career, Kens. It's kind of important to me."

My stomach somersaulted. Right. This wasn't revenge for him, or a way to get out of his normal routine. Convincing people of this relationship affected his career, the game he loved. He depended on me to help him, and for the first time, I wanted to do it for *him,* not just to fulfill my end of the bargain. I tightened my grip on his hand.

"Don't worry, I've got your back," I assured him with a smile. I nudged him with my shoulder. "Go hang with your teammates. I've got this."

With that, I headed to the back of the room, to the intimidatingly large group of women, to convince them Alexei Volkov wasn't actually the wolf he was dressed as. I grabbed a glass of champagne, then nudged my way into the group beside Gemma. She immediately introduced me to the other ten women, all wives or girlfriends of Alexei's teammates.

"Thank you for hosting tonight," I said to Arielle, a tall, leggy brunette in a seventies go-go dancer costume. "I love your home."

"She's amazing, right? Arielle's been helping me design my home," Gemma said. Her newly built home on the periphery of the city would be ready in January. Two months from now. By then, I hoped I would have a place of my own. Maybe I should tackle that item on my list before reaching out to a university to finish my degree.

"Interesting choice of costumes," Maura said, sipping red wine. Winger Paul Coddler's gorgeous wife wore a seafoam green ballet leotard over black leggings, her golden hair pulled up in a perfect, secure bun. For many people, the look would be too severe, but she had the kind of face that could pull off any hairstyle. Paul played with Justin when he centered the top line for the Wolves. "It's almost like you *enjoy* the attention."

"Seriously, Maura?" Gemma hissed.

I placed my hand on Gemma's forearm. "Since we don't have any control over the attention, why not have fun with it?"

Maura scoffed. "No control? Maybe don't hit on your ex's rival only hours after you broke up."

"Have you *seen* him?" My gaze roamed the group, briefly locking with each woman. Gemma discretely winked at me. "If any of you have the kind of willpower to say no to those dimples, I'd love to know your secret. Maybe it could help me finally quit eating Gemma's cookie sandwiches too."

A low rumble of chuckles sounded around the group. "And for the record," I said, allowing a little bite into my tone, "Alexei found me crying because Justin had dumped me and blocked my phone number so I couldn't reach him. He wasn't hitting on me. He made sure I didn't fall drunkenly down the steps or make a fool of myself at the party. That picture was taken out of context."

"Then what *did* happen?" A nurse with red hair asked. Shelly, I think. "How did you start dating?"

Alexei and I had agreed on this story, a variant of the truth. "Gem deserves all the blame for that. She invited Alexei over while I was crashing at her place. He asked me out that night."

"Oops," Gemma said with a facetious shrug. "But not really. Justin Ward was an ass. Did you know he made Kennedy hide their relationship from everyone?"

And so it began. Gemma took the lead on bad-mouthing Justin, which got the truth out there without making me look like a bitter ex. My gaze roamed the room. A few guys were playing Wii golf, others were chowing down at the snack table.

And then there was Alexei, sitting on the couch beside Matt, watching me.

He was every bit the wolf he'd dressed as. One after my own stupid heart.

ALEXEI

All night, Kennedy worked the room, from the wives and girlfriends to my teammates, even to Max and Arielle's cat. I knew she'd done her job well when I came across people she talked to after her. Teammates who played with Justin Ward for years—who never talked to me about our drama—told me they couldn't believe how poorly he'd treated Kennedy. They were glad *I* had been at the party to stop something worse from happening. Several of my teammates' significant others commented on how good we looked together. Kennedy accomplished more in a couple of hours than I'd been able to do in a month and a half.

A winning record smoothed over much of the roughness from the way I'd joined the team and Ward had departed, but other than Matt, I hadn't connected much with my teammates off the ice. Not that I'd tried, but it seemed futile to make too much of an effort when my reputation was a huge mountain to climb.

"Hey," Kennedy said as she plopped on the couch beside me. I posted up here an hour ago to watch my teammates make asses of themselves at karaoke.

"Looks like someone is having fun," I said.

Her flushed cheeks raised as a smile broke across her face. She slid her legs into my lap, holding her skirt in place so it didn't ride up. "I am. Not all of us are grouchy old men who would rather be training."

I laughed, placing my palm on her knee. "Maybe I was missing you."

Her head snapped toward me; her mouth parted. "I am a good time," she said easily, the alcohol loosening her usual tension. Kennedy nestled her head on my shoulder, her eyes closing briefly. "Well, I used to be a good time. You would have liked me then."

Much like the night we met, Kennedy's disparaging words about herself lanced my heart. They weren't a fish for flattery; she meant them.

I ran my fingers along her cheek. Her eyes fluttered open before dipping to watch my movements.

"I like you as you are."

Kennedy sucked in a breath, her big brown eyes lifting to mine.

"You're... magnetic. You draw people to you without even trying. Even when you're actively pushing them away, they can't help it. I can't help it."

"You're different than I thought you'd be," she murmured.

"Alexei." Erik Pomroy's voice broke the moment. Since when was he at this party? "Kennedy."

"Erik," I said as I gently moved Kennedy's legs from my lap and stood to shake his hand. Erik wore a *Top Gun* jumpsuit, his dark shades resting on top of his head. "I didn't know you'd be here."

"I like to stop by if I can," he said.

When Kennedy reached my side, she wrapped one arm around my back and leaned into me. Because of the alcohol or our act, I wasn't sure. "Kennedy Cole, I'm surprised to see you here." His gaze flicked briefly to me before landing back on her.

"Hey, Coach," she said. Her bubbly voice hadn't lost its luster despite her tiredness. "Nice costume."

He clicked his tongue. "Yeah? It's nothing compared to yours."

"Thank you. Do you mind getting a picture of us?" she asked, holding her phone out to Erik before he could answer. "I promised my dad I'd send him one."

Erik took the phone, then stepped back. "He knows you're here?"

Even drunk, Kennedy navigated the situation with skill. I threw my arm around her shoulders, pulling her even closer to me. Vanilla and orange wafted from her, as always. She looked up at me rather than at the camera, giving me one of her wide, genuine smiles. Not in service of mocking, for once. I didn't even care if it was for show.

"Of course," she answered Erik as she patted the fur on my chest. "He told me to warn him if this guy does anything I don't like."

Kennedy had recapped her conversation with her dad for me, but she concealed this warning. I wasn't sure why. It seemed like perfect ammunition for Kennedy's mocking.

When Erik handed the phone back to Kennedy, he said, "Sounds like Cale."

"You ready to go?" I asked her, suddenly wanting to be anywhere but at this party, in a room full of people Kennedy and I were fooling. Including my coach, a man I admired more than almost anyone. "She was falling asleep on the couch," I explained to Erik.

"Sure, yeah. Let me just say my goodbyes," she said before leaving Erik and me alone.

Erik slipped his hands into the pockets of his jumpsuit. "You better know what you're doing, Volkov." The *Or else* was implied. He clapped a hand on my shoulder as he passed by.

A month ago, I wouldn't have thought twice about his words, guided by my motivation to fake-date Kennedy and show everyone I wasn't a piece of shit.

Tonight, we faced a true test, and we made it work, convincing everyone of the realness of our feelings, of our relationship. I should have felt triumphant, well on the way to getting everything I wanted.

And yet, the thought of how simple it was to pretend tugged insistently at the back of my mind.

22

KENNEDY

THANK THE POWERS THAT be for champagne; otherwise, I might not have survived shopping with Gemma for her wedding dress. She tried on ten different dresses. All of them looked amazing on her, but with each one, she became more agitated. *The hem looks weird. This dress is* too *white. My boobs don't look big enough.* And on and on.

As honored as I was to be chosen as her maid of honor, I had no idea how to handle the escalating situation before me. The poor attendants at the shop looked equally worried and kept tossing pointed stares at me. What did they expect me to do? I tried to go into the dressing room with Gemma to talk with her in private, but she snapped that she didn't need a babysitter to remove another hideous dress.

My phone dinged, giving me an excuse to look away from the questioning stares of the staff. You know how to make a guy feel cheap. Alexei's words sent a little ping to the pit of my stomach. He'd landed safely in Philly yesterday, beginning the longest road trip of the season.

My phone dinged again. You sleep with me, and then I don't hear from you.

I rolled my eyes, refusing to give in to the bait of calling what we did *sleeping together*.

You saw me yesterday. I reread my text and realized the words sounded harsher in black and white than they had in my head. I followed up, What did you expect, a full Yelp review on your accommodations?

And flowers and chocolate waiting for me in my hotel room, he answered.

You better lower those expectations or get a new girlfriend.

He said: That's the last time I'm apologizing to you with baked goods.

Those are end of relationship kind of words, I texted after sending a shocked-face emoji.

He sent back an eye roll emoji. You know you're stuck with me. Just like I can't hold it against you that you drool in your sleep.

Stop creeping on me when I sleep, Volkov.

His reply took longer this time, the three dots appearing and disappearing several times. Finally, Thank you for the other night. Seriously.

"What happened the other night?"

I jumped out of my chair at the sound of Gemma's voice. How did I not realize she came out of the dressing room and stood beside me?

"With that grin, it must have been something good."

Flustered, I tossed my phone into my purse. She wore her regular clothes, which explained why she wasn't yelling about another dress. "Nothing happened."

Gemma winked at me. "Y'all looked *very* cozy at the party."

I blew out a breath. "It's not what you think. There was a fight—"

"Yeah, I heard about it from Matt." She twirled her finger in a circle. "Fast forward to the part where you slept with Volk."

"I didn't *sleep* with him," I said in a whisper-yell. "Zach told me Alexei needed company—"

"Oh, I bet he did," Gemma said under her breath.

"So I went over, and he had all these bruises... and I felt bad about it. He said it would be suspicious if I left right away. We cooked food and watched TV and fell asleep at some point."

Gemma shook her head at me in exasperation. "You spent the night in Alexei Volkov's bed, and all you did was watch TV, eat food, and sleep?" She paused, giving me a chance to correct her, but I only nodded. "Oh, Kens, you disappoint me."

She didn't know the little detail of him being only half-dressed when I first got there.

"What, you expected me to jump the guy as soon as we were alone? He was injured."

Too late, I realized I hadn't said I wasn't interested. The knowing smile Gemma wore told me it hadn't escaped her attention.

"Why not? He has two-hundred-plus-pound men slamming him every night. I think he could have handled being pounced on by you."

"Gemma, I'm getting over a breakup."

"Exactly. You deserve to have fun. If you would drop this ridiculous grudge against Volk, I think you'd be surprised by how well you'd get along."

I realized I no longer held a grudge against Alexei. I hadn't thought about it in days. The Alexei Volkov from the media and Justin's stories didn't align with the real live version. He didn't even match his persona on the ice, at least not completely. Arrogant, sure, but—

My phone pinged again, and her smile grew. "Who's it from, Kens? Your *boyfriend.*" Gemma hung onto the last word much longer than necessary.

Reluctantly, I pulled my phone out of my bag, knowing Gemma wouldn't let it drop. I pushed the phone toward her so she could see Deandra's text. "She won't stop bothering me about helping with this Wolves event. She claims someone quit and she's desperate."

"You don't believe her?"

I shrugged. "Maybe? But it could also be an excuse for me to work with them again."

"Do you want to work with them again?" Gemma asked, her voice gentle, tentative.

"No," I said immediately. But then I thought about my list—*Pick a career??* I'd written the words, then promptly ignored them. Some of my happiest memories came from my time working for the team.

But that was *before*—when my mother was still here. I was a different person from the woman who could hope and who knew the future was full of possibilities.

I wanted to be that woman again. "Maybe."

"I'll pick a dress if you help the team."

"Fine," I said, "but only because your wedding dress reign of terror needs to end."

"Let's do this then," Gemma said with a smile. She stalked over to the associates, who plastered on false smiles as she ordered them around.

Before following behind her, I clicked open my phone screen and typed back to Alexei, Good luck tonight. Let me know how the game goes.

23

ALEXEI

THIS WAS MY FAVORITE silence, the kind following the end-of-game buzzer after we'd kicked the asses of our opponents in their own house.

And the fact it had been against the team that released me from my contract last season made this win sweeter. The Bulldogs organization played a tribute to me during a commercial break, a simple one-minute video showing highlights from when I played for them. I expected the divided fan reaction, receiving both applause and boos, but not anything from management. I *wanted* nothing from those assholes after how they dumped me.

"You look happy tonight," Flip Carlson said when I sat down in front of the camera for a virtual postgame press conference.

"Opposed to how I usually sit here, scowling at everyone?"

Genuine laughter filled the room through the speaker. Maybe my displeasure about moving to Palmer City showed all over my face from the moment I stepped into the town. I thought coming back to New York would fuel the resentment and remind me of everything I lost. But tonight, beside my new teammates, gratitude consumed me. They had my back out there. No one needed to say a damn word for me to know their rough play, their extra fire to win, had everything to do with me.

"Two weeks until your next big showdown," another reporter whose name I couldn't remember chimed in. "Are you ready to face off with Justin Ward?"

I gritted my teeth. Ward and I would face off twice this season, but I hadn't realized the first time would be so soon. "I'm focused on our next game. But I'm never not ready."

"All right, thanks, Volk."

"Thank you, all," I said, then flew off the seat as if it were on fire. I had enjoyed media appearances when I first came into the league. People wanted to debrief with me on the game? Talk over how I felt as I scored goals? Great. All these years later, getting through a media appearance felt like a slog, especially when we lost. The last thing any athlete wanted to do after losing a game was talk about all the ways the team fucked up.

Matt came into view as soon as I stepped into the hallway. The media had tapped him for an interview tonight after he'd shut down the Bulldogs' offense and made an incredible save when our goalie was out of position. "Hey, man, you good?" he asked.

I hated how transparent I was, that people could tell a mention of Justin fucking Ward got under my skin. "I'm great. Thinking about going out tonight."

He raised his eyebrows. "Like, with people?"

"Yeah, with people," I said, as if I hadn't spent every road trip this year holed up alone in my hotel room. Matt had pressured me into a hot tub pizza tradition after home games, but on the road, I stuck to myself. I wasn't an asshole about it, but my teammates stopped asking because they knew the answer. "You in?"

"I'll find you after this." He nodded toward the room, suppressing a smile.

We didn't have a game tomorrow, which was the only reason I let Matt drag me to a lounge, a popular spot with my old teammates. I had been tempted to go back to my room, but I needed to do something to settle this adrenaline pumping through me. Running in the hotel gym could have done it, but I still hadn't shaken those stubborn feelings of gratitude.

So that was how I ended up sitting in a roped-off VIP section, pounding shots with Briggsy and Matt. Drinking for the first time this season. I would regret it in the morning, but right then, I didn't give a shit.

I proved every fucking person in that organization wrong tonight. My cause for celebration.

"Did you know he could be fun?" Briggsy leaned into Matt, trying to ask the question in secret, but his drunk ass had long lost its perception of reality.

Matt's gaze darted to me for a beat before returning to Zach. "Yeah, Volk and I go way back."

"Was he always so serious? Because living with him can be *scary.*" Zach spewed his words faster than usual, defying laws of nature. "The only time I've seen him smile, you know except for scoring goals and winning games, was when Kennedy stayed over last week. He didn't even notice I left all my stuff downstairs because I fell asleep while playing video games—"

"Oh, I noticed," I cut in. "It's hard to ignore piles of trash in the middle of my house. I just didn't say anything."

Zach pointed at me. "See! It's like he had a brain transplant or something. He always used to yell at me to pick up after myself, and rinse my dishes before putting them in the dishwasher, not anywhere but the specific places he told me to put them and stop taking naps and go to sleep at a reasonable hour and—"

Matt cleared his throat over Zach's verbal vomit. "It's because he's getting laid, jackass."

I wish.

"Your sentimental side is overwhelming." I knocked back another shot.

If I had to talk about my situation with Kennedy, I needed more alcohol. Since the night boy-wonder invited her over, nothing had been the same between us. Or at least, that was how I felt. I had no idea if Kennedy would agree.

Before that night, I would have described our relationship as cautiously friendly. But then Kennedy came over and stayed over, and I didn't want her to leave. Not when I saw her in my doorway. Not when she ran her hand down my chest. I could have woken her up after she fell asleep, but I liked having her in my bed. I liked waking up next to her even more. Even if it did make me freak the fuck out, because feelings for Kennedy were not baked into our agreement.

"You're getting laid by *Kennedy*," Matt clarified. "That's why you've stopped being an insufferable grouch."

Two months and we were done. I had to hope whatever feelings I had would leave along with her. Focusing on my career—and not letting a woman reel me in only to leave me again—made my life simpler. If I didn't have to put on this front of being in a happy, committed relationship, I would find a woman to bring back to my room and remind myself why *casual* was what I needed.

"Maybe that's the secret to why sun shines out your ass," I said, signaling to a server for more shots. "But my good mood is all thanks to our winning season."

"I'll cheers to that," Zach said as he thrust his shot glass in the air.

"Isn't that Graham Sutter?" Connor Lepel, another Wolves winger, shouted. A woman sat in his lap kissing his neck. She didn't pause at his distracted attention.

Sure enough, my old teammate, Graham, weaved through the throngs of people. Although he was drafted after me, he'd worked his way up to captain of the Bulldogs. Not long after the team dumped me, they signed him to a monster seven-year contract and handed him the keys to what was supposed to be my kingdom. When he saw us, he stopped walking and said something to the blonde trailing him.

"But they lost!" Zach shouted. I would have laughed my ass off if Zach's voice carried to Graham over the volume in the club. Graham and I got along fine, not friends but solid teammates. He ignored the noise around me and my reputation, and focused on the game. He never gave me one reason to dislike him.

Until now. Because that blonde on his arm? That was Cora.

She marched up to our table, pausing between me and Matt. Her short hair made her look formidable. I vaguely recognized the disco-ball colored mini dress she wore. Cora favored standing out in a crowd, so most of what she donned sparkled, used flashy colors, and showed off her body.

"Cora," I said.

Matt's gaze shot up to her face with recognition.

"I didn't expect to see you." *With my former teammate, no less.*

"Hey, Volk." She slipped her hand into Graham's. "I'm surprised to see you too."

"We're out celebrating," I said before introducing Matt and Zach. "Graham, I think you're well-acquainted with these guys."

Graham's bun bobbed with his nod. "Hard to forget the toughest defenseman in the league. Man, you were brutal tonight."

"Hey, you got one," Matt said. "You know our rookie, Zach Briggs?"

Briggsy shot up in his seat, back ramrod straight. "Mr. Sutter, you are one of my favorite players."

Jesus Christ. If he asked Graham for an autograph, I might kick him out of my house.

Graham laughed. "Always happy to meet a fan. I see a long career for you, kid."

The words silenced Zach, something I had never seen. If he hadn't blinked, I would have worried he'd slipped into an open-eyed coma.

"It's good to see you happy," Cora said suddenly. "You and I were always trying to force it, you know?"

I scoffed. "I didn't realize you felt that way until *after* my contract was terminated."

"Volk." Cora softened her tone, dropping a hand to my shoulder that I wanted to shrug off me.

But I realized none of the emotions I would expect to feel when confronted with my ex-fiancée and her new boyfriend had surfaced. In the aftermath of the breakup, nothing I did tempered my anger at losing my contract and my girl. For a week, I drank hard and ordered enough food to feed a small army. Eventually, I felt enough like shit to change tactics, to train harder than I ever had, which helped me claw my way back into the league.

"We weren't right for each other. I'm sorry about how it happened, but you weren't easy to deal with after..." She looked at Graham, who gave her a small nod. She flashed her hand at me, displaying a massive diamond on her finger. "Anyway, I figured I should tell you myself. Graham and I are engaged."

The fuck?

"I know it's fast, but when you know, you know." She snapped her fingers. "Like you and that girl."

"Kennedy and I aren't engaged... eight months after we broke up."

I checked my watch for the date, and it hit me. Tomorrow, Cora and I were supposed to get married. The realization crashed over me with the force of being slammed into the boards.

My wedding was supposed to be tomorrow.

I shot out of my seat, towering over her, eye level with Graham, who looked like he would rather sink into the floor than be present for this conversation.

"But, Cora, you're right. Kennedy isn't the kind of person who would ditch me at my lowest point. She doesn't care about superficial shit like what team I play for or my contract. So thank you for showing me exactly what I *don't* want in a partner. She's a much better fit for me."

Cora's mouth fell open. I threw back one more shot. "*Great* to see you both. Boys, I'm heading back to my room."

I didn't wait for anyone to respond before pushing my way past our guests and getting the fuck out of this place.

The sound of my vibrating phone amplified the buzzing in my head. I groped around the nightstand, knocking over a couple of empty cans that rattled to the floor before finally landing on it. Unlocking my phone revealed a series of texts from Matt and Briggsy in our group chat, checking on me. I quickly responded I was fine and would see them in the morning.

Then I saw the messages from Kennedy. She sent something hours ago that I missed, nothing important, just another message in our string of sharing our days and whatever was on our minds. This photo was of me—a poster board version of me I sent to the McIntyre house as a gift to my new biggest fans and as a way to poke at Kennedy, a habit I enjoyed too much.

The words accompanying the photo were As if I didn't see you enough.

You can't get enough of me and you know it. I clicked send without a second thought, thanks to the alcohol swimming in my veins.

Immediately, the three dots appeared. It was past two on a Friday night, and Kennedy did not stay up this late. Because of her job, her internal clock was hardwired to wake up at the ass crack of dawn. What was she doing awake now? Could she have been out with someone?

I let my head fall back to the headboard, hoping the thud against my skull would fix my broken mind. Of course she wasn't out with anyone, because the only man she could date was me. The reminder brought only small comfort. She didn't choose *me*, only this convenient solution to our problems.

You're mistaking me for one of those drooling waitresses.

I laughed out loud, the action loosening tension still lingering in my body. It's not the same without me there, I replied. Admit it.

Kennedy called, and I instantly picked up. This closeness with her would make it worse once our agreement ran its course, but I wanted to hear her voice. I had only known the sound for two months, but it had quickly become my favorite.

"I'll admit," she started without preamble, "I have felt a lot less annoyed over the last week. Coincidence?" Her voice came through without a hint of sleepiness.

"Well, you have me to watch over you at work."

"You outdid yourself."

"I bet the kids love it."

"Of course they do." She sighed. "And they move it from room to room. I never know where you're going to pop up."

My unexpected presence seemed to be as problematic as these stupid feelings I couldn't ditch. They flared at unpredictable times… like now, when I could hear the smile in her voice because of me. Because of something I did or said. I wanted to believe she felt at least a shred of what I was feeling, but I remembered her words after she agreed to fake-date me, *Don't forget I'm pretending.*

"I'm sorry, is this a bad time?"

I became aware that I'd been silent far longer than I realized, stuck in my head with my slowing senses.

"I know it's late—"

I muscled myself to a sitting position. "No, I like that you called. I'm in a weird headspace."

"Because of hockey?" she asked earnestly, drawing a genuine laugh from me.

"You know I care about things other than the hockey, right?"

Hockey had forced us together, but it also kept us at a distance. Kennedy's father owned my team. Her connection to Ward. Her retreat from the sport she'd enjoyed with her mother.

Hockey held an important place in my life, but it wasn't all I was. I wanted her to know that.

"I was supposed to get married today," I said finally. "We have the day off tomorrow. We're in her hometown, the place we met. My teammates would all be here. She always wanted a fall wedding in Central Park with colorful leaves as a backdrop to her photos. It worked out perfectly. Except that she didn't want to marry me."

Cora, I realized, hadn't known me well enough to make that decision. If she had, she would have known I would never want to get married during the season. That I wouldn't want a massive wedding. Something intimate would have been my speed, something less performative.

But Cora never loved *me,* only what my star power brought to her life.

I had been through a series of short breakups before I met her. She could be pushy when it came to what she wanted. But she *stayed*. She had no problems with the demands of my job. It was easy to look beyond anything bothering me.

"I... I had no idea," Kennedy sputtered. "You never... um, told me why you broke up."

She knew, but still she asked, giving me the space to open up to her if I wanted. I sighed, long and deep. "My contract getting dropped put her in an awkward spot with our friends. The press coverage was ugly, and I wasn't easy to be around. Plus, Cora wanted a *star*. I wasn't one anymore. Seems fucking fitting that she hooked up with the team's current captain."

I wanted to vomit thinking about the three years I wasted with her. I could have used it to build my game; maybe if I had, I would have Graham's contract today.

"Graham Sutter?"

"Please don't twist the knife and tell me you have a thing for that guy."

The statement revealed more of how I felt than I wanted her to know. I hoped she wouldn't look too closely. Picking up the phone inebriated meant a risk of saying something I shouldn't. And I couldn't find one part of me that gave a single shit.

This thing with Kennedy didn't need to mean something greater. We could help each other bounce back from our shitty relationships. Fighting my feelings for her took too much energy. Once I gave in, the novelty would wear off. We could have a friendship, we could hook up, and in two months, we would separate like the mature adults we sometimes were.

"The guy does have great hands, but no, I wouldn't want him for anything other than my fantasy hockey team."

"You have a fantasy hockey team?"

"I used to," she said. "But don't think you can change the subject. How do you know they're dating?"

"Oh, they aren't just dating." I let out a short laugh. "Cora showed me her engagement ring tonight."

She gasped. "You saw her?"

I blew out a breath. "Oh, yeah. We were out celebrating, and she came up to me with Graham to announce it."

"I'm sorry, Alexei. That's shitty."

"It's good it happened before we got married," I said, wholeheartedly meaning the words. I wanted to get married once, to someone who would have my back no matter what. Cora didn't have the stomach for it or the necessary feelings for me to weather it. "But it... reminds me of what I don't have."

"What's that?"

"Someone who I belong to." Part of me regretted speaking the words. Something about keeping them trapped inside me made them easier to ignore. But tonight, talking to Kennedy three hundred miles from each other, sitting in this dark room with alcohol flowing through me, warming me, I was able to say my most coveted desires out loud.

Our phone line momentarily went so silent I checked that the call remained connected. Still there. "Fuck," I said on an exhale. "I can't believe I said that."

"You will find it," Kennedy told me, her voice ablaze.

"Is that what you want?"

"What?" Kennedy said.

"To find someone."

"Doesn't everyone?" I saw her expression in my mind, the careless smile she had no idea caused so much havoc for me.

"That might be the biggest nonanswer you've ever given."

"I don't know what I want."

I didn't know if she would say more, but I stayed quiet, willing her to. I wanted to know more.

"You know how it is, you have a plan for your life, then something happens and it's... gone. Sometimes, it doesn't feel real."

"What doesn't?" I asked.

"That this is my life," she continued, saying to me sober the words she'd drunkenly shared during our first meeting. "I never finished college or figured out a career. I don't have a place to live. My work is a routine that marks time. Oh, and don't forget, my boyfriend is fake. Sorry, I didn't mean to turn this into my personal bitch sesh."

"It's fine. It distracts me. And you never talk about yourself. I like learning about you."

"Oh, I'm sure."

"I'm serious."

"Okay." Challenge filled her voice. "What else would you like to know?"

I paused, thinking over everything I still wondered about her, from hearing more about her mother to what life was like before she died to her feelings for me. But I didn't want to focus on heavy subjects tonight. I only wanted to settle into my bed and let her voice wash over me, to paper over this weird fucking night.

"You have a scar across your collarbone. How'd you get it?"

Kennedy laughed airily, confirming I chose correctly. No more focusing on loss or disappointment. Just two friends trading silly stories about their lives. And that's what we did, even as we became progressively more tired, our voices growing lower and slower.

"Are you still there?" I asked after a prolonged silence.

Kennedy muffled the word. "Yes."

"Good." Part of me worried that ending this call would break whatever spell had been cast over this night. "I'm going to need you to tell me something happy so I can go to sleep." I flipped from my right side to the left, taking the phone with me, leaving it on speaker in front of my face. "Please," I prodded.

"Gemma finally found her wedding dress."

"Did you find your dress?" I asked, tracing patterns on the white sheet with a finger.

"Not yet. Why?"

"It's before the end of the year," I said slowly.

Going to a wedding with her had sounded like a chore before. Instead of hooking up with a hot friend of Gemma's who lived nowhere near me, I would be saddled with Kennedy Cole, who hated my guts. But now...

"I'll need to match you."

"Oh. Right." She cleared her throat. "I'll, um, let you know."

"You look good in dark green." Later, I could blame the alcohol, but all I wanted was to tell her something true, even if the words sliced a hole in my chest to reveal my rapidly beating heart.

Kennedy huffed a nervous laugh. "What?"

"I like you in anything, but something about that color on you… it's stunning."

"No one is listening. You don't need to say things you don't mean."

"I mean everything I say to you, Kennedy."

She swallowed audibly. "Oh. Okay."

I could read nothing in those two words.

"This is the part where you tell me what I look good in," I said, steering us clear of discomfort. We could say anything we wanted as long as we were joking. It didn't count.

"Oh my *God*." She rewarded my efforts with a self-conscious chortle.

I could mentally see her expression again, the way this would cause her to blush and her eyes would roll. My breath caught, imagining it.

"On that note, I'm going to go."

I laughed, deep and unrestrained, soaking in the perfection of this conversation. "I'll see you when I'm back."

Only two more days; it couldn't come soon enough.

24

ALEXEI

IT WAS ALMOST MIDNIGHT when our plane landed in Palmer City.

The warm air hit me as soon as I stepped onto the tarmac, making me regret not removing the coat I'd needed in Boston before exiting the plane. We walked silently toward our cars, all the adrenaline from winning our last game on this road trip earlier tonight drained from us.

Except for Briggsy, of course. I wished I could bottle his energy in moments like this. If I weren't worried he'd be distracted by a squirrel and run us off the road, I would ask him to drive us the twenty-minute trip home.

"Can we stop at McDonald's?" Briggsy asked when we reached the car. He bounced on his feet, waiting for me to unlock the doors. *Christ.* This must be what parents go through on a daily basis.

"You want to eat now?" I asked, fully realizing I sounded like an old man, but it had been a long trip. I dreamed of collapsing in my bed as soon as I walked in the door. The first night back from a trip felt so incredible, I usually slept several more hours than usual.

"I'm hungry."

I fired up the car and waited for Zach to secure his seatbelt. He fussed with the music, having already synced his phone.

"Won't you sleep when we're home?"

"I'm not tired."

Translation: Briggsy would spend half the night playing video games, dirtying up my living room and yelling at the TV. I took a moment to get my grumpy tendencies under control before responding. When I opened my doors to Zach, I knew it would shake my routine. That was half the reason I did it. As much as I complained about him being sloppy and loud, my house felt less like a museum with him there.

"Sure, we can go," I said finally, stifling a yawn. "But maybe stop taking so many naps so you can sleep at a normal hour."

Thirty minutes later, I drove into my driveway. "Did you leave the light on again?" I grumbled as I pulled the car into the garage.

I had a programmed light system, but some of the lights on weren't part of it. Briggsy slurped his milkshake and shook his head. I sighed—nothing signaled no one was home better than a lit house all night. I was too tired to care. I didn't grab my bag from the trunk. It would be tomorrow's problem.

"Surprise!" I heard the words as soon as the doorknob turned, but I didn't see Kennedy until I walked through the door from the garage and spotted her in the kitchen, standing beneath a sign that read "CONGRATS ZACH!" which she had strewn across my kitchen cabinets. She held a cake with Zach's picture on it; in it, he wore an enormous smile and had both arms out wide, ready to accept an incoming hug from his teammates.

He'd scored his first NHL goal on this trip, something worthy of celebration. Even more important, he'd played solid in every game. No way could they send him back to the AHL now.

Briggsy dropped his bag, almost on my foot, and rushed to Kennedy. "Sick! You made this cake for me?"

Kennedy smartly slid the cake onto the counter behind her before Zach knocked it out of her hands. "I might have had help."

Zach flung his arms around Kennedy, saying something to her I couldn't hear before quickly moving to grab a plate and eat his cake. She finally looked over to where I stood rooted to the spot. I'd thought a lot about what would happen when I saw her again. Would this road trip mark a change for us?

Walking into my house to see her standing there—in a dark green tank top—I knew what I hoped would happen. But I couldn't get ahead of myself. She was here for my roommate, not me.

"Where's my cake?" I asked in lieu of hello.

Her shoulders visibly relaxed as I slipped us into our teasing dynamic. Nothing wagered, nothing risked. "Do something impressive and maybe you'll get one."

"Do I need to read you my stats from this trip?"

"Only if you want to bore me so much I'll physically never have the strength to bake again."

I barked out a laugh. "I'm still not sure you had anything to do with this cake."

"Hey," she said, cracking a smile. "I labored over this cake."

Zach looked up from his plate. "So good," he muttered as he chewed, not bothering to cover his mouth. He cut another piece of cake and took off to his lair. "Thanks, Kennedy!" He fell back onto the couch, then turned on the PS4 and TV. Those would be his last words for the evening.

"You're going to give the poor kid a crush if you keep doing stuff for him."

"Oh, please. That's not even close to true. Watch this."

She slipped her shirt over her head, revealing a black bikini, and let it fall to the chair beside her. I fought to keep my eyes from slipping to her chest for too long; to not let them linger for a moment would have made me a candidate for sainthood.

"I'm going to use your hot tub," she said, sauntering straight across the room, directly between the kid and his TV. Zach didn't spare a look at her, only moved his head to look around her at his game.

Kennedy turned back to me, a victorious smirk on her face, but it only lasted a moment. Whatever she saw when she looked at me sent her scurrying out the door to the hot tub without another word.

Like hell I wasn't going to follow her. Exhaustion be damned.

25

KENNEDY

I DIDN'T THINK THIS through. That was the thought flashing through my mind when I saw the heated look on Alexei's face.

We had been in near-constant contact over the last week and a half, but the distance made it easy to pretend that we were talking to someone else. Someone other than controversial hockey star Alexei Volkov and Kennedy Cole, owner's daughter and overall mess. The distance made it easy to forget how this started, that Alexei and I were forced together by strange circumstances.

And I realized I liked talking to him. That, more than anything, scared me.

Our animosity kept me safe, impervious to Alexei and the deep tenor of his voice, the smolder in his glare, the dimples in his cheeks. I needed the animosity, but it felt so far out of my grasp, I couldn't even remember why I once felt that way.

It was also hard to hate someone who looked at you like he wanted to push you against a wall.

It wasn't only that I'd stripped to my bathing suit top in his kitchen. No, I hadn't properly thought anything through since I came over and found him half-naked in bed, bruised from his fight on the ice. Something shifted that night. Maybe if I'd left the room after checking on him rather than hanging out, everything that followed—the texts, the phone calls, my idiotic idea to be in his home when he got back from this trip—wouldn't have happened. Maybe I wouldn't have lost control over this entire situation.

But I stayed that night, and I exchanged flirty texts and traded secrets with him.

And now I sat in his hot tub.

The door to the house slid open to reveal Alexei dressed in a Wolves T-shirt and a pair of black swim trunks. He locked eyes with me as he walked across the deck, sending my heart into overdrive, the same rhythm as during my morning run. A powerful thump, thump, thump that made me feel alive. Alexei kept eye contact as he lifted his shirt, not dropping it until the shirt eclipsed his face. The raw strength of him sent a shiver down my spine.

I watched shamelessly, something he was well aware of once he tossed his shirt to the side of the deck and refocused on me. I expected a snide comment and a devilish smirk to signal he knew the power had shifted. I couldn't deny he had me in the palm of his hand. Not with the way my body tingled in anticipation of him joining me in the water, of what would happen after he did.

I tried to calm down, slowly counting backward from twenty as I exhaled as quietly as possible. It had always worked in stressful situations, but apparently, it was no match for a half-naked Alexei Volkov across from me in a hot tub, looking finer than I'd ever seen him. Even with a residual bruise under his eye. Oh, who was I kidding? That bruise made the sight hotter.

"Seems like I've impressed you now," he said, one side of his lips quirked into a smile.

Right, the cake. It took me a moment to remember our earlier conversation, that he would have to impress me to get me to bake something for him. Distraction is a bitch.

"I don't know if I can be responsible for messing up this whole thing you got going on."

"What thing?" he said, all false innocence.

I motioned to him. "You know, this whole..."

Alexei took a few steps until he hovered in the center of the hot tub. Too close and not close enough.

"I don't know. You're going to have to tell me."

"Jesus Christ, Alexei," I said on an exhale. "You know how you look."

"Not to you." There was a vulnerability, I realized. With my shameless staring, he couldn't have missed how I reacted to him, but he seemed unsure of himself. That crack in his confidence, something I heard the other night on the phone when he confessed he wanted someone to belong to, made me want to give him the truth.

"It matters what I think?" I asked, swallowing hard.

He nodded.

"Okay. You look so good, it's hard to keep my eyes off you sometimes."

Alexei prowled closer, eyes razor-focused on me. "Why did you come here tonight?"

This situation kept spiraling further away from me, my grip on it tenuous at best. I rolled my eyes, trying to erase our steps as we barreled forward to something I wasn't sure we could recover from.

"Didn't the sign and the cake make that obvious?"

"Don't do that."

"Do what?"

"Make this a joke."

Was that… no, he couldn't be hurt by what I said.

"Alexei—" I stopped abruptly before saying something I couldn't take back. "I don't know what you want me to say."

"What do you want to say? Without anyone in your ear. It's just us here."

Just us here. The words sent a pit to my stomach. Not seeing him for the last week and a half had tortured me. No wonder the anticipation geared me up this much.

"It's not because you wanted to see me?" he asked.

I shook my head, biting my bottom lip to keep the words in.

Alexei followed the movement. "You weren't hoping we'd end up alone?"

"I was proving a point."

"You proved it. Zach didn't look at you. Why are you still here, Kennedy?"

My eyes dipped to his lips as he took one last step forward, putting himself squarely in front of me, close enough to touch. Close enough to kiss.

This was madness. The idea hadn't been there until he moved toward me. I should have escaped before my mind fell further under his influence.

"You're curious."

I couldn't speak, not with Alexei this close. But he didn't need me to tell him what he already knew. It was as if he could read every thought plainly on my face. One of his hands brushed my jaw.

"About me. About what it would feel like if I leaned forward…"

"Have you thought about this?" I licked my lips, feeling like I might combust if he didn't kiss me.

"These days, it's pretty much all I think about," he said, his lips brushing lightly against mine as he formed the words. "When I'm with you, when I'm without you..."

My next words sounded breathless. "You've already kissed me once." Once was all we agreed to.

"Are you saying no?" he asked.

I shook my head slowly.

"Then I don't care," he replied roughly before capturing my lips with his.

I needed no time to react, to match his movements. We went from tentatively feeling out each other's emotions, dancing around what we both wanted, to the most intense kiss of my entire life.

Alexei pinned me against the side of the hot tub, my legs coming up to wrap around his waist, pulling him closer to me. His hands settled on my hips, making those fantasies of mine a reality that far eclipsed my imagination. When his tongue worked its way into my mouth, teasing mine, a rush of desire flooded my entire body.

My hands clutched his back, kneading into the muscles behind his shoulders. My hips bucked toward him, searching for friction to relieve the near painful need growing inside me. Squirming for alternative positioning finally got me what I needed, Alexei's erection between my legs. But my body was more out of control, more desperate for him. Especially after he let out the sexiest groan. I didn't know how much longer I could keep going like this. I moaned loudly, grinding myself against him.

"Alexei, I..." My voice sounded desperate, a whimpered plea.

One of his hands traced an invisible line on my thigh back and forth, back and forth, back and forth, never going higher, not going where I needed him. I opened my eyes to find him watching me, his dark irises wide as saucers, and I gave him an encouraging nod.

That permission was all he needed to move his hand over my bathing suit bottom, once, twice, before moving the material aside and slipping two fingers inside of me. I gasped, throwing my head back against the side of the hot tub, letting him take over.

Alexei kissed up my throat, slowly, reverently, until he reached my ear. "What do you need?" he whispered, rough against my skin.

"Don't stop, *ple—*"

With the increased pressure from his fingers, I could no longer speak.

His question alone almost did it for me. But what I needed wasn't his words. More than anything, I needed to be closer to the man who had asked me what might have been the hottest question I'd ever heard.

I leaned forward until my lips met his, moving as urgently and out of control as I felt. The tension kept building, building, building, one spark away from coming apart.

When he raked his teeth against my bottom lip, the dam broke, forcing out a cry as warmth spread through my limbs.

My grip on his back fell slack, but Alexei's body molded me to the hot tub. His forehead rested against mine. I marveled at how natural it was to have him close to me. I sucked down oxygen, keeping my eyes closed, not wanting to deal with the very real consequences of what I'd let happen.

Too soon, Alexei pulled back, forcing us back to reality, a reality in which our relationship was for show.

So then, what the hell was this?

Alexei didn't seem keen to wait around to sort that out. He swam away from me, then propped one foot on the ladder to lift himself out of the hot tub, a movement that allowed me to see what I'd felt hard against me in the water.

"Wait," I called as he landed on the deck, not looking the least bit self-conscious. Not that he needed to. *Dear Lord.* "Where are you going?"

"To shower," he said, then he looked pointedly down at his crotch.

Oh.

"You don't want me to—"

"This isn't tit for tat, Kennedy."

"I know, but you..." My cheeks were set ablaze as I thought about everything that had unfolded between us. For better or worse, that memory was seared into my brain.

"I'll be fine," he said with a haughty grin I felt in my gut. "You gave me more than enough to think about."

I sat stunned in the wake of Alexei's departure, overwhelmed by his arrogance about kissing me senseless, getting me off, then leaving in a cloud of self-satisfaction. He had been unaffected by what happened, perfectly content to take care of himself. I could have done the same thing, never letting us go beyond an ill-advised make-out.

But I wanted him. Lost in a haze of lust and loneliness. Based on his smug smile, Alexei might have left with a different impression, something I had to rectify immediately.

I launched out of the hot tub, my legs a little unsteady for a few steps until I hit my stride. Surprisingly, Zach wasn't in his usual spot in the living room, which saved me the embarrassment of storming past him as I chased his roommate.

I burst into Alexei's bedroom without a knock, wanting to put him as off-kilter as I felt.

"Jesus, Kennedy," Alexei muttered, clutching a towel hanging from his waist.

"I need to talk to you," I said, refusing to acknowledge that he stood in front of me, only half-clothed once again. This had been a recipe for disaster earlier, but my eyes would not stray this time.

"I was about to jump in the shower."

"It can wait. What the hell was that?"

Alexei's mouth quirked. "First time?"

I wanted to knock the arrogance off his face. My hand spasmed at my side. "Stop fucking with me."

"Are you complaining?"

"No, I'm confused. What did you get out of that?"

He'd said he wasn't using me to get back at Justin, that this relationship between us was to save his hockey career. And I believed him.

But what happened in the hot tub wasn't for show... so was *that* something he did so he could later throw it in Justin's face? I hadn't thought he would use me like that, but...

I felt a mess of emotions about what happened between us.

"I've wanted to touch you like that for weeks."

The naked honesty of his words froze my spiraling thoughts in their tracks.

But we don't like each other, I almost said. *Or at least, we didn't.*

Attraction sometimes didn't have anything to do with a person's likability. He didn't have to have feelings for me to want me. And neither did I. Alexei Volkov temporarily had a role in my life, and I was allowed to have fun with him for as long as it worked for me and for him. It didn't have to be more than that.

"I don't want there to be a misunderstanding."

"About?"

"About what happened," I explained. "And how I feel."

"Ah." Alexei fell quiet, his face unreadable.

"I'm lonely, that's all."

"Right. You would have had the same reaction with any man."

"Well, no."

"Because you can't keep your eyes off me," he said, repeating my words.

As much as I wanted to argue, I couldn't. I struggled to focus my gaze anywhere but his bare chest. I folded my arms across my body, keeping the towel snug against me. "That was a mistake."

"Was it?" he asked, jutting out his chin. "It didn't sound that way."

My face burned, thinking of the way I'd begged him not to stop. "I hate you and your stupid smug face so much right now."

"You're frustrated, but don't tell me you're not turned on."

I stood silent, not willing to acknowledge the feeling that had gripped me in the hot tub had come roaring back.

"Why did you come here, Kennedy?" he asked again, taking a step toward me. "You want to keep this going?"

"What? No—"

"Why not? We're both single, and we can't date anyone else."

"Gee, thanks, you know how to make a girl feel good."

"If you're looking for something more, we should stop. A relationship is the last thing I want."

"I don't want a relationship with you either," I said.

"What's the problem then?"

"What happens in two months? We shake hands and go our separate ways?"

"That was always the plan, wasn't it?"

I walked toward him as I huffed out a reluctant "Fine." I needed to even the score between us, to make it clear this was tit for tat and nothing more. "Sit down."

Alexei hesitated a moment but didn't resist as I guided him toward the bed. I dropped to my knees.

"What are you doing?"

"This is what you want, right?" I reached for his towel, pulling it out of his lap without interference. I made no disguise of eyeing his crotch. "Sure seems like it," I said, projecting confidence despite my heart beating out of my chest at the idea of taking his thick length into my mouth.

I took a breath. Waiting, building his anticipation, was psyching me out.

Before I could grip him, Alexei interrupted. "Wait." He leaned back, grabbing a pillow and handing it to me to slide beneath my knees.

"Thank you," I said.

Then, before I could overthink it, I wrapped my hand firmly around his dick, pumping up and down. The sound of Alexei's groans did a number on me, but all I could do was clench my legs together and try to ignore the pounding want inside me.

I watched him watch me as I replaced my hand with my mouth. But then he lay back, flat against the bed, grasping the arm I placed on his stupidly toned stomach. Every strangled moan and those spasms as he got closer to coming amplified the spark of desire inside me. By the time he finished, I felt so turned on, I wanted to keep going, to wait until he was ready to go again… but then he sat up, hitting me with that double-dimple grin of his.

It was too much.

Quickly, I scrambled to my feet and gathered my towel from the floor. "I'm gonna head home."

Alexei frowned. "Is something wrong?"

"No, no. Nothing's wrong," I said as I walked backward to his bedroom door. *Not unless you counted enjoying tonight's sexual encounter with my fake boyfriend entirely too much.* "But it's two a.m., and I've got work in the morning."

Alexei's expression remained furrowed. "You sure that's it?"

"Yes, this was..." I grasped for something casual and light to convince him nothing was wrong. "Fun. We should do it again sometime. If you want."

"Okay."

My hand rested on the doorknob behind me, but I couldn't get myself to leave. *Okay?* That was his response to an offer of future sex. That was the response you give someone when they invited you to an early morning run. "Is something wrong?"

Alexei placed his hands behind his head, the picture of self-satisfaction if there ever was one. "Oh, I'm great." The mask of bravado returned, but two could play that game.

"Great!" I answered with false cheer as I finally pulled the door open. "See you later, then."

The insistent pounding between my legs outlasted my walk home, through my nighttime routine, until I was tucked into my bed. Every time I closed my eyes, all I could see was Alexei's expression of bliss as I closed my mouth over him. The mind-blowing orgasm from earlier tonight did nothing to ebb the desire coursing through me.

I had to take matters into my own hands—twice—to relax enough to fall asleep. It was his fingers working me over, his name repeating in my mind each time I fell apart.

I had never been more screwed.

26

ALEXEI

I LEFT BRIGGSY AND Matt in the hot tub during our postgame recovery pizza party and headed over to see Kennedy.

Days had passed since Kennedy surprised me after my road trip, since the night we hooked up and complicated our relationship. I couldn't have cared less at the time, not after I tasted her full lips, so intoxicating I forgot every reason to stop before we started.

And then she wrapped her legs around my waist, trapping me against her in a vice I didn't want to leave. And Christ, when she followed me upstairs and got on her knees... the details of that replayed every time I got into bed.

Falling asleep took longer than usual these last few days.

Gemma opened the door after I rang the doorbell. "Hey stranger," she greeted, dropping a kiss onto my cheek. "Surprised to see you remembered where we live."

"Don't tell me you're hurt I missed dinner."

She looked at me pointedly. "*Two* dinners, Volk."

"I've been busy."

Gemma made a sound that told me she didn't buy the bullshit I was selling. But I did make other plans because I was too chickenshit to see Kennedy, not wanting her to confirm what I feared to be true. Her parting words—*This was fun. We should do it again sometime. If you want.*—made it clear that night meant something very different to her than it had to me.

Gemma smiled knowingly. "Oh, I've noticed. You've done more in the last few days than I've seen you do since you got here. Couldn't help that none of your plans involved my girl tho—"

"Gemma," Kennedy interrupted. She stood halfway down the stairs, dressed for work in her standard outfit of leggings and a T-shirt. She wore her hair pulled back in a messy bun. "Hey, Alexei."

"Kennedy," I said, giving her a quick nod, forcing my eyes not to linger too long on her.

Gemma blew out a breath. "How the two of you convince anyone you're dating is beyond me."

"They haven't been convincing anyone of anything lately," Deandra called from the other room.

I hadn't expected her to be here, but maybe Kennedy had rekindled their friendship.

"And before you ask, yes, the internet has noticed you haven't been spotted together in weeks."

Kennedy's eyes found mine for only a blink before she headed toward Deandra.

Don't watch her walk away. Don't watch her walk away. She almost made it completely into the other room before I lost my willpower. Those leggings left nothing to the imagination, sealing themselves around the ass I had an overwhelming desire to palm... again.

Gemma's knowing smirk told me she saw the entire thing.

"Don't say a word," I muttered.

Kennedy always commanded my attention, all the way back to the first night we met, but my awareness of her was painfully amplified. That night, she was an outline in the dark, someone I didn't know but wanted to come closer to see. But now I knew how it felt to have her body pressed against mine, the way she tasted, the sound of her moan. I struggled to shake the jolt of adrenaline when her name showed up on my phone during my road trip, and when I found her standing in my house after I got back. It was the moment of anticipation before the puck hit the ice.

"The team is winning, that's the story. No one cares about that old picture," Kennedy said, perched on the arm of the couch.

Deandra slid her phone across the couch to Kennedy. "That's not what the internet says."

Kennedy's eyes scanned the screen, getting larger at whatever she read. "People like drama, but that's all died down, hasn't it? Maybe we... quietly end this."

I gritted my teeth against the tightness in my chest. We agreed to three months, but she wanted out now. If the bolting from my room after we hooked up the other night didn't make it clear, her wanting out of this arrangement hammered her feelings home.

She regretted what happened between us, while I lived in those memories. Losing this complication I couldn't afford sent a ripple of panic through me. I needed more time to figure out what it meant.

If we ended our arrangement now, we would never talk about what happened between us. We'd lose whatever relationship we built. And there was *something*. Otherwise, we wouldn't have texted night and day while I was on the road. It would have died out eventually, but neither of us let it.

"You think attention is going to *die down* just before Justin Ward comes to town?" Deandra laughed as she snatched her phone back.

Kennedy straightened. "He's... when is he coming back?"

"Next Wednesday. Two nights after the fundraiser."

"We should go together," I said carelessly. Desperately. At least my voice sounded casual. I stopped hovering in the kitchen and strode into the room where they sat. "Think about it. If we're pictured there together, someone will ask Ward, and he'll spout off at the mouth like he always does. It'll drum up our rivalry right before the game, and more people will want to be there."

Deandra clucked her tongue. "You know, Volkov, sometimes I like you."

"But do you need all of that?" Kennedy pressed. She spoke to Deandra rather than me. "Hasn't winning helped with attendance and with Volk's image?"

Her use of my hockey nickname scraped my chest. "Not enough," I said, unable to stop myself.

Kennedy's eyes didn't stray from Deandra, wanting her to confirm what I said.

"His press coverage has improved, but we need more time. And the extra attention for the team won't hurt either."

"You want to keep faking this?" Kennedy asked, addressing me for the first time.

I smirked. "It's not all fake, is it?"

Her mouth parted in surprise. She didn't dart a glance at either of her friends but instead kept her gaze on me. "My feelings of annoyance aren't."

I huffed out a laugh. *Feelings of annoyance* was one way to characterize what existed between us. But there were plenty of other nonfake things happening. I wasn't about to reveal that in front of anyone else though. There would be other opportunities, with us alone, to confront her.

Gemma sat uncharacteristically quiet, observing the entire exchange. She briefly glanced at me, but I couldn't read her expression.

"We agreed on one team event," Kennedy reminded me, as if I had forgotten.

"But up to three dates a month," I replied. "And we haven't had *any* dates this month, unless you count—"

Kennedy shot off the couch, pushing me out of the room. "Fine, I'll go. And now *you* can leave so we can get work done."

We stopped moving as soon as I offered a smidge of resistance. "You're working? On what?"

"It's nothing—"

"Kennedy is helping with the fundraiser after my good-for-nothing employee quit with no notice," Deandra explained. "We would have been screwed without you, Kens."

Her face revealed nothing, even as I said, "I didn't know you were working for the team again?"

"I'm not." She was still avoiding my gaze. "I'm helping out. It's not a big deal."

Gemma rested a hand on Kennedy's shoulder. "Can I talk to you for a minute? Alone."

Kennedy followed Gemma into the other room. They walked down the hallway, huddled close together, their lips moving quickly.

"She's never talked to you about coming back?" Deandra appeared at my side, breaking my concentration and making me realize how long I'd stared after Kennedy. "To work for the Wolves," she added.

"No, she's... not very open."

"She hasn't been the same since her mom died. But she kept that secret about Ward before then. Maybe I never knew her as well as I thought I did. I wouldn't have been able to keep a secret like that. But that's Kennedy—she'll hurt herself before anyone else. She gave up school to help her parents, and she loved school. She had big plans. She's wasting her talent. You'll see at the fundraiser."

"You're good at convincing her to do what you want," I observed.

"Pot meet kettle." Deandra narrowed her eyes at me.

I schooled my features to blandness, not wanting to give anything away.

"Anyway, dating you, planning a party, I think she'll survive."

Maybe she would, but I worried I wouldn't.

27

KENNEDY

THE NIGHT OF THE Wolves fundraiser, a classic, out-of-nowhere southern storm moved in. Alexei rang the doorbell, holding an umbrella with the Wolves insignia, but it did barely anything against the rain coming down in buckets. I waved him in before heading to the kitchen with my phone to my ear as Deandra recounted the alternative setup for the night. Swimming would be out, but she moved the photo booth to the foyer, the third food station into an unused hallway, and cleared the furniture out of our main room to create a bigger space for a dance floor. I would have been there to help with the last-minute scramble if I didn't need to arrive at the party with Alexei.

After hanging up, I turned to find Alexei leaning in the doorway, watching me, wearing the same heated gaze as the night we ended up in the hot tub together. "You look beautiful."

Out of habit, I glanced at my body, covered tonight in a little black dress paired with black strappy sandals, a silver necklace with an emerald heart charm, and hoop earrings. I tucked my loose, straight blue-black hair behind my ears, giving myself a moment to recover from the compliment and escape his look—like he wanted to skip the party altogether and keep me to himself.

"Thank you. I, um, like your suit."

He gripped each opening of his navy-blue-plaid jacket and flicked it out. The flaps fell against the black polo shirt underneath. A perfect mix of formal and casual, like me. "I can't let you steal all the attention."

I rolled my eyes. "Oh please. When I'm next to you, I might as well not exist."

Alexei strolled over to me, offering his arm. I snatched my wristlet off the counter as I hooked my arm in his.

"When you're next to me, you're the only person who does exist."

I nudged him in the side, opting to joke to avoid acknowledging exactly how those words affected me. "Save it for the party, hotshot."

He looked down, his infuriatingly handsome smirk in place. "Don't worry about my game, Cole."

Unbidden, his words from the other night popped into my head. *I've wanted to touch you like that for weeks.*

Oh, he had lines for days, and every single one of them worked their magic on me.

I insisted on driving my truck since Alexei's flashy sports car wouldn't do well in this storm. Even with the windshield wipers on full tilt, I could barely see. After reaching the highway, I kept my speed slow and my hazards on, knowing I would never live it down in Palmer City if I injured their newly anointed star winger. As we reached the exit for my dad's house, the music stopped abruptly and my Bluetooth announced Justin Ward was calling. I ignored the call, willing the music to distract from it. And maybe it would have if Justin hadn't called again.

"Why is he calling you, Kennedy?" Alexei asked as I declined the call. The music blared back into the car until Alexei turned it down.

"I don't know," I said, keeping my eyes on the dimly lit road.

"You don't know," he repeated, a hint of skepticism in his voice. I could feel his gaze on me.

"No," I snapped, my hands tightening on the wheel. "Did you want me to answer so the three of us could work out the root of our problems in the middle of a rainstorm on the way to my dad's house?"

"Shit, I'm sorry, Kennedy. The game's in two days... I'm in my head." He took a deep breath. I said nothing. The game had hung over us for the last week. Everything played out as predicted. Justin ran his mouth online, presumably after seeing recent photos Alexei and I posted together. The media asked Justin and Alexei about their rivalry at their press conferences, and each of them hyped up the game, as if they were two fighters about to step into the octagon.

When I didn't respond, Alexei said, "You're not... back in touch with him?"

"No, I'm not back in touch with him. Not that it should matter to you bec—"

My words halted as I let out a blood-curdling scream, slamming my brakes to avoid the deer running into the road. The quick action caused my truck to hydroplane. I quickly turned the steering wheel, trying to keep us on the road, but I only managed to send water into the air. I slammed on the brakes again to prevent us from smacking straight into a tree after the car went into the downward-sloping grass.

My breath came in labored gasps. Alexei removed his seat belt and leaned over me, one hand on my arm, the other on my face, turning it toward him.

"Are you all right?" he asked, his big, wild eyes scanning me. "Kennedy—"

"I'm fine, just shaken," I said. "You're okay?"

He nodded. "I'm an asshole. I shouldn't have distracted you like that."

"It wasn't your fault. I was paying attention. It just happened so fast."

His hand remained on my face, his fingers tracing back and forth on my chin. When his gaze dropped to my lips, my breath caught. Was he going to kiss me again? Did I want him to kiss me again?

I told him only once, and we already broke that rule. But still, my eyes started to flutter shut...

Wait—no. *No*. I did not want him to kiss me again.

Neither of us wanted a relationship, and soon, we would part ways, as if nothing happened between us.

But I didn't know if I could do that. When it came to Alexei, the valve I'd placed on my emotions failed.

"Kennedy," he said, his fingers moving up to caress my cheek. His chest moved quickly, intent clear in his eyes.

No, this could not happen again.

Alexei would move on from me. Maybe I would want that, but maybe I wouldn't. I couldn't risk being tossed aside, especially not when I would have to continue to see him because of his connection to Matt and Gemma. It would hurt too damn much. We needed to make the smart choice and stop whatever we'd started the other night in its tracks.

I said the only words guaranteed to kill the growing tension between us. "Why do you hate him?"

Alexei blinked, as if emerging from a trance, pulling his hands back from me, the loss of contact so stark I almost regretted ruining the moment. He flopped back against his seat.

"We should get to the party."

"Fine," I said, not disguising my annoyance. I turned the key in the ignition and put the car in reverse as soon as it came to life. But when I pressed the gas pedal, we didn't move. The tires spun and spun, stuck in the mud left by the storm.

"I'll get out and push the car while you back up."

"No way. You can't show up to the party covered in mud. All of this will be for nothing. I'll call Triple-A."

"That'll take an hour."

"Then it takes an hour," I said.

The dial tone blared through the car speakers effectively ending our conversation. Alexei answered with an exasperated sigh, louder than the phone, something that satisfied me after he blew off my question.

It did nothing to quell my inconvenient desire to kiss him though. Two months ago, I didn't think I could convince people of our relationship; as hot as Alexei was, I had no interest in a self-important ass who prioritized himself over his team and demanded attention at every turn.

But that wasn't Alexei, despite what Justin and the media described. The Alexei I knew—the one who would inconvenience himself to make his rookie roommate comfortable, who made me feel like a priority even when he was on the road, who looked to satisfy *me* while expecting nothing for himself—was someone I liked. And *that* complicated everything.

"Are we really going to sit in silence?" I finally asked.

Alexei's head rested against the seat, his eyes shut. "You're the one who established we wouldn't talk about Ward. I've been following your lead."

"You brought him up first tonight," I pointed out.

"It surprised me, okay?" The words tore out of him, loud and frustrated, as if wrenched from a place he tried, and failed, to keep a lid on. "I can't believe you're talking to the asshole who called you his leftovers."

"I told you, I'm not talking to him."

"Then why is he calling you?"

"I don't know." I threw my hands in the air. "Look, I haven't talked to him since the day we broke up. He texted me once—So that's how you want to play it. I never responded. Not that this is any of your business."

Alexei's frantic breath filled the car. On instinct, I reached over to take his hand. He flinched before relaxing into my touch. We remained like that, silent, until his heaving chest calmed to its normal rhythm.

Gently, I asked, "Are you going to tell me why you hate him? The real reason."

He shifted in his seat. "Justin and I played juniors together, did he tell you that?"

"Yeah, I think so." Though part of me knew he hadn't. Justin and I didn't have that kind of relationship, though somehow I managed to convince myself we did.

"Justin was seventeen and captain of the team," Alexei said, his eyes still closed. "I was fifteen, here alone and could barely understand anyone. Even though I was one of the youngest players, Ward felt threatened by me. He was better than me, I'm not too proud to admit that, but my ceiling was higher than his. He must have realized it, otherwise he wouldn't have iced me out. The rest of the team followed his lead, by the way. And then one night, I saw him on the ice with his father. You know his story, right?"

He cracked open one eye, turning his head toward me. I nodded, though I didn't know much. Only that Justin obsessively took care of his body, afraid he might suffer the same career-ending injuries his father did.

"His dad abused him, physically and verbally. Justin had been a dick to me since I joined the team, but I felt for him at that moment. Not that it excuses it..."

Abused. It made so much sense, explained so much about Justin.

"I told him what I saw, Kennedy, but Ward shut it down. I think he couldn't stand that I had seen him weak. That's when he came after me, for learning his secret. He tampered with my equipment. Played dirty during practice. Said shit to my teammates that I didn't understand, but I knew couldn't be good because they would laugh, openly, in front of me."

My stomach clenched, thinking of Alexei in a new country, all alone and suffering. He tried to do the right thing—he tried to help—and Justin's cruelty had been his reward. I knew what that was like too well. Because for all Justin did for me and as much as I loved him, he'd turned on me too, plenty of times. Even when my intentions were good. Even when I didn't do anything wrong.

"What was I supposed to do?" Alexei continued, the words coming easier now. "I needed to get drafted. I didn't want anyone to think I was a problem or I couldn't hack it. The odds were already impossible, so I stayed out of his way. Kept my head down. Never said anything to anyone. Until you."

It felt like that night we talked on the phone while he was on the road. As if we could say anything to each other in this bubble, without fear of judgment.

"Ward was gone after one season, drafted into the NHL in the first round like he wanted. When we next faced each other, he still targeted me. It spiraled from there, because I was no longer a gangly fifteen-year-old kid he could push around. I came at him just as hard. He's still the only player I've ever wanted to hurt."

His anxiety over the upcoming game finally made sense. Sure, Alexei wanted to win and to show Justin up after all his shit talk. But the real source had been the battle he knew he would have on his hands, thanks to their past, but also because he'd poked a wasp's nest.

I squeezed his hand. "Why did you want to do this if you knew it would make things worse?"

He spun his head toward me, his eyes now open. "I'm not going to let him take anything from me."

I nodded my understanding; those words weren't only his explanation but a call for me to not let him do the same. How he had known I needed to explain, I didn't know, but I didn't dwell on it. I opened my mouth to finally say what I'd kept inside since the breakup.

"I let him take too much," I admitted. "Or rather, I gave in too much. To his rules and routines. But I knew how to navigate it, even if I didn't like it. I don't know, it probably sounds weird to you, ceding control like that."

"Your life felt out of control after your mom died. He imposed structure. I understand why you wanted that."

The rain continued to patter on the windows, a calming presence. I didn't know how much time had passed since I called for help, but I found myself wishing for them to never show up. To allow Alexei and I to exist like this a little longer.

"Getting this distance and... meeting you, I realized I made the easy choice by staying with him. There were a lot of problematic parts of our relationship I ignored. I think I knew it, but I kept shoving it away."

"You wanted it to work, so you made it work."

"Exactly."

Alexei turned away again, this time dropping my hand. "Gemma wanted to set us up. Did she tell you that?"

The abrupt change in subject hit me like whiplash. "What?"

Gemma hadn't said anything to me, unsurprisingly since she knew my stance on Alexei Volkov and that I'd hoped to soon move in with my boyfriend.

He let out a small, short laugh. "She thought we'd have something in common."

"That sounds like Gemma, aggravatingly vague."

"Maybe she wanted us to find out for ourselves."

I thought back to what Alexei told me about his last relationship, how he stayed long past its expiration and understood his point. "What? We're both damaged in the same way."

His gaze fell on me again, dark and serious, whooshing the air straight out of my lungs. "That we're the same. We will do anything to make things work, even when we know they won't. Even if it hurts us."

I snorted. "So we're both idiots."

"When we're with the wrong people. Sacrificing for someone who takes and takes burns us out. But for another person like us, there would be balance. Reciprocation."

"Nice theory," I said, deflecting the weight of his statement with the expert shield I'd learned to wield over the last year. "But Gemma's matchmaking is almost always focused on proximity. I wouldn't read too much into it."

A couple of raps on my window from Triple-A helped me escape the conversation. He told us he would pull us back onto the road with his tow truck.

Soon, we would arrive at my father's party, hand-in-hand, beaming smiles on our faces, as if we were smitten with each other.

Pretending it was true no longer felt like the most difficult part.

28

ALEXEI

So much had changed since the last time I stood in front of Cale Cole's house. But there was one constant—staying on my game and convincing the people at this party I deserved to be here, that the team made the right choice in giving me a chance.

"You did all this?" I asked as we walked into the foyer.

Deandra hadn't oversold Kennedy's abilities if she helped pull this event together. Throngs of people filled the house—all elegantly dressed—as servers moved through the crowd, carrying drinks and food, pausing every so often. Soft classical music played below the din of conversation. Fairy lights hung from the walls, making the rooms dim and cozy. And beside us, near the front door, sat a large poster board showing the progress in raising funds for this year's chosen charity, an organization that supported underprivileged kids in playing sports.

"It's a party. Don't sound so awed," Kennedy said, though I watched as she surveyed the room with pride. She leaned into me. "I think we should start with my dad."

"Lead the way." I reached for her hand.

It didn't take long to spot Cale Cole near the bar, surrounded by several men in suits. He waved us over, drawing interested glances from his companions who began whispering to each other. Kennedy squeezed my hand tighter as we approached.

"Kenny," Cale said, stepping forward to wrap his arms around her.

"Hey, Dad," she said into his shoulder.

He pulled back from the hug, his gaze roaming over her face, as if he needed the reminder she was okay. Knowing he lost his wife not that long ago, it broke my heart. "Deandra informed me you had a large hand in pulling this event off. It's incredible. Thank you."

Kennedy beamed under his praise. "Dad, you remember Alexei Volkov, right?"

He barked out a laugh, the kind that lingered for a beat too long. His companions tittered at the cheesiness of the joke.

"I guess that date went well after all," he said to Kennedy, forcing a blush to creep into her cheeks.

I sucked in a breath as Cale's attention fell on me. The last time I talked to him had been in this house when he told me to show everyone why they made the right decision in signing me. He told me to lead this team and to avoid drama.

Not to get photographed with his daughter, and certainly not to date her.

And yet, I detected no anger in his expression as he stuck his hand out to me. "Always good to see you, Alexei. Even if you're accompanying my pride and joy."

There it is. The subtle warning didn't take long.

Kennedy hissed, "*Dad.*"

I relaxed my features, my breathing, wanting to appear at ease in front of the father of my fake girlfriend, the man who also happened to write my paychecks. As if I had done nothing wrong.

Kennedy knew the truth though. I couldn't hide the slickness of my palms from her unless I dropped her hand. I wouldn't; opportunities to be close to her like this shrunk with each passing day.

"If it makes you feel better, she doesn't make anything easy for me," I said.

He jutted his chin out in pride. "Good," he said simply, appraising my expression. Whatever he saw must have answered his questions, because he turned back to his companions. "Let me introduce you."

The next twenty minutes turned into a series of questions for me about the season. I answered all of them thoroughly, with more enthusiasm than I mustered for the media. When Kennedy stifled a yawn, I told them, "Well, I think we've bored Kennedy enough."

Her father waved a hand. "Nonsense, my daughter loves the game. She used to go to every one with her mother and Deandra. Same seats, center ice, behind the team bench. Even though they could have been in my box, that's what they preferred."

"I keep hoping she'll show up to one of my games." My gaze bored into the side of Kennedy's face, but she refused to look at me. Dropping my hand sent the message clear enough.

"Kenny," her dad chided.

She shrugged. "I'll show up when he earns it."

A chorus of *oohs* rang out from the group. I elbowed the air, playing along with what only I suspected wasn't fully a joke. "See what I have to deal with?"

"Okay, well, *this* has been fun but we really should—"

Cale interrupted Kennedy's attempt to end the conversation. "She's always been like this, ever since she was a kid. You remember your thirteenth birthday party, Kenny? I think I still have the video—"

"Okay, okay!" she shouted. "No one needs to see that."

"As much as I'd *love* to see that," I said, sharing a knowing glance with her dad, "let's not make her too angry. It'll be a thing for days."

"Good call. We don't want it to bleed into the holiday." Cale paused, deliberating his next words. "Do you already have plans for Thanksgiving, Volk?"

Kennedy's head snapped to her father, quick as a whip. "Dad, it's—"

He held up his hand, speaking loudly over her objections again. "I've never met any of her boyfriends. Clearly, you're important to my daughter, so we should spend more time together."

She groaned loudly and muttered under her breath, "Kill me now."

I replied without looking at her. "Yes, sir. I'll be there." Then I held out a hand to Kennedy. "Dance with me?"

She wrinkled her nose in the adorable way I loved. She stared at my hand, refusing to take it. Hesitation was her power move, but it would take more than that to get me to back down. "Come on, Cole. Don't tell me you can't dance."

"I can dance, smartass," she snapped, finally slapping her hand into mine.

Cale laughed as he returned to his spot against the wall. "Have fun, kids."

Kennedy elbowed me in the side as I pulled her to the dance floor. The hit didn't even register, but it allowed me to tug her closer into a slow-dancing position. "What are you doing?"

I rested my hands on her hips. "It'll be easier to talk to you this way."

KENNEDY

"Talk to me about what, exactly?" I asked, placing my hands on his shoulders, which took a bit of stretch given his height. I said the words to his chest, not trusting myself. The desire to kiss him crowded out any rational thought.

He tipped my chin, forcing me to meet his gaze. Desire pooled low in my gut, distracting me entirely from any annoyance at our last conversation, at any apprehension of what he might ask me next. All I thought about was how his tongue had parted my lips in the hot tub, his fingers running along the inside of my thigh, his groan when I slid his dick into my mouth.

My breath came quicker now, my want for him mirrored in his dilated, near-black pupils. He tightened his grip on my hips as I shuffled even closer to him.

"Fuck, Kennedy." Alexei broke eye contact, his gaze trailing around the room. He let out a long breath, breaking the moment and giving us both time to collect ourselves.

After a silent minute, I said, "I didn't know he was going to invite you to Thanksgiving. Does this mess up your plans?"

He smirked. "You mean with my *Russian* family, who don't celebrate Thanksgiving?"

"Oh. Right."

"My mom is visiting though, because we have a couple of days off and a home game stretch. She'd love to meet you, I'm sure."

I tried to ignore the little flutter those words gave me; the line between real and fake was becoming harder to discern. There had been real moments between us, like the one in the car ride over here, but too much had been scripted for me to always tell the difference. Like now—did Alexei want to come to my family's house for Thanksgiving and introduce me to his mom? Or was he only playing along?

"And your dad?" I prompted.

"He's staying in Russia," he replied. "My parents are separated. They have a complicated history."

From the set of his jaw, I should have backed off, but I couldn't help myself. I wanted to know more about him. "What does that mean?"

His gaze focused on a spot over my head. "My dad has taken my mom for granted his entire life. His dreams were always more important than her. He's managed to always be there for me. I've had to set their relationship apart from my own with him, otherwise we wouldn't have one." Alexei swallowed hard, his throat bobbing. "The thing I hate most is that I've turned into him. In every relationship I've ever had, I've been told I made them feel second place in my life, second to my career. I want... a family, someone I can come home to. An us-against-the-world type of love. But I don't think I'm cut out for it."

The heavy confession hung between us as we continued to sway slowly to an upbeat song. Sharing this with me at this crowded party was suboptimal, but maybe that was why he did it. He had to hold it together here, and if the conversation veered in a direction he didn't want to go, he had an easy out. There were hundreds of people he could escape to talk to instead.

"You haven't been that way with me."

"This doesn't count, and you know it." An edge crept into his voice, almost as if he resented my words.

I swallowed, knowing my next words would offer more than I wanted. "It meant something to me," I admitted. "I think it's been fairly obvious I've had a rough go of it. You've made it easier."

Easier and harder, but I couldn't admit *that* much.

This gave Alexei the opening to ask what we'd avoided addressing the last two weeks. "You bolted out of my house like it was on fire," he said, studying my expression. I offered him a small nod. "Care to explain?"

"You didn't do anything wrong."

I expected him to grin haughtily and make a joke about his sexual capabilities, but he remained quiet, staring intently at me.

"I don't have much experience with this whole casual thing. So I—"

"Panicked?" He scoffed. "Yeah, I got that."

"I hope I didn't bruise your male ego too hard."

"Not at all. Or did you forget how you moaned my name earlier in the night?"

I threw up my hands. "And there it is," I said, trying to step away from him, but his strong grip on my hips kept me in place. Every time I thought a moment between us was real, Alexei, or the universe, reminded me it wasn't.

"Hold on," Alexei said. He threaded one hand through mine. We danced in an old-timey position, our entwined hands held away from our bodies. "It was a stupid joke. I'm also new to this."

It was my turn to scoff. "Oh please. To casual hookups?"

"With a woman I'm pretending to date. Yeah." Alexei took a deep breath and let it out slowly. "I would never have... gone *there* with you if I thought it would screw this up." He tucked strands of hair behind one of my ears. "You're different than I thought you'd be," he said, repeating my words from the Halloween party.

“For the record, you didn’t screw anything up. I got into my own head.”

One side of Alexei’s lips turned up into a small smile. “I’m familiar with that problem.” He opened his mouth once then closed it, warring with himself over his next words. I offered him a smile, feeling for the first time that maybe, *just maybe*, we battled the same feelings. “Do you want to get out of here? I’ve been waiting to watch the end of *The Nightstand* until I was with you.”

“After this song,” I said, leaning forward until my face rested on his shoulder.

29

ALEXEI

KENNEDY DRUMMED HER FINGERS against the steering wheel as we sat at a red light before turning into our neighborhood. We'd spent most of the drive in comfortable silence with music playing in the background. She caught me looking at her once and held my stare, offering me a small smile. But with the proximity of my house, her relaxed state changed.

"You don't have to be nervous," I told her.

"What?"

I nodded to her still drumming fingers, which immediately put a stop to the motion.

"I'm not nervous. What would I have to be nervous about?"

"I don't know," I said, overenunciating the words. "You know what happens in the show. It couldn't be because we'll be alone again."

Kennedy laughed, giving me the sound of pure joy I loved. "Someone is mighty full of himself."

But as she pulled up in front of her house, her laughter ebbed, and she hit me with a look full of heat, her gaze roaming from my face to my lap. She unbuckled her seat belt before inching her dress up to midthigh.

My eyes tracked her movements, drawn to the smooth creamy skin on display before me. Without a word, she swung one leg over the console, creating enough momentum to propel her entire body into my lap. She flushed at her clumsy movement, maybe at the boldness to surprise me like this. I pushed her hair over her shoulders before settling my hands on her hips.

"I told you I wasn't nervous," she whispered, those big brown eyes snaring me. She rolled her hips, pulling us closer and eliciting a groan from me. Her eyes widened at discovering exactly how much my body craved her, hard for her in moments.

"I can see that." I scanned the length of her, from her flushed, wild-eyed gaze to where she straddled my waist. Not making a move took a ridiculous amount of self-control, but I wanted to see what she would do next.

Her parted lips remained inches from mine as she exhaled, long and slow. "I've been wanting to do this for hours," she said, finally placing a hand on each side of my jaw and closing the space between our lips.

I kept my mouth still, allowing her to kiss my top lip first before moving to suck my bottom. When she deepened the kiss, sliding her tongue against mine, I lost my grip on self-control. She moaned into my mouth when I moved my tongue against hers, ratcheting up our pace.

Everything after that became frantic movements. The desperate slide of our lips, over and over, her fingers pulling at strands of my hair, my hands tracing her thighs beneath her dress, her hips bucking into me, making it impossible for me to think at all.

Time became meaningless.

"Alexei." Kennedy pulled back just enough to separate our lips. Her words came between panting breaths. "I want you now." Her shaking hands fumbled with my belt, the clanking sound reverberating in the silent car.

I placed my hands over hers to still the movement.

"What? Do you not—"

"How can you ask that?" I said, moving her hands slightly south. A move I regretted because it made it that much more difficult to exercise restraint. "But not here."

She glanced around the car, as if suddenly remembering we were parked on a public street where anyone could stumble upon us. "Right. Sorry. I got... carried away."

I laughed, tipping her chin so she could meet my stare. "Never apologize for coming on to me. Ever."

Kennedy climbed off my lap onto the driver's side of the car.

"Are you worried people might see you parked in front of my house?" I asked, wondering why she parked here instead of at my place, which was where I assumed we were headed. Matt and Gemma would be home any minute, and I had no desire to talk to them about whatever was buzzing between Kennedy and me.

"No, but I figured..." She trailed off, fiddling with the keys hanging from the ignition. "I didn't want to be in the way..." She smiled shyly.

Tomorrow morning when I leave for practice. She planned to stay the night, not bolt like last time or sneak out after I fell asleep.

"Now who's mighty full of herself?"

"I hate you," she groaned.

"You know, I won't believe those words from you ever again."

"Why, because I pounced on you?" She rolled her eyes, facing me to make sure I saw it. "Don't let it go to your head."

"No, not only that." I reached out to rest my hand on her arm, a gesture to get her to look at me. "This entire night... I don't talk to other people like I talk to you. I don't *share* with anyone. And I don't think you do either."

You lit up when people acknowledged our relationship.

You rested your head against my shoulder while we danced.

You came home with me.

I didn't dare say the words because they could mean nothing at all. All part of our act mixed with a heavy dose of lust. The guests at the party weren't the only ones buying the narrative though. She made me believe it too. Either she acted her ass off or some part of her had blurred the lines between fake and real, like I'd done.

She shook her head slowly as she opened her door. "No, I don't."

I followed her lead, climbing out of the car, hoping my confession didn't freak her out. Kennedy yanked her dress into place but didn't bother fixing anything else—the strap that slipped from her shoulder, her tousled hair, the smudged lip gloss across her lips turned thoroughly pink from kissing me. Once she reached my side, she gasped in surprise. I followed her line of sight, spotting the shadow rising to its feet on Matt and Gemma's porch. Instinctively, I stepped in front of her.

"Kennedy?"

Motherfucker.

The shadow took several steps until the streetlight slanted across his face, revealing that the worst possible end to my night had, in fact, come true. Justin Ward paused halfway through the yard as he realized who else stood in front of him.

Kennedy didn't move a muscle, not to walk toward him or to give a single inkling on her face of how she felt.

"What the fuck are you doing here?" The words flew out of my mouth before I could stop them. I was prepared to meet him on the ice in two days. Not here. Not in my personal life. Professionally, I would continue to see Ward until one of us retired from hockey, and that was too damn often.

"Kennedy," Ward repeated, ignoring me. He didn't so much as look in my direction. "I need to talk to you."

"How did you know where I was?"

"Lucky guess." He grinned, as if this was part of their history, an inside joke.

I wanted to knock his teeth in.

She looked at me, and before she said anything, I knew our night was ending. Never mind he trash-talked her to the media, she would choose him. Jump because he deigned to show her an ounce of attention.

"Talk to him," I said loud enough for Ward to hear, so he knew he hadn't won this round. "Find me after."

"Bold of you to assume there will be an after," Ward sneered.

Kennedy scowled at him. "I'll only be a couple of minutes," she whispered, leaning into me. "I'll—"

"Don't bother," I whispered back, my voice all ice. "I don't have time for distractions before the game."

Kennedy flinched. "You're right. You're not cut out for it."

I fixed my expression in neutral, not wanting her to know how much it bothered me to have my confession from earlier thrown in my face. Why should it matter if Kennedy thought I wasn't cut out for a relationship? We would never have one. After one more month, she would let herself be dragged back to Ward. That the first steps toward that outcome were happening earlier than expected was the only surprise.

She pasted a smile on her face, one I saw her flash plenty of times tonight, and said loud enough for Justin to hear. "I'll see you in a bit."

Playacting, that was all we were.

"Can't wait to see your ass on the ice, asshole," I said to Ward before stalking toward my house, refusing to give either of them another look.

30

KENNEDY

Tonight, Justin Ward would return to Palmer City to face off against his old team. Everything led to this moment—the trade, the picture of Alexei and me, our fabricated relationship, the antagonizing press conferences. Deandra gleefully texted this morning to share that the game had the highest ticket sales of the season, nearly selling out for the first time in half a dozen years.

I hadn't watched a hockey game since my mom died, but tonight, I would tune in from home.

Everything played out exactly as we'd intended. The Wolves had a winning record. Media coverage was boosted. People filled the arena. Alexei led the team in goals.

And in a month, we'd part ways after successfully milking everything we could from this "scandal."

The idea of pulling this off should have filled me with a glimmer of happiness or a sense of accomplishment. The team wouldn't move, not after the way this season electrified Palmer City.

Dating Alexei made Justin jealous, a small punishment for how he'd treated me. He wore the emotion all over his face the other night. Not that I could celebrate it. After Alexei stalked off, I couldn't think of anything but what I snapped at him. I refused to talk to Justin, instead storming into the house like the coward I was.

Guilt sat like a rock in my stomach.

"And here we go," one of the announcers gleefully stated as the ref dropped the puck and Justin won the faceoff. "The game we've all been waiting for."

I drank in everything about the game—the electric way the players glided across the ice, the sound of skates scraping and players slamming into the boards, the familiar music blaring through the arena, the team that belonged to my family. The game my mother loved.

I loved it too.

I forgot how much joy it brought me. Or maybe I buried it deep to avoid what I'd lost. That connection to my mother, to something bigger than myself. I remembered the giddiness of game day when I worked for the Wolves, how Deandra and I would change into our jerseys in the bathroom after work, the ones emblazoned with our last names. Sometimes we swapped, so I sported Collins and she wore Cole. We waited in long lines for overpriced beer and too-salty pretzels.

It wasn't only that my parents owned the team. I loved that my work contributed to the event playing out in front of me, connecting people. It allowed them to escape from their lives for a couple of hours. My work mattered, not in some larger cosmic sense—I wasn't curing cancer—but people showed up to support and love the organization I worked for.

Please tell me you're watching this. My phone buzzed with a message from Gemma after the first scrum between Justin and Alexei with three minutes left in the first period. Alexei had gained a step on

Justin while in the offensive zone, and Justin hacked at him. It took him off his skates and sent him sliding into the goal. Alexei popped onto his feet and charged Justin. Soon, every player got in on the action, taking swings or pulling players back.

I'm watching, I texted back.

Your little rivalry is heating up.

In the penalty boxes, Justin and Alexei shouted at each other. Justin smirked, enjoying every moment of their fight. Alexei looked the opposite, his expression murderous before he covered his face with a towel to dry his sweat and the blood from a cut on his chin. The cameras remained on them until the game resumed.

Not my rivalry. This hatred had existed long before I came into the picture.

The game was tied when the third period began, amping up the undercurrent of tension humming through the arena. The tension ignited when Alexei and Justin fought each other along the boards for the puck, an extended fight that ended with Alexei shoving Justin and Justin taking a swing at Alexei's face.

The crowd erupted in cheers, screams, and pounds to the glass as they dropped their gloves to trade punches. Justin snagged Alexei's jersey, limiting his range of motion as he continued to deliver hits. Alexei struggled to break free but used the momentum of his body to slam Justin backward onto the ice before falling on top of him. That prompted the refs to break it up and send them both back to the penalty boxes for the rest of the game.

Or what would have been the rest of the game, if someone had broken the tie.

Overtime didn't last long. During the first shift, Justin shoved Alexei, the move annoying him enough to activate another gear. He hustled after the puck as it was passed to Justin, intercepting it and dodging a hit with a midair spin, to push the puck ahead to Briggsy, who put the game away. Zach skated along the edge of the rink with one leg in the air as he thrust both hands up. Alexei slid into his arms, an enormous grin on his face, before the rest of the team enveloped them both.

That was a hug Gemma would, no doubt, appreciate.

As if on cue, a text from her arrived a moment later. My heart can't take this, Kennedy. MY HEART.

For once, I could relate. Not only because my stomach did a little flip when the camera found Alexei's unbridled expression of joy, but also because I made it through a game. I'd missed it more than I realized, but I also missed her. My mom would have gone wild for that goal—shooting right out of her seat into the air, slapping the hands of people around her, screaming loud enough for teenage Kennedy to shrink away in embarrassment.

Alexei waved to the crowd as they chanted his name, over and over again, as he sat on the bench waiting to be interviewed after being crowned the game's first star. *Volk, Volk, Volk, Volk.* Nothing stopped their chants.

The interviewer proceeded anyway, asking Alexei what this game meant to him.

"This is validation," he answered, still breathing heavily. "No one thought we could win. They called it a rebuilding year, but this team has proven everyone wrong. And we're going to keep doing it. Hopefully, in front of more amazing crowds like the one here tonight." Screams rose again. Alexei smiled. "You all made the difference."

I shut the TV off.

I wanted to feel like I did before. To feel excitement in my life. A sense of purpose. The joy that lit Alexei's face after they scored the game-winning goal. But I had no idea how to get back to a place of such hope.

Hope felt reckless after all I endured.

Living without it, though, felt dim.

My life had been reduced to safe routines—living by someone else's rules, working a steady but less-than-fulfilling job, closing my circle to a handful of people. I couldn't go back to my old life. That life belonged to someone else.

But it didn't mean I had to settle for the one I'd been living.

After slipping into bed, my mind wouldn't stop replaying what happened the other night. Alexei called me a distraction. It cut deep, the reminder our relationship had been an act. And yet, part of me knew that wasn't all it was.

You're not cut out for it. My words back to him haunted me. I hated myself for saying it.

I pushed out of bed, threw on jean shorts, a tank top, and a hoodie, slipped into flip-flops, and made my way to his house. The doorbell brought no one to the front door. After a few minutes, I used the key Alexei had given me. My call of *anyone home*? was met with silence, so I ventured further into the house until I found myself standing on the deck, watching Matt and Zach in the hot tub, eating pizza and drinking beer off two pool floats. A closed pizza box sat on the edge with a cooler, no doubt filled with more beer.

"Kensie!" Matt called, setting down his beer can. "What brings you to our recovery party?"

"I'm looking for Alexei."

A goofy smile crossed Matt's face. "Ah, of course. Our fearless leader isn't here. He's blowing off steam."

Blowing off steam. The idea of him with someone else made me want to lose my dinner.

I couldn't blame him. I'd started something we never finished. And he won one of the biggest games of his career tonight. Of course he wanted to celebrate.

"Oh no, he's not—" Matt rushed to say, accurately reading my expression. "You don't need to worry about that with Volk. He's skating, trying to burn off the adrenaline."

"You mean anger," Zach said around a bite of pizza. "I've never seen him so pissed, and I've almost burned his house down, like, five times."

"But he won the game."

Zach pushed himself against the back of the hot tub, propping both arms on the ledge. "You watched the game?" he asked, not pausing for my response. "What did you think?"

"You played well. A little sloppy in the neutral zone in the first, but your aggressive offensive zone forecheck made up for it in the end. Nice goal, by the way."

"Wait..." Zach's mouth fell open, and he dropped a bite of pizza into the water. "Have you been, like, studying hockey to impress Volk or something?"

Matt snorted. "I don't think she has to resort to talking shop to impress him. She's got that pretty well in hand."

My heart jumped into my throat. Had Alexei said something to him?

"You don't watch hockey. How would you know—"

"I've been on this team for nearly half your life, Briggsy," Matt answered for me. He'd only been on the Wolves for five years, but he never missed a chance to razz Zach. "Kennedy and her mom came to every game and cheered, even when we got our asses kicked."

I sent a pointed look Zach's way. "I didn't say I *never* watched hockey, only that I don't watch it much."

Zach sported a shit-eating grin. "But you watched tonight."

"What woman wouldn't tune in to see two guys beat each other up over her?" Matt tipped his beer can at me before taking a long swig. Of anyone, I realized, Matt had the most insight into this situation. He was friends with both Alexei and Justin and engaged to my overly perceptive best friend.

"They weren't fighting over me."

"You're right. You're the latest in a long-running list of shit between them," Matt said. "I heard Ward was waiting on our porch when you got home from the party the other night."

"Alexei tell you that?"

"Yeah, right. Don't tell me, Kensie, that you're having a hard time telling your boyfriends apart."

"Don't make me come in there after you," I warned.

Matt gestured me toward him with both hands—a taunt.

"You know I would, but I have somewhere important to be." I turned on my heel to head inside.

"Say hi to our grump-ass winger," Matt called after me.

31

ALEXEI

Silence in the arena stood out more than the screams and cheers from tonight's sellout crowd. The crowd that had long ago left the building, along with my teammates and our coaching staff. Leaving me alone on the ice with a bucket full of pucks.

Usually, the crew would have removed the goal by now, but no one bothered me or asked when I would go. Not that I had an answer for them. Adrenaline still pumped through my veins from the overtime goal. If that had been it, I would have left the ice long ago and gone home to celebrate with Matt and Briggsy, who had probably commandeered my hot tub. But the simmer of anger hadn't receded enough for me to be in anyone else's company yet.

I smacked another puck into the net, turned toward our bench, and spotted her.

Fuck.

Kennedy and I hadn't seen each other since I retreated to my house, leaving her with Justin fucking Ward. Probably to talk about how he wanted her back, if his taunts tonight were any indication.

I can take her from you at any time. You get that right? She's only with you because I haven't asked.

I tightened my grip on the stick. "What are you doing here?"

"Heard you were here," she answered, seemingly unbothered by my tone.

Matt and Zach should have kept their mouths shut. They knew I wanted to be alone. Though I hadn't told them about the issues between Kennedy and me since our relationship needed to project perfection.

"You know, some people would be happy about that win."

"Oh, I am," I said. "But it was one game. We still have sixty to go."

"Not tonight. You won the game and the fight. Your arena sold out. What else could you want?"

I wanted you here watching me.

I wanted you in my bed the other night.

I want you in a way I can't have you.

Ward's taunts all game annoyed me from repetition alone, especially when combined with his constant shoves and pushes. He got away with more than a few penalties tonight. The refs seemed keen to let us play on, so I upped my physical play, which, for me, said something. Around the league, people knew me as much for my goal-scoring as for my hits. But I couldn't fight back against Ward's claims. He didn't need to steal Kennedy from me. Because she didn't belong to me.

I wanted to hit another hundred pucks at the net.

But Kennedy had come to see me, despite how I charged away from her after calling her a distraction. The least I could do was talk to her.

"So you'll come here to check on me but not for a game?" I said before rearing back and hitting another puck.

"I'm not talking to you about that."

"Were you *bored* by the game tonight?" I continued, repeating the lie she initially told about why she didn't like the sport. I knew the truth about why she wouldn't go to the games, and it was beyond fucked-up to press her on this, but I wanted to fight with her. I wanted to stop feeling anything for her. Since that was impossible, I chose anger.

"Alexei, stop."

"Stop what?" I asked, skating two lengths toward her. "You wanted to talk to me. We're talking."

She shook her head, rising from her seat. "I came here to check on you. But I guess you're fine..."

When Kennedy turned, I snagged a puck and hit it at the glass in her direction. A loud thwack sounded through the arena, making her jump.

"What the hell?"

"If you're making the rounds," I taunted, "I bet you could still catch Ward's plane on the tarmac."

"If you want to know what happened between Justin and me after you left, just ask."

"I don't give a shit." I reared back again. *Thwack*. "Do whatever you want with Ward. Settle for someone who doesn't deserve you. Let history repeat itself. It's not my problem."

"You sound like Gemma. She fill you in on all the big bad Justin Ward stories?"

"Don't be mad at her for being protective. She thought we'd done the whole shared dating history talk since we're 'dating.'"

"Except we're not really dating, Alexei," Kennedy said. "This is all for show."

"Is it?" I spun toward her again. "You showing up tonight to check on me is all for show? Because no one is here, Kennedy."

"This was a mistake."

She turned to leave, but I couldn't let her walk away from me. Maybe I couldn't have her the way I wanted, but I wasn't ready to let her walk out of my life.

"Why did you come here, Kennedy?" I asked again, all the fight leaving my voice.

She blew out a breath. "I don't know. I thought you could use a friend. You won this game... and you're here alone." Her gaze circled the empty arena before landing back on me. "I thought being friends, being there for each other could be the one benefit of this fake relationship thing."

"Not the only benefit." It didn't take much to conjure the image of Kennedy straddling me in the front seat of her truck.

Kennedy's blush crept up her neck and added more pink to her chilled cheeks. "That was a lapse in judgment we shouldn't repeat."

"Why's that?"

"It'll confuse things. Make this feel like something it's not."

"But you coming here doesn't?"

"I thought we were becoming actual friends, but I guess I got that wrong."

"That's what you want?" I asked. "Friends?"

Part of me wanted her to see reason, to see there was no way we could be friends. Forcing us to ignore the crackling chemistry between us was self-imposed torture, but the more rational part of me knew that being friends would stop her from breaking me into pieces when she went back to Ward.

And by some miracle, if I was wrong and she didn't go back to him, it wasn't like something between Kennedy and me could ever work out. Why even go there when it would blow apart? It might start perfect, but it wouldn't be long until she complained I was never around and didn't pay her enough attention. We would slip into stilted conversation and frustration over remembering what we used to have but no longer did.

She smiled, her shoulders dropping a centimeter. "Don't you?"

"Someone has to raise Zach," I said, avoiding her question. "God knows how long that's going to take. Guess what I caught him doing the other day?"

Kennedy moved toward the bench as I skated closer to her. Tension deflated between us. "Tell me."

"He microwaved metal, then left the room like it wasn't going to cause a fire. I walked into the kitchen when it started sparking."

She laughed, tilting her head back. Winning a laugh from her felt as good as the overtime puck in the net tonight. I didn't know if I could be only friends with her, but the thought of a clean break, drifting back into strangers, killed me. Somehow, in two months, Kennedy had become a person whose presence in my life I relied on. I pushed it out of my mind; that decision was weeks away.

"Seriously?" Kennedy asked. "What did he say?"

"He said he's done it his whole life, and it's never caused a fire before."

She let out a high-pitched laugh. "Of course he did."

"I invited him to Thanksgiving. I hope that's okay."

Kennedy's small smile grew into a wide grin. "Our holiday got a whole lot more interesting." She stood again, teetering her weight on one foot before shifting it to the other. "Are you done? Because I know a spot where you can get pizza and beer and sit in a hot tub."

I skated to the bench and pulled the door back to stand in front of her. Her eyes studied me, roaming over the cuts and bruises on my face. Ward looked worse than I did. Kennedy had been right, I won that fight handily. I wanted to break his nose again, for every way he made my life more difficult, and for how he took this wonderful woman who stood in front of me for granted.

She moved so quickly, taking two steps forward and wrapping her arms around my middle, I didn't have time to react. Not until the choice became wrapping my arms around her or standing stock-still. I dropped my stick and gloves, and pulled her toward me, my hands resting on her midback. She laid her head against my chest, as she had when we danced at the fundraiser. There was no way to disguise that my heart wanted to beat straight out of my chest. I hoped she would chalk it up to postgame adrenaline.

"It was the first game I've watched in over a year," Kennedy said, so softly I wasn't sure the words were for me. The anger at not having her here tonight bled away. She'd pushed through that block to watch me. "I forgot how good you are."

My hand tugged lightly on a strand of her hair. "I like the direction this conversation is taking."

She laughed again, all in one puff of air. "You never get tired of people telling you how good you are, huh?"

"Some people," I said and rested my chin on top of her head.

Kennedy pulled her head back to look into my face. "Maybe I'll tell you more at the recovery party."

"You've already sold me, Cole," I said, sliding my arm around her shoulder, nudging her to walk in front of me. "Lead the way."

That was how I planned to spend this last month with Kennedy—following her, for as long as she would let me.

32

KENNEDY

"How do I look?" Zach's high-energy voice reverberated off the walls as he scampered down the steps two at a time.

My dad and I didn't celebrate Thanksgiving last year, at least not in any traditional sense. We stayed home, as we had for most of the two months since my mom died, and soundlessly ate a ready-to-cook meal in front of the TV, barely absorbing anything on it.

This year, I expected a more traditional affair with catered food and elegant tablecloths and china, especially since we'd invited guests.

Zach stood at the foot of the steps, looking expectantly in my direction. He looked dressed for game day in a gray checker-patterned suit with a maroon tie. His usually floppy, light brown hair was slicked back, not one strand out of place.

"You know we're only going to my house, right?"

He surveyed my outfit. "You're wearing a dress."

I didn't need to look to confirm it, but I did anyway. Stupid habit. My dark gray sweater dress hugged my curves. Without my polka dot stockings or gold chunky necklace, it would have looked plain, but it looked fancy compared to the casual clothes Zach usually saw me in.

"This is the only dress I put on," I argued. "You've changed your suit three times. Each time, you looked fine. And no offense, but my dad won't care."

"So I can put on something more comfortable?" Alexei appeared halfway down the steps, knocking the breath straight out of my chest. He wore a maroon suit, expertly tailored to fit snugly across his broad shoulders, with a gray cotton shirt beneath the jacket. No tie. His hair looked the same as always, a bit of a swaggled mess, strands falling onto his forehead that he hadn't, and likely wouldn't, brush aside.

Zach groaned. "If Volk changes, I'm changing."

"And they say women have a hard time leaving the house." I rolled my eyes.

Alexei fiddled with his cuffs as he made his way over to me. He leaned forward, brushing his lips against my cheek. "You look..." He lost his words as his gaze skimmed over my face, down my chest to where my dress met sheer stockings, to the black boots below my knee. The heat simmering in his eyes caused my mouth to go dry.

Friends, Kennedy, dammit. Although it would have taken every bit of strength not to be affected by the way Alexei looked at me.

Zach made a gagging sound. "*Come on*, guys. I need to be able to eat in an hour."

Our petulant guest would keep Alexei and me from blurring any lines. We'd decided on friends, and I was resolved to keep us squarely in that zone. No sliding into his lap. No resting my face against his punishingly strong chest. And definitely no kissing.

Lingering looks. Cutesy banter. Shared smiles. That was the line, even when we had an audience. Anything more than that was too confusing, at least for me.

"Someone's got a weak stomach."

Zach responded by sticking his tongue out at me. Petulant child, indeed.

Alexei drove the familiar route to my father's house in his flashy sports car. Zach rolled down the back window, sticking his head out like a dog. The choppy wind and the blast of music Zach played kept our drive otherwise silent.

Part of me wanted to ask Alexei about what to expect when I met his mother, but that was something a real girlfriend would ask. Instead, in my head, I nervously practiced possible answers to questions she might ask. *How did you meet? What do you do for work? What are your intentions? How* do *you feel about my son?* I stumbled over the last two but kept running through possible answers in my head, resolved not to miss a beat.

Alexei parked his car in our cobblestone driveway behind a small gray rental. "My mom beat us here," he said, confirming my suspicions. He glanced at me, head cocked to the side. "Ready?"

I opened my mouth to speak, but Zach popped his head in between us. "Aw, Kenzie Wenzie, are you nervous?"

"*Never* call me that again, Zachary," I ordered.

"It's Zach, Briggsy, Ten, or hot-ass rookie to you."

Alexei stifled a laugh. "No one calls you hot-ass rookie."

"Read the comments section of Twitter, Volk. You'll see." Zach leaned back in his seat. "Actually, *don't* read those comments. People say the nastiest stuff about you." His stress of the A in nasty made the word sound worse. "And I mean nasty as in—" Zach stopped abruptly to make vague sexual gestures with his hands.

"Yeah, we got it," I said curtly, not needing a reminder of Alexei's desirability.

Alexei grinned at me. "Is someone jealous?"

"Of internet randos wanting to..." I trailed off, not knowing how to voice Zach's proclamations or wanting to use his terrible hand gestures. "I'm the one who has you at my house for Thanksgiving. What is there to be jealous about?"

That one day he'll belong to someone else, the stupid voice in the back of my head unhelpfully supplied.

Alexei tapped the steering wheel once with an open palm, then stepped out into the sunlight, leaving Zach and me to trail behind him. Alexei waited for me to open the front door. My father yelled "In here" from the main room as soon as it opened. Alexei slipped his hand into mine before we reached the room.

The little zing from that contact quickly turned to dread as he tightened his grip almost to the point of discomfort after seeing *both* of his parents sitting with my father in front of a lit fireplace. I'd seen his mother in pictures—tall, beautiful, blonde—but not his father, though I could have picked him out of a crowd due to their resemblance.

Alexei spoke in Russian, which sounded fast and angry, but I couldn't be certain given that I didn't understand a lick of the language. He gestured toward his father with a pointed finger, which led his father to jump in the conversation between Alexei and his mom. Alexei's face turned slightly pink, his voice raising several decibels to be heard over his dad's deeper, booming voice.

Zach leaned into me. "You're right. No one cares what I'm wearing."

I slithered my hand out of Alexei's grip and pulled at Zach's jacket sleeve to guide him away from the Volkovs. My dad rose from the couch to embrace me in a big hug. "Kenny, Happy Thanksgiving."

I wrapped my arms around him, taking every ounce of comfort he offered. *Safe.* If anything went wrong, I would be taken care of. Not everyone was so lucky. "Happy Thanksgiving, Dad."

"Sir," Zach interjected, pushing his hand toward my father. His voice was all business with no trace of his usual playfulness. "Thank you for inviting me to your home."

I elbowed him in the side. "Cut it out, Briggsy. You don't need to put on a show."

My father's eyes danced with amusement, but he accepted the business handshake from Zach. "It's commendable that he wants to make a good impression. It's good to see you, Zachary."

I coughed, trying to hide my laughter at my father's use of the name Zach had just ordered me to never call him. Zach didn't correct him.

"Did you know Alexei's father would be here?" I asked.

"No," he answered. "They arrived fifteen minutes ago. Is this... going to be a problem?"

I looked back at the Volkovs, who all stood in a close circle, still speaking away in Russian.

Not wanting to intrude, I quickly turned back. "Maybe. It's complicated."

My father's forehead wrinkled. "Is he... is he treating you well?"

We didn't have practice discussing my romantic relationships. I never brought anyone I dated home to meet him, unless my prom date—a boy I went out with only once more—counted.

"I wouldn't bring him here if he wasn't." And that, I realized, was true. Not like with Justin, who I clung to as a lifeline, even though he offered me the barest of minimums throughout our relationship.

Lying to my dad about my relationship with Alexei didn't feel good. The least I could do was tell the truth about the details. Though, *I'm trying to stop wanting to kiss his face off every time we're in a room together* wasn't the kind of truth I ever wanted to tell my dad. Instead I offered, "Don't worry, I'm happy."

He nodded, those wrinkles scrunching even more. "You went to the arena for him."

"How did you—" I stopped abruptly, realizing he'd seen the photo someone snapped of Alexei and me hugging in the middle of the Wolves bench, looking the picture of a happy, supportive couple. "I didn't know you had social media."

"Deandra showed it to me when we had lunch the other day."

"You had lunch with Deandra?"

"She's a real go-getter, that one. She cornered me in the hallway and asked me to lunch so we could talk about her marketing ideas."

That sounded like something she would do, all right. If only my dad knew how far Deandra's creativity extended, like conjuring an entire relationship into being for damage control. If it didn't involve his daughter, I had no doubt she would have told him, and he would have appreciated the effort.

"And I came up how?"

"Well, she made a good point about letting fans get to know our players a bit more personally. She says your relationship with Alexei has attracted a lot of attention. We should do more of that if we want fans to feel like the team is their family."

Zach nodded like a bobblehead. "I'm all for it."

"People did like that video of you nearly burning Alexei's house to the ground and me saving your ass." I grinned sweetly at Zach. Deandra had gleefully used the footage Alexei supplied in an in-game entertainment video as a prank on Zach.

The accented voice directly behind me made me jump. "One of those videos is enough for a lifetime."

More than anything, I wished Alexei and I spoke a language no one else in the room did so he could tell me what the hell had been happening for the last ten minutes. When he brushed his hand against mine, I realized, with a start, we did have our own language. *Everything is fine*, he seemed to say with that quick contact. If it wasn't, he would have lingered more or pulled me out of the room for a breather.

When did I start to know him so well?

"Kennedy, I want to introduce you to my parents."

His father stood stiffly, hands in his pockets, while his mother's gaze roamed over me, assessing me. Both had forced smiles on their faces. "My dad, Igor, and my mom, Marina."

"It's great to meet you." I gave them a pathetically small wave. "How was your trip?"

"Long," Marina answered, her accent stronger than Alexei's.

Her husband—ex-husband? once again boyfriend?—hummed his agreement.

"Of course," I said, this line of questioning falling flat. I thought travel talk would buy us a few minutes. Another brush of fingers, this time across my lower back, told me to relax. "Well, we're glad you could make it. It's our first Thanksgiving since my mom died—well, the first one we've celebrated."

Alexei's fingers stilled. I surprised myself with the admission, how easily the words came without me having to steel myself to say them.

Marina's pinched face softened. "Alyosha told me about your mom"—she glanced over my head—"your wife. Loss is never easy."

"No," my dad agreed. "It isn't."

When the doorbell rang, I asked, "Are we expecting anyone else?"

No one answered. Moments later, Gemma's voice cut through the air. "Y'all got room for two more?" She appeared at the wide-open entrance to the room with Matt at her side.

I rushed to her. "What are you doing here?"

"There's a huge snowstorm," Gemma explained, opening her arms to me. "Our flight got cancelled. You'd know that if you answered your phone."

I hugged her tightly, grateful to have her here to help weather the shitstorm Alexei's parents blew into our holiday. I worried about him shutting down during dinner, or the argument with his parents cropping up again.

"It's been a little frosty here, as well," I whispered in her ear. "I haven't had the chance to look at my phone since we arrived."

Alexei introduced Matt, Zach, and Gemma to his parents. Igor's stern expression broke into a wide smile when he met Zach, talking to him about his overtime goal the other night. The tension melted as long as everyone focused on hockey, so Alexei kept that conversation going until dinner.

After taking our seats, Alexei's hand found my knee, drawing my eyes to his. *I'm glad we're in this together,* I imagined his expression saying.

I hoped he could read mine. *Thank you for being here.*

33

KENNEDY

"I UNDERSTAND FROM MY son that you met at a party in this house?"

The conversation, apparently, could not remain on hockey all night. Or maybe it could, but Marina didn't want to talk about her son's career. She came here to meet me, the woman who entered his life in a flurry of drama. The first woman since his engagement fell apart.

I expected her questions. I practiced for these questions. And yet, I shrank in my seat as all eyes swiveled to me.

"We did," I said, placing my fork on the table. I would continue eating after the interrogation. "A couple of months ago."

My father added, "I throw a kickoff party at the start of every season. It's a nice way to remember we're all part of a team, and we all need each other for the organization to succeed."

"Did you go looking for him that night?" Marina asked, altogether ignoring my father's contribution. She didn't care about the organizational culture in the slightest. Her gaze remained razor-focused on me. "To get back at your ex-boyfriend?"

Ah, so that was her issue.

"Mama," Alexei hissed, his fork clanging against his plate. He said something in Russian.

"No." What the hell? Maybe she would respect honesty. "I didn't want anything to do with Alexei. I thought he was an asshole."

Gemma spat wine back into her glass, and silence descended on the rest of the table.

"An asshole," Marina repeated.

"Well, yeah. I got one side of the story from Justin," I explained. "And I mean, no offense, but he does come across as a little *too* self-assured, you know?"

Alexei laughed quietly beside me. "No offense, but you thought I was an asshole and too self-assured. That's great."

A ghost of a smile graced my lips as I turned to him for the first time since we sat down. I'd waited in agony for this line of questioning and barely paid attention to any of the conversation before this. "Well, what did you think of me? It couldn't have been much better."

He shifted in his seat. "You seemed unhinged, remember? The loud cursing, the rambling..."

"In fairness, I was just dumped and drank way too much champagne."

"But I wanted to know you."

The tender words froze me like hardening concrete.

"I hadn't felt anything for anyone in a long time, and you... you made me feel... something."

The words he shared felt too private for the audience. Is that why he chose this moment to say it? Because I couldn't brush it aside? In front of an audience, we were supposed to be falling in love, and that declaration should have made me moony-eyed.

"What? A throbbing headache?" I deflected.

"You tested me, for sure, but that's what I needed. Someone not to take my shit or walk on eggshells around me. I don't know if I would have... bounced back if I hadn't met you, Kennedy."

Gemma made a choked sound at the other side of the table. "I'm sorry." She used her napkin to dab at her eyes—dramatically or because she needed it, I wasn't sure.

"You're ruining their moment," Matt whispered, but in this quiet room, where a hair follicle hitting the floor might have made been audible, we could all hear him.

My eyes found Alexei's again because he never stopped looking at me. "I didn't realize."

"You are what I'm thankful for this year."

Not being signed by the Wolves. Not his winning team record. Me. I bit my lip, trying to tamp down an unexpected swell of emotion.

And thanks to that unspoken connection between us, Alexei swung his gaze to his mother, shifting the attention off me. "Does that answer your question?"

A smile slowly bloomed on her face. "I'm thankful you make him happy," Marina said to me before turning to Alexei. "All I want is your happiness."

"I'd like to make the playoffs," Zach announced grandly. Every single head spun in his direction. "What? Someone had to say it."

"You're supposed to say what you're grateful for, jackass," Matt said. "This isn't a birthday wish."

"Fine," Zach said. "I'm grateful Volk hasn't evicted me."

"Yet." Alexei pointed at Zach, the heaviness of his conversations with me and his mom replaced by mirth. Zach naturally brought that out in everyone, sometimes at the exact right moment.

I was thankful for the laughter filling the room. I hadn't been sure laughter would ever fill this house again.

ALEXEI

Kennedy found me in the backyard a couple of hours later, in the exact spot she'd stood in two months ago.

My father being here for Thanksgiving with my mother almost made me leave. They had been through this countless times before—breaking up and making up, arguing until they hated each other, my father disappearing to live on his own. I couldn't stand to watch it unfold again. He cared more about himself and his own aspirations than what it took to make it work with my mom.

And I was just like him. As much as I didn't want to be, things always went sideways in my relationships. There would be a commitment I missed because I stayed too long at practice, or I would zone out because I was thinking about a game the next day. I would forget to call. I made decisions about my life without consulting my significant other.

The worst part? I recognized this pattern in hindsight, but never in the moment. That was how immersed I became in my own shit.

I partially blamed my parents. They raised me to look out for myself, to have blinders on to reach the goal I desperately wanted, to shove everything else aside.

"Fancy finding you here," Kennedy said, no tinge of embarrassment or annoyance in her voice. I half expected it after putting my feelings out there in front of everyone. She probably thought it was all part of the show.

"I knew you'd know where to look."

"So you're not avoiding me?" she asked, taking a seat beside me on the top step of the stairs to the backyard. The stairs she sat on the first night we met. "Who then?"

I shrugged my shoulders, not in the mood for our usual banter. "I needed air."

"Dinner went okay, I think." When I said nothing, Kennedy bumped her shoulder with mine. "This is the part where you tell me what you think."

"It went fine."

She rested her head on my shoulder. Her sleeves were bunched in the palms of her hands, maybe a nervous habit or the chill in the night. Either way, I shrugged off my jacket and draped it around her shoulders. She tossed me a grateful smile and settled back into me as I hoped she would.

"I was supposed to go back to college last year. Right before my mom died. I didn't want to leave after what happened with my dad. Besides, all my friends had graduated. But my mom wouldn't hear it. She insisted I go back to school. We were driving home from a shopping trip when the accident happened."

Kennedy took a deep breath. I braced myself for the words that would follow, knowing she had to work herself up to them. I wished more than anything I could save her the pain of having to relive it. Something told me she needed to tell this story, that she sought me out to do so.

Her pause lasted a minute but felt like an hour, so long I thought she wouldn't continue.

"I don't remember much because we went straight into the highway median. I woke up and she didn't. Some people would've taken that as a sign to live life to the fullest... but for me, it was the opposite. The world dimmed. I became painfully aware of how easy it was to lose what mattered most. Everyone wanted me to get over it and move on with my life."

"You're never going to get over losing your mom, Kennedy." My arm went around her shoulders, my fingers tracing the top of her arm. "I think you should do whatever you need to do. It doesn't matter if someone else understands or approves. You know what's right for you."

"I wish I could move on. Not so I can do what is expected of me, but... I miss how I felt before she died."

"How did you feel?"

"Full of possibilities." She lifted her head to meet my eyes. "I'm thankful for you, Alexei. For shaking up my routine. Arguing with me. Bringing me out of my shell. Making me feel everything I'd shoved down."

I leaned my head against hers, wiping away a single tear falling down her cheek.

"Two months ago, on this spot, you told me I had some nerve to insult you after what I'd done. A lot can change in two months."

"A lot *has* changed in two months," she corrected. "And it will change again soon."

The statement sat like two-day-old milk in my stomach. The reminder of our impending end felt wrong after today, after this moment between us.

"You know I'm not going anywhere." Her eyelashes fluttered, moisture reflecting on them in the light from the back of the house. "Friends after this, remember?"

Friends. Part of me still didn't know if I could do it—remain her friend—but I knew I couldn't pretend I never knew her, that we hadn't shared moments like this. I wasn't sure what would be worse—her fully gone or still in my life like a ghost, someone I couldn't let go. Eventually, I would learn the answer.

But not tonight. No, tonight, I would sit under the stars, snuggled against my fake girlfriend, my friend, the woman I was falling in love with.

34

ALEXEI

The entire Wolves hockey team descended on the small mountain town in upstate New York that Matt and Gemma had chosen for their wedding ceremony, barely beating the predicted snow.

After an ass whooping in New York, no one seemed up for celebrating, though Matt sternly ordered us to put on a good face at the rehearsal dinner. Usually, rehearsal dinners included only the wedding party and family, but since we all traveled as one unit, every member of our team had a place at the table.

We settled into our rooms before going to dinner, something I did alone since Kennedy already left the room we were apparently expected to share. A room with only one bed. Gemma had taken her meddling up a notch, but it was her wedding so no way in hell would I say shit to her.

"Enjoying the view?" Matt's voice pulled my attention away from Kennedy, who stood talking with Gemma and her parents near the windows. She wore a tight green dress that barely reached her knees, immediately vaulting me back to our phone call while I was on the road. *I like you in anything, but something about that color on you... it's stunning.*

"The snow is a nice touch," I replied.

He clapped me on the shoulder. "We do what we can for our women, right?"

"Like divert an entire team from a road trip to get married?" I wanted to celebrate my friends for finding each other in this impossible world, but the words *our women* grated on me. Kennedy wasn't mine. "Sorry, man—"

"It's fine. You're always a crabby ass after losing," Matt said, though I could tell my words bothered him. "Gemma wanted a winter wedding. She told me when we first met, before she knew how impossible it would be given our schedule. She would've waited until after the season, but I didn't want to. Her dreams come first."

I elbowed him in the side. "Way to set the bar high."

"It's the only way relationships work, if you both want what's best for the other person more than what's best for you."

Matt clapped me on the shoulder, excusing himself to find his family. I headed to the bar to avoid the emotions pushing to the surface. I stayed away for as long as I could, until servers brought food to the tables starting with a fancy shrimp appetizer and tomato soup.

"There you are," Kennedy greeted me as I slid into the seat beside her.

"Here I am," I said hollowly, picking up my spoon. My need to eat was less about recovering after that intense game and more about distracting from her. That she wore the color I liked most had affected me in ways it shouldn't.

"Sorry about the game," she said quietly. We'd started talking hockey after she watched us play against Ward. I hadn't asked if she watched any other games. "But you're still top of the division. You'll get 'em next time."

Her hand landed on my thigh, squeezing once. I placed my hand over hers before she could pull back. Her eyebrows rose in surprise, maybe concern.

"I want to have fun tonight," I found myself saying.

Soon everything would change between us. Kennedy and I would "break up." Gemma and Matt would move to their new home, and Kennedy would no longer be a quick, two-minute walk from my house any time I wanted to see her. Not that I would have the ability to see her whenever I wanted. We would go back to our usual routines.

But for tonight, for the rest of the weekend, I didn't have to focus on that. We were on a snowy mountain without a tinge of real life.

"Well, it is a wedding," she answered, half smiling. "And there is an open bar."

She lifted her glass to clink it against mine. I followed suit, gulping my drink down. "You should get through your speech before you hit that bar too hard."

She flashed me a wicked grin. "Why? Worried about what I might say without a filter?"

"Since Gemma will kill you if you ruin this night for her, yes, I'd say giving your maid of honor speech plastered would worry me. *Outside* of that, no. I will always want to hear what you say."

She pointed a finger at me. "You say all the right things, you know that?"

"You know that's not true," I said, thinking of the night in her front yard when Ward interrupted us.

Her smile slipped a moment, the reference dawning on her. "I didn't mean what I said that night. You're cut out for this." She motioned between us as she said the words.

My throat bobbed. "You don't know me well enough to say that."

"Is that a challenge?" she asked in a lilting tone. "Because you know how I feel about challenges."

I wondered if there wasn't a situation she wouldn't stubbornly take on to prove she could—including showing me I could be an attentive partner, even if it meant sacrificing herself to do it. I would lose her from my life before I ever let that happen.

Before I could let that thought take root, I replied, "And we all know how I've beaten you at every single one of our challenges."

She scoffed. "I bet I could get someone to offer to take me upstairs tonight before you do."

"This room is full of hockey players," I said. "The numbers are on your side. Besides, I don't know if you realized this, but Gemma put us in a room together."

"What? But there's only one bed in that room." Kennedy's eyes snapped toward the head of the table where Gemma was aggressively kissing Matt. "What a *fucking* meddler."

"Bringing other partners to our room tonight might be crowded."

She turned her gaze on me, her nose adorably wrinkled on its bridge. "Well, there's always their rooms."

"Not a chance," I said.

"Fine. Let's see who lasts the longest."

I nearly spit out my drink. "What?"

"At the party," she clarified, failing to realize the direction of my thoughts. "Whoever gets tired and wants to go back to the room first, loses."

I held out my hand to her, which she grabbed. Going back to the room meant Kennedy and I would sleep beside each other. Which meant, by losing this bet, I would also win.

"You're on."

Kennedy tried to pull me off the dance floor by one arm. Her blue-black hair fell behind her like a cape as she struggled without success. After dinner and her speech, we spent the next few hours rotating between the dance floor and the bar, which landed us in a perfect state of feeling loose and carefree.

"Come on," she said. "I want to take some pictures."

I finally moved with her, shifting my weight forward, slow enough so she didn't fall on her ass.

"Why is this even here?" I asked, nodding toward an old-school photo booth in the corner of the room.

She shrugged. "Gemma's nontraditional, or did her scandalously low-cut gold wedding dress not tip you off?" Kennedy covered her mouth. "Shit, pretend you didn't hear that. Act surprised tomorrow."

I climbed into the booth behind Kennedy who slid her legs across my lap as soon as I sat down. She inched toward me until her arms wrapped around my neck. "I haven't been in one of these since I was a kid."

"I've never been in one," I said.

"No?" Kennedy's brown eyes grew wider. "I'll show you the ropes." She hit the start button. "Smile normally first." The camera flashed, blinding me. "Okay, now a silly one." I glanced over at Kennedy who stuck out her tongue and held up a peace sign. The camera flashed again; I assumed I only had a grin on my face.

"Now what?" I asked.

She responded by planting one hand on either side of my face and kissing me.

Her lips landed softly against mine. When the camera flashed again, I expected her to pull away but instead, she opened her mouth wider, inviting me to kiss her back. The camera flashed again as I slid my lips against Kennedy's, slowly, waiting for her to end it. But she only continued to move against my mouth, pushing closer until my lap bore most of her weight.

One of my hands moved to the small of her back, securing her in place as the other traced patterns on the side of her calf. When Kennedy captured my tongue with her lips, any trace of restraint left me. I pulled her until she straddled me. My lips left hers to kiss down her neck, bringing the soft sound of her pants to my ears. She smelled so good, the maddening scent that always clung to her, to any place she had been, a mixture of vanilla and orange. I could—

"Alexei," Kennedy said with a sigh before taking my ear lobe into her mouth; my vision temporarily went black. "I want to go upstairs."

The magic words to end our silly challenge for tonight, which would also conveniently put me out of my misery. I would have stayed here with her, lapping up the torture of having her close without being able to take it farther. But fuck was I glad she wanted to leave. I pulled back, studying her face. "Are you sure?"

She nodded vigorously. "Yes."

I gripped Kennedy's hips, lifting her until she stood on her feet, ducking her head to avoid hitting the ceiling. Her dress slid back down her thighs as she ran her fingertips through her hair to straighten her ruffled locks.

"Head to the elevator," I told her. "I'll grab your bag."

35

ALEXEI

MY BREATH CAUGHT AS I turned the corner and found no one standing in front of the elevator.

"Took you long enough," Kennedy said behind me.

"Someone's antsy to get upstairs." I teased to fight off the terrible gut-punch feeling when I thought she disappeared. She linked her arm through mine, calming my panic, then hit the up button to summon an elevator. "Never thought I'd see you eager to surrender, especially to me."

Her eyes sparked as the elevator dinged and the doors opened to an empty box. "You know... maybe I'm getting a second wind after all. We should go back..."

Kennedy gestured to the party behind us, but as soon as I lifted her, she wrapped her legs around my waist.

"Not a chance," I said, hitting the elevator button to close us off from the rest of the world.

The door hadn't even closed before her hands were tangled in my hair, her lips pressed against mine with all the desperation of our last kiss. She kissed her way to my jaw and down my neck, likely feeling my pulse pound out of control. I moved toward our room with her in my arms, fumbling in my pocket to find the key, desperate to hear the door opening click.

Kennedy's legs loosened from around me after I pushed inside the room. Her feet hit the floor as I flipped on the light.

She didn't move. Only stood in front of me, looking.

"Don't tell me you've changed your mind." Part of me expected her to say we were going too far, us being together like this was a mistake.

Instead, she turned her back to me, lifting her hair so I could unzip her dress. "Does it look like I've changed my mind?" she asked over her shoulder with a coy smile.

I tried to mask my shaking hands as I slowly dragged the zipper down her back to the seam at her waist, revealing smooth skin and no bra.

"You *look* fucking incredible."

"Took you long enough," she said for the second time tonight, again revealing her impatience for me. It was addictive. She quickly shimmied her arms out of the sleeves before turning to give me a full view of her breasts.

Fucking incredible didn't even come close to covering what I thought of her.

"Fuck, Kennedy, I—"

My words were cut off when she pushed herself against me, slamming my back into the door. She smashed her lips against mine as I moved the rest of her dress down her body, needing to touch her.

But as soon as she stepped out of the dress pooled at her feet, she walked backward away from me. "Your turn."

She bit down on her bottom lip, watching as I followed her slowly, peeling off my jacket first and tossing it onto the table. My gaze remained on her as I unbuttoned my shirt, enjoying the way she soaked in each movement. When the shirt fell, Kennedy's gaze roamed over my bare skin.

"Damn, you look better than I remembered," she said, her tone almost angry.

Having lost track of her backward pace, she gasped when her knees connected with the bed behind her. Two eager strides, and I stood before her. She made quick work of unbuckling my belt, all while looking up at me through her lashes, her chest rising and falling in rapid breaths.

One of my hands covered hers, stilling her movement. Two instincts warred; a hungry one, desperate to be inside her, as close to her as I could be, and a rational one that wanted to remember this, to make this last.

Kennedy's eyebrows drew together. "Is something wrong?"

I trailed my hand down the side of her face, settling it against her jaw. My fingers brushed slowly over her warm skin, already flushed. Her throat bobbed.

"You are the sexiest sight I've ever seen."

This moment, I would remember. Eyes locked, choosing each other.

"I need you out of your pants now," she said, her voice breathless.

"Show's over, then?" I smirked, drawing my zipper down before stepping out of my pants, leaving them discarded with the rest of the clothes on our hotel floor.

She licked her lips, eyeing the tent in my boxers. Before she could spring me free, I lifted her by the waist, hauling her further back on the bed, covering her body with mine.

Kennedy actually beneath me beat all of my fantasies. Her breasts rubbed against the hard planes of my chest. Her legs coiled around my waist. Her eyes devoured me, all heat.

My hand skimmed a path down her body, starting at her collarbone, between her breasts, down her stomach. I stopped when I reached lace, dragging a frustrated sigh from her.

"So impatient," I murmured, before drawing her lips into mine.

Kennedy moaned as I rolled my hips, teasing her with my dick, over and over, building the tension between us.

"Off," she finally said as she tore at my boxers. She didn't wait for me to comply before reaching beneath the fabric and wrapping her hand around me.

Our kisses turned frenzied. Her hand moved roughly up and down my shaft, the feeling so good, I almost lost it. My hips soon matched her movements.

I was beyond lost in this woman.

"Just one time," Kennedy said suddenly, breaking our kiss and my heart a little.

She pulled back from my lips to meet my eyes.

We promised each other a weekend of fun. This night together was part of that promise, to finally scratch the itch plaguing us since we met. To satisfy the attraction beneath the exasperation.

She wanted to get this out of her system—to know what it was like to be with me—so in two weeks, she could have a clean break.

"Just one time," I agreed.

And when I kissed her, it wasn't a frenzy. It was languid so I could prolong this moment as long as possible. So I could commit every second to memory—from the taste of her on my lips to the way she sighed as I pulled down her panties, palming her ass lightly before slipping a finger inside her.

She rocked against me, craving more friction, as she kissed me roughly, our movements a mash of lips and teeth and tongue, all desperation.

Still, I took my time, working her with one finger, then two, not wanting to rush a single second, even as my body tightened painfully, needing release from this torturous tension.

"Alexei," Kennedy said, her voice soft and curt. "Now. I need you now."

"How?" I asked, pinning her with a meaningful stare.

"What?"

"How do you need me, Kennedy?"

If she wanted this only once, I would give it to her exactly how she wanted it, how she imagined it between us.

It took a moment for her to understand, but when she did, she inched away from me. "Lay back," she said, gesturing to the headboard.

Before following her direction, I lunged for my bag beside the bed.

At the sound of the condom wrapper, Kennedy said, "I'm on the pill, and I've been tested."

"Me too," I said, still holding the condom, not wanting to pressure her. I didn't care how I had her tonight, only that I did. "But we can—"

"I'm okay without it as long as you are."

I nodded, then moved into position, my head against the pillow, my entire naked body on display before her, for her. My fingers twitched, wanting to touch her, to make her feel so good, she would never forget this night. But I would follow her lead, even if it pained me.

"As much as I enjoy watching you ogle me, you're *killing* me here."

"Is that right?" She ran a fingertip from my ankle up the inside of my calf. Her lips parted as she reached my knees, placing a hand on each one, then sliding slowly up. "Unfucking real..."

I smirked at her naked adoration, especially after how long it took for her to admit it.

Kennedy leaned forward, her lips grazing my inner thigh.

"Hey," I said, reaching to pull her up to me. "Kens, you don't have to—"

"I *want* to."

I dropped my hands at the fire in her voice.

She continued to kiss a trail along my thighs. "*This* is what I need."

"Kennedy." I closed my eyes, overcome by need for her. "A little help here..."

"You mean like this?" She grinned before sliding her mouth over me, taking me in one quick movement and pulling back before my groan even finished.

"Don't tease..."

She pushed herself flat against my body, my length pressing against her stomach. She kissed me, her hand tightening against the back of my neck. "But it's so fun," she whispered before sucking my earlobe.

My breath shuddered. "You... are... evil."

Kennedy laughed. I reached for her shoulders, wanting to tug her back to my lips, but her eyes flicked to mine. "Hands off, hotshot. I'm not done."

Reluctantly, I pulled my hands back, resting them behind my head, elbows flared to the side.

But then she gripped my shaft, pumping once, twice. "Kennedy—" My warning was cut short by the blinding pleasure of her soft mouth replacing her hand.

Thank fuck, this time it wasn't a tease.

I threaded my fingers through hers, watching as she bobbed up and down. She met my gaze as her tongue licked its way to the head of my cock. My body jerked, and she pulled back.

"You are too good at that," I said slowly, my breath heavy.

She smiled. "We have all night if you need to—"

"No," I said. "I need to be inside you. Come here."

I tugged her close enough to kiss, for her to settle beside me so I could reach between her legs. The wetness that met my fingers... "Fucking *Christ,* Kennedy," I muttered against her mouth.

"I know," she groaned.

Kennedy climbed on top of me, easing my dick inside her, and I almost came from that amazing sight alone. She moved slowly down, moaning as she adjusted to my size. Her lips parted, her eyes half-shut, mirroring how I felt with her on top of me. She pitched herself forward, kissing me again as she ground against me, her movements excruciatingly slow.

Kennedy leaned back, resting her hands on my chest. "Hey," she said.

That flushed smiling face of hers as she rocked against me—fucking gorgeous.

"You feel so fucking good." I sat up, taking one of her nipples into my mouth, sucking lightly. "So fucking good."

"Alexei, I'm close..." she whimpered, increasing her pace. I wanted to watch her, to touch her, to tease her, but she grasped each side of my face and claimed my mouth—never breaking, only sliding lips and clashing tongues until Kennedy cried out my name as she fell apart on top of me.

When I tried to take over, she placed her hand on my chest. "No, I like you like this," she said and resumed moving her hips.

"You like having total control over me?"

Kennedy lifted her hips, inching higher and higher, before slamming back down, knocking the smirk off my face. I bucked my hips up, finding a rhythm with her, the sound of our slick skin slapping together mixing with our heavy breathing.

"Fucking hell, I'm—"

At one last swivel of her hips, my body spasmed, a hot pleasure flooding my blood. Kennedy kissed me once, long and slow, before falling against my body, keeping me inside her as she rested her face on my chest. This level of comfort with another person, to stay like this, was new... but right.

When she finally slid off me, the pain of her absence began, an absence that would grow after tonight. But I pushed it out of my mind, inviting her into the crook of my arm when she returned from the bathroom.

"Can you tell me what you're thinking?"

"I'm not thinking." A half lie. I couldn't share how much I wanted to keep doing this with her, which was the only thought in my mind. *Again* chanted every muscle in my body. "I don't know when I'll be able to think straight."

She covered her mouth with a hand, suppressing a smile. "I've never..."

I shifted to my side so we could look at each other. "What?"

"Felt that bold, I guess."

I pushed a strand of hair behind her ear. "Well, it suits you."

You suit me too. The words sat on the tip of my tongue. Not telling her I'd long moved past pretending meant I could have her a little longer like this, imagining this relationship was real, pretending she felt the same.

I was a fucking coward.

"There you go, saying all the right things again."

"I am only telling you true things," I said, strumming my fingertips along her arm. "It's okay to be scared—everyone is, whether they admit it or not—but I wish you wouldn't let it rule your life. You deserve more."

Kennedy placed a finger on the tip of my chin, then traced up to my bottom lip. She seemed as helpless as I was against this pull between us. "Are you going to take your own advice? Stop thinking you can't have what you want because people in the past made you doubt you could?"

"I'm lousy at relationships. I'm—"

She nudged herself into a sitting position, still tucked into my side. "Do not say you're not cut out for it."

"So bossy." I laid my hand on her waist, atop the sheet covering her. "I think you've let all this control go to your head."

"Stop trying to manipulate me with those dimples."

"Dimples?" I asked, snagging her around the waist and pulling her tight against my body. "What dimples?"

"As if you don't know," she gasped.

I began kissing her neck, sucking lightly each time. Not enough to leave a mark, though some wild part of me considered it.

"They're honestly so dangerous, you should have to register them."

I laughed against her skin. "You're one to talk, with those big brown eyes."

"No one's ever said that to me before."

"If you want me to compliment other parts of you," I said, moving down to tease the soft skin of her breasts. "That is not a problem."

She rested her hand under my chin, stopping my movement south, guiding me back to her lips. "You're so stupid." Her lips formed the words against my mouth.

I grinned against her. "So stupid."

I was stupid—giving into this overwhelming rush of lust, especially when what sat alongside it was more feelings than I could accept. My heart would break in the end.

And yet, I wouldn't stop, couldn't stop myself from spending time with her.

When I rolled over the next morning to find Kennedy still here, peacefully sleeping beside me, my heart expanded in size. *I love her*, it said with each beat. I wanted, more than anything, to kiss her awake and whisper the words to her in the morning sunlight, to slide in and out of her, to hear her moan my name.

But I did none of those things.

Just once, she said. It would never be enough for me.

Still, I put my hand on that hot stove, thinking if I pulled back quick enough, the burn wouldn't fuck up my skin for life.

So fucking stupid.

36

KENNEDY

"I CAN'T WAIT TO get this dress off," Gemma said as we entered the bridal room at the venue.

She walked to the mirror, her long gold train trailing behind her. Gemma insisted on this dress, but she also knew her love of pictures would not outlast her annoyance at carrying around five pounds of fabric.

"I've got you." I dropped to my knees to find the six clips to release the bottom half of her dress.

Gemma glanced over her shoulder at me. "If you and Alexei weren't so terribly smitten with each other, I would push you toward Jeff tonight."

"I have no interest in dating Matt's brother," I said, ignoring her obvious fish for information about Alexei and me. She didn't deserve to know after the same room, one bed meddling of hers. Even if it had ended well for me. Twice.

"Of course not, since you're taken."

"Or maybe I was distracted by the disgustingly loving words your husband vowed to you." I released the last clip, pulling the dress away from her and laying it flat on the table.

"He totally ruined my makeup." Gemma touched her fingers underneath her eyes, though there was nothing to fix. "I did a pretty good job getting to him too."

"You got us all, trust me."

Gemma dramatically curtsied, her arms held out wide, holding an invisible skirt. "We do our best. Anyway, are you ready to get back out there? I'm sure *Jeff* is waiting to escort you in."

"We do not need to make an entrance."

Gemma hooked her arm through mine. "It's *my* wedding, Kennedy."

I rolled my eyes. "Yes, and that's why I'm not scolding you for once again meddling in my life. Yet."

Gemma fluttered her eyelashes. "Whatever do you mean, Kens?"

"Two words—one bed."

"Well, it worked, didn't it?" We walked into the hallway to find Matt and Jeff waiting for us. The rest of the wedding party stood in a circle down the hall. "I saw you two this morning. There was an afterglow."

I said nothing; I didn't trust I could deny the claim without my face lighting up like a Christmas tree. Even if I wanted to tell Gemma about my night with Alexei, I didn't know if I could find the words. Obviously, sex with him was mind-blowing, the best of my life.

But she would want to know how I felt.

Waking up this morning, my head on Alexei's shoulder, my leg tangled between his... it felt *right*. Pure terror shot through me because our night was an end rather than a beginning, but my heart didn't get the memo, beating double-time as soon as our eyes locked. And it wasn't only because Alexei slept shirtless and woke up with rumpled hair, looking like a sin.

I thought back to what he said to me last night, the way he'd encouraged me this entire time to go after what I wanted, to stretch for more because he thought I could.

Fake-dating Alexei was a risk in itself. We could have been caught and made to look so, so pathetic in the public eye, but it also pushed me toward completing items on my list. I went to a party full of strangers and worked the room. Alexei taught me how to cook. I dyed my hair. I contacted UPC to find out the process for applying for admission and transferring my credits from Prescott.

I did most of those things myself, but he helped me. I liked the person I was when I was with him.

That person, she was brave and honest. She didn't sit on the sidelines of life. She would tell Alexei her feelings, even if it amounted to nothing. Even if it broke her still mending heart.

Because I could survive. It wouldn't be easy, but I was strong.

And I wouldn't let myself forget that any longer.

"What are you two talking about?" Jeff sidled up next to me.

Gemma backed into Matt's arms until she rested flush against his body. His arms wrapped around her waist. "Just how Kennedy's *boyfriend* is stupidly in love with her."

"No, that's not—" I tried to interrupt before Matt cut in.

"Don't think we didn't see you make an Irish exit well before the party ended last night."

"So what?" I said. "Sex doesn't mean love. Maybe your old married asses have forgotten that."

Gemma raised her eyebrows comically high. "Sex, you say?"

I groaned and tossed my head back. "Please stop."

"Kens, stop holding out on me! I need to live vicariously through you, remember?" She flashed her shiny diamond rings.

I tossed Matt a meaningful look. "This doesn't bother you? Gemma's unhinged love for your teammate."

Matt shrugged. "Honestly, I get it."

"You're so hot when you agree with me." Gemma tilted her head toward Matt who leaned down for a kiss that held for an uncomfortably long time.

I glanced at Jeff. "I never thought I would say this, but I'm ready to make my entrance."

Jeff insisted we needed to do something funny, but we didn't like each other's ideas. The reception doors opened before we could compromise, so Jeff swept me off my feet and into his arms like a damn damsel in distress.

"I'm going to kill you," I hissed, but Jeff ignored me, smiling as laughter filled the hall. He finally put me down on the dance floor. The attention shifted to Matt and Gemma, who were announced as the Harrises for the first time. They came into the hall to a nineties song—*C'mon N' Ride It (The Train)*—while doing the ridiculous dance.

"I'll take over." The familiar deep-accented voice came from behind me, raising goosebumps on my forearms. Alexei pulled me by the waist toward him, my stomach swooping with the move that brought my body against his. He navigated us away from Jeff, closer to the edge of the dance floor.

"I think I'm supposed to dance with the best man, Alexei."

His double-dimple smile hit me deep in my gut, as always.

"Too bad. He's had you all to himself for the last few hours." He moved his hands from the small of my back to the side of each hip, resurfacing memories of last night. My heart pounded, forcing me to look away from him to hide the emotion that no doubt showed on my face.

"Yeah, well..." My voice caught when I noticed the person standing behind Alexei, watching us. My feet stopped moving. My arms tensed around his neck, feeling as stiff as concrete.

"Is something wrong?"

I cleared my throat. "Don't look, but Justin Ward is behind you."

Alexei's hands tensed on my hips, but to his credit, he didn't turn around. "Did you know he was going to be here?"

"No."

"He's here for you, isn't he?"

"I don't know."

Alexei shook his head. "Kennedy, don't bullshit me. He showed up at your place. Now he's at this wedding. And on the ice, he wouldn't shut the fuck up about how you were only with me because he hadn't tried to get you back yet."

That was what Justin taunted Alexei with during the game?

"It's true, isn't it?" Alexei prompted when I said nothing.

"What?"

He watched me intently, looking for whatever sign in my expression would reveal the truth.

"Is that what you think of me? That Justin could snap his fingers, and I would run back to him? Give me some fucking credit."

"I don't know what to think."

"Neither do I," I said. "You're acting like a jealous boyfriend when we both know you have no right."

Alexei scoffed. "What happened to not wanting to make the easy choices, Kennedy? You blame it on your grief, but you're afraid. And

Ward?" Alexei spat out Justin's name as if it were stale beer. "He won't support you. He'll let you keep hiding. You should want more."

My heart squeezed.

What, like you? The man who I'd tried to resist, but he managed to make me like him anyway. The man who pretended so well, I never knew what he felt and what he faked. Was he pissed at the idea of me going back to Justin because he hated Justin? Because it would mean he lost this game of theirs? Was his concern because we became friends? Or had he developed feelings for me?

That was the problem with lies; they were hard to untangle.

"I'm failing to see how this is any of your business," I said, pushing away every last confusing thought to focus razor-sharp on what was true. Alexei held no permanent place in my life. His judgment wasn't something I had to tolerate. "If I go back to Justin, if I tell him to fuck off, it makes no difference to you. In two weeks, this arrangement of ours is done. So I can continue *blaming everything on my grief* without your freaking judgment."

Alexei took a step back, his grip falling slack, a painful reminder of how close we had been last night, how different we had been with each other. *Delusional,* that was what we had been. I should never have let it go so far.

"Because I say something you don't like, you're going to shove me out of your life?" he asked.

"As if you're any better. I close myself off from people, but you do too. You blame it on hockey and being afraid to ruin someone like your dad did with your mom, but the truth is, you're afraid you'll be left behind. Like you were with Cora. And that's why you're alone. So don't pretend that you're better than me because—"

"I let *you* in, Kennedy," he whispered.

"Because this isn't real!" I hissed, keeping my voice low. "It's easy to let someone in when you know they won't have the power to hurt you."

"You would know," Alexei fired back, his voice as low as mine. "You didn't love Ward. I saw you the night he left you. You were pissed off at him, but you weren't heartbroken. You pinned your life on that asshole instead of doing anything for yourself because you couldn't muster the courage."

"You should walk away from me," I said, my tone deathly calm. I dropped my hands to my side, taking a step away from him. A moment later, he finally removed his hands from my body.

There we stood, two people who started as strangers armed with enough knowledge to hit each other squarely in the Achilles heel. This morning, sunshine illuminated his naked body beside mine, and his grin sunk a pit in my stomach in an entirely different way than this angry expression.

Twelve hours could make all the difference in the world.

"It's done then," he said.

"Fine by me."

Alexei walked away from me, maybe for the final time. I waited for the relief at ending our lie. It didn't come.

Despite what Alexei said, I would figure out my next steps in life, and I would do it without the weight of having to fake my way through a ridiculous relationship. Before I could grab my phone to fire off a *We're done* text to Deandra, another man slid in front of me.

"Trouble in paradise?"

Justin had enough sense not to pull me to him, as if my agreeing to dance was a foregone conclusion. His blue eyes shone against his dark blue suit. I noticed that about him when we first met. That, and how easily he made me like him. A smile. A laugh. The way his forehead wrinkled into lines. His hand on my arm. I never stood a chance with the irresistible pull into his orbit.

I waited to feel it now, the instinct to forget what he'd done so I could have his approval.

But it didn't come.

"What the hell are you doing here?" I said, crossing my arms over my chest.

"I came to talk to you."

"So Gemma and Matt's wedding is a sideshow?"

He shook his head. "You aren't going to make this easy on me."

"You don't deserve anything from me."

"You're right." He held his hand out to me. "But I'm going to ask anyway—dance with me? I rented a car and drove three hours to get here after my flight was canceled."

Lord. "What did your coach say about that?"

Justin looked at his watch. "He'll find out in about twelve hours."

He expected this gesture to make a difference to me because he had done less in the past, and I forgave him each time. He ignored me for a week while on the road after a stupid fight I couldn't even remember, and he gave me a magnet from each of his stops, as if to say he thought about me even while we fought. When he snapped at me after the first and only time I questioned why we couldn't just tell people we were dating, the next time we saw each other he had my favorite takeout waiting even though he hated it.

He might have upped his gesture game, but his offense was far greater.

I didn't take his hand.

"I see you're still with him." Justin nodded in the direction Alexei retreated.

I refused to look, not wanting to see Alexei's face. He shouldn't have to watch us talk after our argument. Our breakup of sorts.

"That's none of your business." I walked toward the door to the outside of the property. Snow blanketed the expansive outdoor space, but the venue had cleared its patio. It did nothing to protect me against a sharp chill permeating my bones.

Justin closed the door behind us, then shrugged off his jacket. At my simple "No," he wordlessly slipped it back on.

"You've put it all over the internet. It's not like you, to be that showy. That's why I don't believe it."

"Believe what?" I asked.

"That you're legitimately together."

Shit. Even if Alexei and I ended our charade, anyone finding out would lead to disastrous PR. Another strike against Alexei and an embarrassment for the entire organization.

And for the rest of my life, people would call me the fake former girlfriend of Alexei Volkov. Excuse me if I wanted more for myself.

"Well, I had sex with him last night, so I'd say we're pretty together."

The look of pure shock on Justin's face almost felt worth the stab of pain in my chest at the reminder that less than twenty-four hours ago, Alexei and I went back to our room together. That he kissed me slowly, as if he wanted to make time stop, to preserve the moment. That even though I tried to resist it, I felt more for him than pure lust last night. Something I'd now have to shove down deep and wait for it to go away.

Justin laughed with no humor, only a sharp angry edge. "I'm gone for three months, and you open your legs to just anyone? It's not only your hair color that's changed."

Adrenaline flew through my blood, lighting every limb, urging me to strike him. "I've also miraculously developed the ability to come without having to take care of it myself."

His nostrils flared, both hands clenching into fists. He took one deep breath, then expelled it along with the visible anger in his posture.

I blew out a breath. "What is the point of this? Why are you here?"

"You and Volkov spun this entire story in your favor. You waited less than four hours before hooking up with my old teammate, and everyone is on your side. I look like the jackass."

Of course. The point was to paint himself as the victim in this situation.

"That's because you *are* the jackass. You left me behind like I didn't matter. All you cared about was making sure I returned the keys to your realtor."

"Kennedy, I was mad. You knew I would get over it."

"And what? You'd send for me when you were ready?"

Justin moved a step closer and lowered his voice. "I would have, if you hadn't taken up with my enemy."

"So instead, you told the whole world I was *leftovers*?" The word still stung. "And this is the part where you tell me you didn't mean it."

He reached for my face, but I took a step back before he could connect.

"I was angry," he repeated, dropping his hand to his side. "Of course I didn't mean it."

"What about when you told me I wasn't the same person you fell in love with? That too?"

"It was a shitty thing to say."

"But you meant it," I pressed. "So why are you here now? To prove you can take me away from Alexei?"

He made a clicking sound out of the side of his mouth. "He told you about that, huh?"

"We have an open and honest relationship."

"It doesn't look like you have much of a relationship at all anymore."

I glared at him, wondering what I had ever seen in him to make me accept so little. So much less than I deserved. "And neither do we."

When I turned to go inside, Justin grabbed my arm. "Don't throw this away. We were good together once. We can be good together again. Do you remember what we were like in the beginning?"

I shook my arm, but couldn't free myself from his grasp. "You mean when you pretended to be my friend, biding your time until I was single?"

Justin laughed as one of his fingers moved along my jaw. "No. I meant the summer we spent together, fucking and lying by the pool. How'd that summer compare to your sex last night?"

I swatted his hand away from my hair. "There is no comparison. I'm much happier now."

"You love him? Because that's how you felt about me three months in."

Something unpleasant unfurled in my gut. How could I sort through my feelings for Alexei when I didn't know what had been real and what had been fake? There was something between us, something I ignored because there was no point in looking too closely. Nothing could come of it.

"That's none of your fucking business."

"You need someone to take care of you. I'm ready to do that now." He motioned toward the reception hall. "Volkov isn't built like that. He'll get tired of being the only one going somewhere. I won't. I'll take care of you."

Three months ago, that was all I wanted—someone to protect me from everything in the world that could rip me apart. I might have felt unsatisfied with my little life, but at least it was safe.

"You liked when I was a doormat, fragile and obedient. But that's not who I really am, at least not anymore." I slammed my heel on the top of his foot.

Justin winced, letting out a pained curse. The move freed me from his grasp.

The thrill of pulling off the Wolves fundraiser had made me remember the satisfaction of an accomplishment. Watching hockey again made me realize how much I missed working for the Wolves organization.

And last night with Alexei, I connected with someone again, *really* connected, something that hadn't happened with Justin in a long, long time.

"Kennedy, what are you doing? This isn't you."

"What isn't?" I spat.

He hesitated. Whatever he saw in my expression truly was different from the woman he had known. A flash of anger poked through before he schooled his face into nonchalance. "He's got you putting your entire 'relationship' out in the public for his benefit. He's taking advantage of you, Kennedy. And when he's gotten what he came for, you'll be alone."

I shoved away the anger because he was right. I did end up alone.

Pushing my shoulders back and jutting out my chin, I straightened to my full height. "*He* didn't make me do anything. Just like *you* didn't. I've *always* chosen. I let you convince me I was weak because my mom's death devastated me. I wasn't strong because I struggled. And it was a gift that you overlooked those things, that you kept me in your life. No one else could understand or accept the broken version of me. Not even you in the end. Until now, of course. Lucky me."

Justin sank back on his heels, stuffing his hands into his pockets. Speechless. He didn't recognize me, because I wasn't the person he knew. This person wasn't so easily manipulated.

"You've changed," he said finally. "And it's not attractive."

"Good," I spewed. "Because I never want to attract another bastard like you. I'd rather be alone than with someone who makes me feel less capable than I am."

37

KENNEDY

I DROVE BACK FROM the wedding, straight to my childhood home.

One of Alexei's parting lines before he walked off the dance floor, out of my life, played on repeat. *You blame it on your grief, but you're afraid.* The words hit too close to the mark, to the part of myself I'd started to share with him. He told me I should do what felt right, but he clearly felt the same as everyone else.

I should be able to move on.

As empowering as it felt to finally confront Justin, the drive back had me going to that dark place again. Maybe no one could ever accept this new version of me. Part of me still didn't.

"Dad, I need to talk to you," I said after knocking on his open office door.

He sat behind his desk, typing away, but he paused and stood, a broad smile gracing his face as soon as he saw me. It faded when he processed the expression on mine. He didn't walk to me as he usually would, instead gesturing to the chair in front of his desk. "What's wrong, sweetheart?"

I want to come home. The words sat behind my lips, begging to come out. *Solve my problems for me.*

He would never turn me away. A blessing and a curse to have that security, always.

"So much is wrong," I said, slumping into the seat.

He sat back in his, interwoven hands resting on his desk, patiently waiting for me to go on.

"And I... I don't know if I can fix any of it. I don't know if I'm capable of fixing any of it."

"I highly doubt that. Since you were a girl, you've faced down everything with strength and conviction. Whatever—"

"Until she died, Dad." The words ripped out of a place deep within me. "I'm not the same anymore."

My father launched out of his seat to the chair beside me.

"I know you think it too," I continued. "You preferred the old me, when I was in the world, accomplishing things rather than bumming around your house."

He reached for my hands. "I'm happy you're here, Kenny." He sighed. "I'm relieved you're okay. *She* would know what to do if our roles were reversed. You got left with the wrong parent."

"No, Dad—"

"I'm working on it, though," he cut me off. "With a pain-in-the-ass therapist."

I lifted my head. "You're in therapy?"

"I went back four months ago to do it for real this time. I wasn't ready before, but I am now."

I sucked in a breath, gathering the courage to say the next words, steeling myself against the tide of emotion headed my way. "I miss her so much."

Pain flickered across my father's face. His eyes glistened, and he made no effort to hide it.

"It's unfair she's gone," I continued. "Sometimes, I wonder what the point of anything is. We make plans and life has other ideas for us. Why should I want anything when I can lose it at any time?"

"The point, Kenny, is the time you have when things are going right. I wouldn't have traded a second of my time with your mother, even knowing how my heart would break in the end. I didn't want to push you, but it hasn't been easy watching you sleepwalk your way through life this past year. I want you to be happy, kid. Seeing you at Thanksgiving was the first time I thought maybe you were."

His words made me cry harder, tears streaking down my face. I let them fall.

I'd anticipated hating every moment of her not being with us on Thanksgiving. And I missed having her there—baking pies the day before as she grilled me about my life, shopping online as we sipped hot chocolate, decorating for Christmas as soon as we closed the book on Thanksgiving. But I hadn't wanted to crawl into bed and never come back out again like last year.

And I knew why. *I'm thankful for you, Alexei.*

I swallowed the lump in my throat and took deep breaths to calm down.

"Did something happen, Kennedy?" Dad asked.

Nothing unplanned.

I thought about lying to him—I was *supposed* to keep lying. But if I had any chance at happiness, I had to stop hiding how I felt.

"I need to tell you something, and you're not going to like it. Alexei and I weren't dating for real. Alexei did it for damage control, and I... I was pissed at Justin, and wanted to make him jealous and realize what he was missing. And it worked. Too well. At a certain point, it stopped being pretend. But I screwed it up, Dad, and now we're... nothing."

I slumped back in my seat, spent from venting all these emotions. After an extended, silent moment, I asked, "Aren't you going to say anything?"

"Kennedy," my dad said, a smile spreading across his face. "You don't need me to say anything."

"No, I really do. Aren't you disappointed I lied? Multiple times, to your face."

He shook his head slowly, chuckling lightly. "Oh, kid, I don't think you ever lied to my face." He stood abruptly and rested a hand on my shoulder for a moment before heading to the other side of the desk. "And you know exactly what you need to do."

My stomach roiled, but it wasn't enough to make me go backward. It wasn't enough to ask to move back home, to run from my problems like I had in the past.

When I made it back to Gemma's, I changed out of my clothes into a sleepshirt and leggings and crawled into bed. I pulled up the DVR and turned on the Wolves game from several nights ago. Relief hit me acutely, but in the way scratching scabbed-over skin did. It eased pain temporarily, but healing would take longer and maybe leave a scar.

But as I watched him glide across the ice, checking players into the boards with an aggressiveness I couldn't help but find sexy, I found I didn't care. Someday, it would get easier, but for now, I would go at my own pace.

As I always had. Two steps forward, one step back.

38

ALEXEI

Two weeks passed in a blink following Matt and Gemma's wedding. I fell back on my old tried-and-true habits to forget what happened—physically pushing myself beyond the point I should.

At least, I wasn't in it alone this time. Briggsy took pity on me, abandoning his routine of video gaming and naps to go in early to run and lift before practice, to stay after hitting pucks well past when everyone else left. Erik took notice, but not in a good way. He banned me from the arena outside of practices, which was hypocritical given the way he lived at the gym.

But he couldn't stop my home workout regimen.

"It's Christmas, dude," Briggsy called from the doorway as he watched me pedaling uphill on the stationary bike. "You can take a day off."

He knew, better than anyone, that this had little to do with my dedication to hockey.

"I have five more minutes," I said.

"We're supposed to be at Gemma and Matt's in a half hour." Briggsy couldn't go home since we had a game the day after Christmas.

"I've got a call with my parents. I'll come by after."

"Don't bail. She won't be there until later tonight. She's with her dad." He had gotten scarily good at reading me.

"I said I will be there." I gritted my teeth, turning my attention away from him to focus on my climb. In my periphery, I saw Zach give me the middle finger and leave his post.

An hour later, I sat at my kitchen counter, waiting for my parents to call. They would celebrate together today, but it wouldn't last. It never did. My father screwed up again and again, and I did the same.

In many ways, I wanted to be like my father. He'd chased his dreams with dogged dedication until he got them. I watched and learned from him, surpassing him as I achieved the dream he never did, playing in the NHL. But I had one thing he never did—parents who would sacrifice anything to make my dream happen. So despite my frustration over how their relationship played out like a damn soap opera, my gratitude always outweighed it.

My mom's glowing, wide-smiling face filled the screen when I accepted her call. "Merry Christmas, Alyosha. I like your decorations," she said in Russian.

I'd had nothing to do with my decorations. Zach took it upon himself to deck out the entire house in wreaths and Santas and a ginormous tree Matt helped him set up. "Merry Christmas, Mama."

"No Kennedy today?" The reminder of her absence chafed like sandpaper on my skin. I expected her to come up in this conversation, but I didn't realize I'd be hit with the question in the first minute.

"I don't think you'll be seeing her again."

She looked genuinely apologetic before I watched the emotion slough off her face. "What did you do?"

"Why do you assume *I* did anything?"

"Because I saw the way you looked at her."

Not the way she looked at me. Another reminder of how I was the fucking idiot who caught actual feelings in our pretend relationship.

"He doesn't need the distraction," my father chimed in, his face appearing over her shoulder. "This season is too important. You're off to a good start, but there are a lot of games left. You can't lose sight of the goal."

A distraction. The exact word I used with Kennedy after Ward showed up in her front yard. As if I needed more proof I was my father's son.

"She's been a big part of my success this year." Not only because she helped me turn the tide of public opinion, but she'd been there with me, every step of the way for the last three months.

"Why aren't you together anymore?" The accusing set of Mom's eyebrows told me all I needed to know. After one meal with Kennedy, she realized what I'd fought all along—how right she was for me. But it didn't matter, not when I was fucking useless to her. Not when...

"I'm not sure she's over her ex," I said.

Justin fucking Ward showing up at the wedding doused our weekend with reality. We had kidded ourselves, pretending we could live in a bubble for one weekend, as if nothing else mattered. Not my reputation. Not her unresolved feelings for Ward. And not the fact that I couldn't be what she deserved.

"And I am not cut out for a relationship."

My mother's eyes softened. "Why would you think that?"

"Because I've fucked up every relationship I've ever had. Always putting me and my goals first. Even with the woman I thought I would spend my life with, I couldn't prioritize her over myself. I'm like him." I nodded in my father's direction. "In all of the good ways and in all of the fucking flawed ways—"

My father raised his voice over mine. "Hold on—"

But I plowed forward, needing to say what I'd danced around all these years. Ignoring how their relationship affected me allowed me to keep a close relationship with my father, but it also ate at me. "I don't want to make someone I love feel like a second priority. To make them question their worth. To waste their time when someone else out there could give them the attention and support they deserve."

My mother reached behind her, presumably to grab my father's hand, communicating silently for him to let her handle this. By some miracle, he complied. Probably because this was the stage of their relationship where he was still on thin ice.

"For most of your life, you never said anything about your dad and me, but I always could see it, Alyosha. The disappointment each time he moved back into the house, not because you didn't want him there, but because I kept allowing him to come back after we separated. It can take time to get it right. I don't regret any of it."

I let the words wash over me. She didn't regret a single moment of their complicated relationship. She would do it again. That was how much she loved my father, enough to wait for him to figure it out. It should have filled me with something other than dread, because she thought the pain had all been worth it, but I could only think about the fear that I would inflict it on another person.

She continued, "Yes, you have big dreams, and dreams like those take dedication, but it doesn't mean you have to go through life on your own. Neither has to be sacrificed. And if you're worried you can't see when you've got tunnel vision, find the person who won't hesitate to call you on it."

Kennedy would do that. She had no problem unloading her opinion on me or asking questions I never would've answered for anyone else.

And I meant what I told her—Justin Ward wasn't the right person for her. He wanted to stifle her growth, to keep her in the same place she'd been, which she said didn't make her happy. She deserved more. When I pushed her on it, it wasn't to give her a hard time, but to make her see that.

I was the kind of person she needed. Someone who wouldn't let her shy away from something good in life because of her fear.

And she would never tolerate me pulling away from her, from becoming too focused on myself.

"It's inevitable," Mom continued, "you will hurt each other, sometimes when you don't mean to, but you have to be willing to figure it out. That's the secret to making it work."

"I fucked up," I whispered, my head in my hands.

"Then you need to fight for her. The same way you fought for your hockey dreams your entire life."

I shook my head. "I don't know that she feels the same way about me."

"Feelings like that are hard to hide. They have a way of shining through."

An image of Kennedy opening her eyes beside me in bed the morning of the wedding flashed in my mind. Sleep clouded her eyes as she turned toward me. She smiled, small and shy, and I wished—no, I knew—she liked me beside her. Liked it more than two strangers who reluctantly fake-dated and became friends. The night before, she'd kissed me, again and again, never letting our lips come out of contact, as if she couldn't stand to part us. It was more than getting it out of our systems.

Still, it didn't mean a relationship with me was something she wanted.

But I had to know. I had to fight for her and the life we could have together if she would allow it.

"I've retired," Dad announced, pulling me back to the moment. A twinge of bitterness laced his words. Not at the retirement, but at me. He wasn't used to me calling him out on anything, and he didn't like it. Still, he looked me in the eyes, and I saw he cared. "That was what I needed to do to get the life I wanted with your mother, to prove to her I was serious. There's *something* you can do to show Kennedy the same."

"What does that mean, exactly? You retired?"

"I'm no longer coaching the junior Olympic team," he replied. "I'm moving home. I'm thinking of private coaching. It's not like we need the money, not with what you've given us. I only coached because I loved it. But I love your mama, and I'm choosing our life together going forward."

I blew out a breath. This was... new and unexpected. He'd never said he would quit before. Could it be that after thirty years of screwing up, they'd finally gotten it right?

"I... don't know what to say," I stumbled, grasping for something to acknowledge what they shared. "I'm happy you're both happy."

I left out *I hope it lasts* because of the adoring way they stared at each other. The same shared look of adoration I'd seen between Matt and Gemma too many times to count. It hit me in the gut each time, because I wanted what they had.

Maybe that had been the issue all along. I hadn't met the right person. The person who would make it worth risking everything.

Until I did.

39

KENNEDY

I SAT IN MY car for far longer than I would ever admit.

Although Alexei's car remained parked in his driveway and lights were on in his house, he could still be inside Matt and Gemma's place. I needed to get used to seeing him around because of his friendships with them. At least through the end of the season. Who knew if Alexei would stay longer than that? With the way he was playing, he would likely have his pick of teams.

When I pushed open the door, Gemma called out, "You're home!" No hint of nervousness in her voice, which I took as a good sign.

Walking deeper into the house, I saw no Alexei, only Gemma, Matt, and Zach in front of the TV.

"Your cookies are in the tin by the oven."

"Aw, you saved me some?" I said, dropping my bag onto one of the countertop stools.

"Of course," she said. "I expected there to be more, but you created a monster. I had to take them away from Volk before he inhaled them all."

Less than a minute. That was all it took for someone to mention Alexei.

I focused on eating my cookie, moving as slowly as possible to avoid acknowledging Gemma's comment.

"It was a nice Christmas, then?" I asked, taking a seat in the corner chair, facing the sofa where the three of them sat.

"Zach got along famously with my nieces and nephews," Matt said.

"Where are they?" I asked.

"Ice-skating downtown."

"I'm surprised you didn't go," I said to Zach.

Gemma ruffled Zach's hair. "Our boy is tiiiired."

Zach swatted at Gemma's hand. "You'd be tired too, if you were held hostage by a bunch of kids for hours. And I also didn't want to leave..." He trailed off.

"You can say his name."

Zach let out a breath. "Sorry, this feels like my parent's divorce all over again. I'm the only layer of defense between Volk and his favorite coping mechanism. I'm worried about the stationary bike. The poor thing can't take much more."

"Dude." Matt smacked him on the back of the head. "What did we say about oversharing?"

"What? Oversharing with family is fine."

Gemma side-eyed Zach before turning her attention to me. "I heard you found yourself an apartment."

"How?" I asked, staring straight at Zach. We hadn't told anyone we planned to be roommates yet. I'd wanted to tell Gemma and Matt myself once it was a done deal, mostly because I worried they would try to talk me out of it.

"Your new *roommate* has a big mouth. Kennedy, this is like your version of cutting your hair super short."

I brushed crumbs from my chest into my palm. "What are you talking about?"

"You're pulling a Felicity. After a bad breakup, women cut their hair super short. It's a thing. But your decision, instead, is to move in with a man baby."

"Hey!"

Gemma patted Zach on the shoulder. "I mean it in the nicest way possible, Zachary."

He scowled.

"He's not that bad. He's been housebroken." At least I hoped. Zach had learned to do his laundry, cook his food without causing a fire, and even vacuum his room on a semiregular basis. "And my breakup wasn't..." I almost said *real.* "That bad."

Zach scoffed. "My aching muscles call bullshit."

I stared at him, waiting for him to explain.

"Because I've been a great friend, and teammate, *and* roommate, working out with Volk and it's... a lot. It's cutting into my video game and nap time. On an unrelated note, I'm going to head out."

Matt glanced at Gemma. "I'm going to go with him."

The two of them scampered out of the room. "Real subtle," I mumbled. "Did you coordinate that?"

Gemma smiled slyly. "So paranoid on Christmas, Kennedy. Maybe they wanted us to have girl time." I narrowed my eyes at her, not buying a word. "I have something for you. From Alexei." She tapped a white envelope on the table.

"What's this?" I asked, reaching for it. My name was written in black ink on the outside.

"Open it and find out."

Inside, there were two tickets—Wolves tickets—to the game tomorrow night. My breath caught when I saw the section and seat numbers. These were the seats my mother and I sat in at every single game. There was a slip of paper with them. *She would want you to go.* I relayed the gift to Gemma before I folded it up and slipped it back into the envelope.

"What are you going to do?" Gemma asked.

Alexei knew I'd avoided hockey since my mother died. It hurt to think about enjoying it without her. Attending Wolves games belonged to another version of me, one that no longer existed. But I had gone to the arena and watched a game on TV. Because of Alexei. He invited me to tackle the last, most difficult of the activities I avoided—attending a live game in the seats we'd occupied every season since my parents moved the team here.

For the first time since she died, the idea of being there didn't feel impossible. But I hadn't only avoided the games because it would make me sad. Going back would also prove life could go on without her, something so fundamentally wrong.

"I don't know, Gem."

"He's not wrong. Kens, you have to step out of your box sometime. Yes, the world is scary, and it can hurt you, but what you're doing to yourself is worse. You're missing out on what you deserve to experience—rooting for the team you both loved, relationships with people who care about you, finding your passion in life. Your mom wouldn't want this—"

"We can't ask her," I snapped, my voice sharper than it had ever been with Gemma.

"No, we can't," she said softly. She paused, weighing her next words. When she spoke again, they carried Gemma's usual punch. "But as someone who loves you, I think I know her answer. Her death was unfair and devastating, but don't forget you survived."

Sometimes, it didn't feel that way, but I knew Gemma wasn't wrong. The choices I made in the wake of my mom's death muted my life. The world kept on going, as senseless as it seemed, but I made sure my life didn't. Every time I wanted to change it, something held me back.

Gemma continued when the silence stretched too long. "Whatever happens, I'm here. We'll go through it together. And it's not only me." She looked at me pointedly.

"Don't start," I told her.

"Uh, no, I will very much start. Kennedy, I've never seen you happier. Even that first night we met, you remember?"

"Of course," I said, rolling my eyes. "You immediately inserted yourself into my business."

"I saw your feelings all over your face."

Gemma had no qualms asking about my feelings for my ex, even though I was still dating someone else. She somehow saw what I'd denied, even to myself.

"I wasn't wrong then," she said, "and I'm not wrong now."

"Even if I wanted to do something"—Gemma opened her mouth, but I held up a hand to stop her interruption—"it wouldn't matter. It's too late."

She waved the envelope in front of my face. "It doesn't feel too late."

"Gem, he doesn't want to see me. Alexei's only doing this out of the goodness of his heart."

"Give me a break, Kennedy," she said. "Alexei's a good man, but this isn't *out of the goodness of his heart*. Do you see the way he looks at you?"

"It's called acting, Gemma. We were in a fake relationship."

"The only people you two managed to fool were each other." She held up the envelope again. "This is a peace offering. Don't pretend otherwise. It's fine to ignore it, but at least have the courage to admit you know what this means and you're actively choosing not to take it."

My mind snagged on one word—*courage.* Gemma thought I was hiding behind my grief like Alexei accused. I'd never been one of those people who raced toward what they wanted, damn the consequences. My moves in life were measured, sure. But before my mom died, I made moves. I went to school out of state, even though my parents wanted me to remain close. I worked for the Wolves despite the assumptions about how I got the internship.

Slowly, these last few months I started making moves again—calling a university, finding an apartment, even dying my hair. And now, Alexei presented me with the opportunity for two more risks. Neither of which I felt ready for. But maybe no one ever felt ready as they went headfirst toward what they wanted.

I snatched the envelope out of Gemma's hands.

"That's my girl." Gemma pulled me into a hug. "I'm proud of you. I can go with you, if you want."

"No," I said into Gemma's ear. "This is something I need to do alone."

40

KENNEDY

I WALKED TO THE arena in a sea of green and black jerseys—couples holding hands, parents with children, college students out on a Friday night. Everyone else walked toward a night of entertainment, a chance to drink beer, eat fried food, and cheer on their team.

I walked toward the painful memory of nights like this with my mom. She would meet Deandra and me in the same place every time, in front of The Den, which sold Wolves merchandise. It didn't matter how many games she attended or how many times she looked up from her phone to see us walking toward her, she beamed from ear to ear every time.

Tonight, I walked alone into The Den and found Alexei Volkov's jersey, paid for it, and slipped it over my plain black tank top. With fifteen minutes to puck drop, I made my way to section 105, not wanting to miss the opening sizzle reel. The usher's eyes widened upon seeing me, but she didn't say anything, just gave me directions to the seat I could find blindfolded.

A mass of people—in Wolves and Lions jerseys—crowded the glass to watch the end of warm-ups. When the buzzer sounded, players skated off the ice as the crowd headed to their seats.

"I was starting to think you wouldn't make it." Deandra rose out of her usual seat. She wore her green jersey with Collins on the back, like she used to.

"D, what are you doing here?"

Her eyebrows rose. "You thought I would let you do this alone?"

"How did you..."

She took a step toward me and gripped my shoulder to turn me enough to read the name on the back of my jersey. "How do you think?"

"He told you?" I asked, settling into my seat beside her. The seat to my right—my mom's seat—would remain empty tonight.

"He needed someone to get him the right seats."

She turned her attention to the jumbotron as the Wolves video her team designed played on the screen, showing highlights of each player interspersed with them standing in front of a green screen made to look like a forest, primed for battle. The dramatic music made it feel like a movie trailer.

"I suspected there was something between you. What happened?"

"Neither one of us knows what's real," I said as Alexei's determined face flashed on the screen for a beat before the scene changed to him checking a guy hard into the boards and scoring several impressive goals. Each one included the announcer's audio—*Volkov goooooooal.*

She laughed. "Come on, Kens. It's me."

"I'm here to watch the game." I directed my attention to the Wolves storming out of their locker room onto the ice to the cheers of the crowd, bigger than I had seen in years. After the national anthem, Alexei looked over to these seats, checking to see if I was here. When we locked eyes, a grin spread across his face as he skated to his position. Briggsy followed his gaze and waved excitedly at me until Alexei pulled his arm down.

"You were saying..."

"Hush," I warned, bumping against her shoulder.

The first goal scored by the Wolves came in the middle of the second period, cutting the Lions' lead in half. As soon as the red lamp lit, the familiar song blasted through the arena, and fans leaped to their feet to cheer, scream, and dance. I glanced to my right, and in my head, I could see my mother high-fiving everyone around her as she cheered.

Deandra grabbed my hand, noticing the emotion shining in my eyes. She hip-checked me and started to dance, tugging my hand until I did the same.

Tears stung my eyes at the memory of what this celebration used to feel like. *This one's for you, Mom.*

"It's good to see you here, kid," a familiar voice said behind me when I settled back into my seat. Bertram, the friendly older man who held season tickets and always talked my mom's ear off about the team. "Hasn't been the same since."

I nodded at him and allowed a small smile. "Thank you. It's... good to be back."

When Alexei tied the game off a power play at the start of the third period, I needed no encouragement from Deandra to get to my feet. He skated across the ice to Zach, who had perfectly placed the pass that led to the goal. The force of Alexei's hug slammed Zach back into the boards as the rest of their on-ice teammates surrounded them.

The team started to feel like mine again.

Once I was back in my seat, I pulled my phone out of my pocket to send Gemma a text about the post goal hug when I saw an unread message from her. Are you okay?

All thoughts of joking about the hugs left me. Deandra's here, I wrote back.

The three dots appeared immediately as if she'd been waiting for my response. I know.

I shook my head, glancing at Deandra, but she was focused so intently on the screen—scrutinizing something to discuss with her team later—she didn't notice. You fucking meddlers.

What are best friends for?

The two teams battled through the rest of the period, each with several close scoring chances. Every near-goal by the Wolves elicited a collective inhale from the crowd, followed by a groan. With less than two minutes left, Alexei scored the go-ahead goal, deflecting in a puck sent toward the net by Briggsy. The crowd went berserk—Deandra and I along with them.

Alexei had been a controversial signing, one many Wolves fans didn't support. The rallying cry against him grew stronger after the Wolves traded Justin. Now, halfway through the season, the crowd chanted Alexei's name—*Volk, Volk, Volk*—as they named him the first star of the game.

I spun in my seat, looking at the large, screaming crowd. My mom would have loved this.

He sat on the empty bench next to a rink-side correspondent for an interview, grinned at the crowd, and said into the mic, "I love you all."

The crowd's chanting grew louder. Alexei's cheeks flushed, and he gave a little wave.

My heart squeezed—my mom would have loved him too, for this team. And for me.

"Alexei, walk us through that last goal. What was going through your mind?"

He ran a hand through his sweat-soaked hair. "I saw Matty coming away with the puck and pushing it up to Briggsy, so I knew I had to get to the goal. Luckily, I got a good bounce and was able to sneak it past their goalie to put this thing away."

"We've watched you play your heart out for this team all season, but it seemed like you dug deep and found another gear tonight."

He let out a choked laugh. "You could say that."

"Anything, in particular, inspire you?"

"You mean other than this crowd?" Alexei said, a placating statement the crowd ate up like the last piece of cake before a diet. When they quieted, he leaned closer to the mic. "There's someone here tonight who I wanted to impress. I wanted to give her a win."

Deandra nudged me with her shoulder as my breath caught. I didn't want to admit how much I cared about him, afraid to be left behind because I wasn't good enough. But pretending I didn't love him to protect myself didn't make the feelings disappear.

The interviewer opened her mouth to say something, but Alexei tilted the mic in his direction. "That's all I'm going to say about that."

"Can you take me to him?" I asked Deandra.

A devious smile stretched across her face. "Of course I can. Not that you need an escort with your name on the side of the arena."

I bounced on the balls of my feet. "Okay, okay, can we go?" I wasn't worried I would change my mind or lose my nerve, but now that I'd decided to go after what I wanted, I didn't want to wait.

Nerves snuck into my stomach while I stood outside the media room, listening to Alexei charmingly answer their questions. Deandra ran off, I suspected, to get a camera, a thought that made me cringe, but it didn't last. The first sound of his deep laugh made me forget every worry. I wanted to hear that laugh every day for the rest of my life.

"All right, thank you, guys," Alexei said. I heard the scrape of his chair, and suddenly, he stood in front of me, halting his steps as soon as his gaze landed on me. His gray Wolves T-shirt looked fresh, and a green baseball cap sat backward on his head.

I swallowed, taking in his muscular forearms and biceps, pressing the limits of his shirt's short sleeves, until finally, I landed on his face. No trace of smugness lingered there today, only the damned double-dimple grin.

41

ALEXEI

KENNEDY COLE STOOD AGAINST the wall, fiddling mindlessly with the sleeve of her jersey. A jersey sporting my number.

My breath burst from my lungs at the sight of her. Seeing her before puck drop had given my heart stupid hope.

"Hi," she said, glued to the wall.

I took a step forward to allow Connor to enter the press room. He glanced at me then at Kennedy before clapping my shoulder as he passed. *Good fucking luck* was what that gesture said.

"So eating dirt wasn't all that appealing, after all?"

Kennedy's eyebrows rose in confusion.

I gestured to the jersey she swore she'd never wear. "You have no idea what it does to me to see you wearing my jersey."

A smile graced her lips as she looked away. "Did you mean what you said? That you were trying to impress me?"

"Oh, I wanted to impress you all right. Those goals were all for you."

Kennedy pushed off the wall, taking a step forward. "Don't let the real fans hear that," she whispered, pitching herself toward me and cupping one hand around her mouth.

"You are a real fan," I said, tugging a hand at the end of one sleeve before letting my fingers rest on her bare wrist. The contact stoked my need to be close to her, a closeness I worried I might never have again. Kennedy's sharp intake of breath at this barest of contact was the best sound I'd heard in weeks.

"Is that why you came?" I traced my thumb back and forth on her wrist, watched her follow the movement. "Love of the hockey?"

"Yes," Kennedy said. It took a moment for her to wrench her stare from her wrist to my face.

I sucked in a breath as her eyes met mine. She looked so fucking good standing there in my jersey, in the color I enjoyed best on her.

"But there's also the whole love of you thing."

My fingers stilled against her wrist. I watched her, waiting for her to continue, too scared to open my mouth and shatter the moment.

"You were right about me wanting to make the easy choices. Or what I thought were the easy choices. I chose what I thought wouldn't hurt me, but it does. It does because it's caused me to miss out on so much. But I... I don't want to miss out on you. I *can't* miss out on you."

Neither of us moved an inch. A big part of me wanted to scoop her into my arms, take her home, and not leave my room for the next twenty-four hours. But I couldn't ignore the voice in the back of my mind. She didn't know what it was like to be with me.

I loved her, but it didn't mean I wouldn't fuck it up.

"It won't be easy being with me."

Kennedy's shoulders visibly relaxed. "Don't I know it."

"I'm serious, Kennedy. I'm selfish. I get a one-track mind."

"Because sometimes, that's what you need to do to be the best. I get that."

"And I only have a one-year contract."

She nodded. "I know."

"What if I move to another team?"

"Is that... what you're thinking of doing?"

"No." Palmer City had become my home, because of her, because this organization gave me an opportunity no other would. Erik pushed me like no coach in my career had. I wanted to play well for him, for these fans. "And I wouldn't, not without talking to you."

Those words came without a second thought, and they were true. In three months, my feelings for her changed my approach to the rest of my life. Not only about what was best for me and my career, but what was best for us. If she would let me.

"I'd hate myself if I ever make you feel less important than you are. You are my priority. I love hockey—it's where I escape and have my best moments, and it challenges me like nothing else. But it's a game, and it can't give me everything I want."

"What do you want?"

I placed my hands on her waist, drawing us closer together. "You to come home to. To tell you about my day and hear about whatever true crime show you're watching. I want you cheering me on while wearing my jersey. I want to belong to you. I want a future, something we'll decide together."

Her face split into a grin, the sight of it tightening my chest. I wanted to spend my life earning more of those from her.

"A lot of your wants revolve around me, huh?"

My grip on her waist tightened, the desire for her pounding in my gut. "Don't be an ass."

"I would never," she said, reaching to place her hands on my jaw. "I don't want a life without you either. I've hated not seeing or talking to you these last couple weeks."

I pulled Kennedy to me until her body melded against mine and her head tucked under my chin. "Please come home with me tonight," I said.

"Well, only because you begged." She pulled her face back to show me her smirk.

I backed her up until she hit the wall. "I love you and your sarcastic ass too," I said before pressing my lips to hers. Kissing Kennedy had the dizzying effect of being exactly what I needed and not nearly enough of what I needed.

"Once could never be enough for me, Kennedy," I whispered, resting my forehead against hers. Our fingers threaded together at our sides.

"Good," she said, pushing onto her tippy-toes to say the words into my ear. "Because *once* wasn't even close to what I had in mind."

Epilogue: Four Months Later

ALEXEI

I ARRIVED FIRST AT the Wolves practice arena. Today was an off day, coming home from a four-game road trip. We had two days before our next game, a generous break for us, especially in April. Miraculously, the Palmer City Wolves were on pace to clinch a wild card playoff spot, shocking the entire hockey world.

Just got here. Heading inside, I texted Kennedy.

I watched the screen, waiting for her response. A week without seeing her felt like an eternity. Normally, she would have waited at my house for me to return, but she had a paper due today. Moments later, my phone dinged. On my way.

My heart beat faster, knowing I would see her soon, but Kennedy was in class a couple of towns over. *On my way* could mean another twenty minutes. I grabbed my gear out of the trunk and headed inside. The arena was blissfully quiet, and only the sound of my skates across the ice filled my ears. Until I heard another pair.

I stopped, leaning against the boards. "I didn't know you'd be here," I said to Briggsy.

"Kennedy invited me," he said, skating in my direction until he playfully rammed into me. It had become a tradition of ours at every game, something the Wolves filmed and posted on their social media accounts. "Didn't she tell you?"

"I haven't talked to her since I got back. She had a paper due."

"Right, the econ one." Zach skated backward, away from me, toward center ice. "She looked stressed when I got in last night. I went right to bed, and she was still asleep in the morning. No idea how long she stayed up finishing it." He slipped a puck from his pocket and waved it at me. "Care for a game?"

Zach dropped the puck. I didn't know how long we played by the time I spun around him and buried a goal in net and heard cheers from the bench. Relief flooded through me at seeing Kennedy skate my way, arms outstretched. She hurled her body into mine, the force moving us backward on my skates.

"I missed you," she said against my chest, her arms wrapped tightly around me. "I couldn't watch the game last night because of my stupid paper."

I lifted her chin, then crashed my lips against hers. Her soft lips met my quick movements. Kennedy tilted her head to the side, deepening the kiss. The sound of a hockey stick pounding several times against the ice made her jump and look toward the noise. I dropped my head back because that kiss wasn't enough to satisfy my need for her, but there would be plenty of time later.

"Shit, sorry, Zach," Kennedy said as she wiped her fingertips against her mouth.

Zach waved his stick in the air. "I would have been fine with just about anything to shut this guy up from Kennedy this, Kennedy that, all freaking week, but I have to draw the line somewhere."

I shrugged one shoulder. "I might have missed you too."

Kennedy grinned. "I would have preferred to welcome you home properly last night"—Zach made a gagging sound—"rather than writing my paper, but I'm free and clear tonight. All yours."

"Now *that* is what I want to hear." I pulled her toward me, resting my chin on top of her head.

"Guess I'll have the apartment to myself."

Kennedy playfully glared at him. "As if you care. You'll just be in your gaming room all night anyway."

The fact that Zach required their apartment to have an entire room dedicated to his gaming—and that Kennedy went along with it—still boggled my mind. Although, Kennedy also framed and hung the jersey from the night we officially became a couple in their living room, so sacrifices were made on both sides.

"We're here!" Connie called as she ambled toward the ice with Silas in her arms. Gemma trailed behind Izzy, while Matt and Rich remained deep in conversation behind them all. Mason already sat on the bench, preparing to come onto the ice. This morning's meet-up had been Kennedy's idea—bringing all her favorite people together.

"Oh, Kennedy, we've missed you," Connie drawled.

Kennedy glided three strides over to lean against the boards. "Trust me, I would much rather spend my morning with you than recovering from a night of paper writing."

When Kennedy went back to school, she cut back her hours with the McIntyres, only working for them in the early mornings. She'd get Mason and Izzy on the school bus before dropping Silas at daycare before she headed to class. Gemma took the afternoon shift as a "test run" for her soon-to-be role—mother. Matt and Gemma made the announcement last weekend that they were expecting a girl, which thrilled Gemma as much as it terrified Matt.

"Someone didn't want to wake up from his nap," Connie said in a baby voice as she tickled Silas's belly, drawing immediate laughter.

"He made us late," Mason grumbled.

Kennedy laughed. "Welcome to my life, every single morning when you won't listen to me."

"This will be his first time on the ice," Connie said, dropping to the bench to put on Silas's skates.

My father got me on the ice for the first time when I was two years old, despite my mom's protests. He always said the earlier someone learned to skate, the more comfortable they would become. Silas looked at us with his big blue eyes, not saying a word. Probably still in a post nap stupor.

"Izzy's first time too," Rich chimed in from behind the bench. "Did you say hi to everyone, Izz?"

Izzy stood from the bench after Gemma finished lacing up her skates. "They should say hi to me *first*." Already a ballbuster at only five years old.

"Come on, Izz," Kennedy said. "Wanna skate with me?"

Izzy hesitated a moment, glancing at me and Zach before answering. "Yes, but only if we get away from the boys."

Zach burst out laughing. "Richie teach you that?"

Like the rest of the world, Briggsy had the McIntyres in his corner, and not only because he played for their favorite team. The lad drew people to him without even trying. It was hard not to like him, even when he dirtied up your house... or nearly burned it down.

He, like every other person here, was part of a new life I was building in the last place I expected. And I would go through all of the pain and fear all over again to end up here, with this family of mine.

Kennedy stepped forward, opening the door to the bench. "Ignore him."

I handed Kennedy a hockey stick as she helped Izzy to the ice. "She can hold onto this until she gets comfortable."

Kennedy held the stick between them while they inched across the ice. Gemma handed Silas to me when she finished lacing up his skates. I held him underneath his armpits and lowered him until his skates hit the ice. He moved his legs back and forth, blades scraping every so often, but mostly I held him and skated slowly around the rink. Zach trailed behind us with Mason, the only person who could rival Zach's verbal vomit.

I caught Kennedy's eye as she and Izzy passed us and couldn't help the grin that overtook my face at how adorable she looked in her Wolves beanie, teaching this little girl to skate. I wondered if this would be us one day. We had a lot to experience together, and I didn't know if she wanted kids. If she didn't, being uncle and aunt to Matt and Gemma's kids would be fine for me, as long as Kennedy remained in my life. The first time we skated in this arena, I wouldn't have dared to dream I could get her to stop hating me, let alone to fall in love with me.

I never thought I would get a chance at a future with her. Now, it was all I could think about, how much I wanted her never to leave my life.

Every time she left my house, I wanted to ask her to move in with me. But this relationship was too important to rush. Kennedy had only just moved out of her childhood home and into her own apartment, an item on the list she told me about soon after we got together. As I'd guessed, she didn't remember telling me half that list the first night we met.

She also needed time to finish her undergraduate business degree and figure out what career she wanted to pursue. Over the summer, she planned to work for the Wolves again to see if that was what she wanted.

She deserved this time to figure out her life, and I would stand by her side until she did, supporting her and cheering her on.

"I don't know what I did to deserve you," I said as we left the arena together hours later, hand-in-hand, arms swinging.

"It truly is a mystery." Kennedy spun out in front of me, blocking my way to the car. Her grin fell away as she walked closer to me. "You made me believe in myself. You showed me some risks are worth taking. Especially with cocky, too-handsome-for-their-own-good hockey players."

I tucked a strand of her hair behind one ear. "You are so lucky you're cute." I took a deep breath. "If it weren't for you, I would still be alone, feeling sorry for myself, wanting someone I didn't think I deserved."

Kennedy leaned on her tiptoes, her mouth inches from mine. "We're lost without each other, huh?" She pressed her lips against mine before pulling back. "Good thing I love you then."

"Yeah, good thing."

She shoved against my chest but smiled up at me.

"You know I love you, Kennedy."

"Yeah, but I like hearing it."

So I repeated it, again and again, that night and every night that followed.

If you enjoyed Play Your Part and...

... want more of Alexei and Kennedy, visit my website by scanning the QR code below to sign up for my newsletter and receive a free bonus chapter.

Acknowledgements

Thank you to everyone who read *Play Your Part*! Writing this story felt like a blissful escape. I hope reading it has been equally enjoyable for you. I never thought I would have the opportunity to put a story out into the world. I didn't share my writing with anyone for the longest time because I was worried about their judgment. This author journey has helped me value my opinion; if that's all I come away with from this experience, taking the risk would still have been worth it.

AnnaMaria, Sarah, Becky, and Rose – I appreciate the time you spent reading drafts and revisions. *Play Your Part* benefited from your thoughtful, honest, and insightful feedback. Thank you for caring about Kennedy and Alexei's story. It's a better story because of you.

To my editor, Rachel Shipp – thank you for your thorough review. Your edits made my manuscript shine without it losing my voice. I'm so grateful for how enjoyable you made the editing process and how much I learned from you.

Mary Scarlett LaBerge – thank you for creating this gorgeous cover. I was nervous to work with a designer because I didn't have a specific vision. Somehow you translated my sometimes vague feedback into the perfect representation of this story.

Thank you to **Eddie and Rose** for their legal guidance, and **Maria** for answering all my Russian questions.

I want to thank **my parents** for supporting me throughout my entire life. Without your sacrifices, guidance, and love, I could not have taken a risk like this. I'm grateful for the life you created for me every day.

And to my husband, Mike – I love you so much. When we met twelve years ago, I lacked confidence and felt insecure. You've helped me learn to accept myself. I also appreciate that you brought hockey into my life, which yes, I have made a big part of my personality these last few years. No regrets. Let's go Canes!

About the Author

Kathryn Kincaid writes contemporary romance featuring sports and characters finding the love they deserve. She lives in North Carolina with her husband and four adorable but high-maintenance cats. When she's not working or writing, she spends her free time devouring books, binging TV shows, cheering on the Carolina Hurricanes, and getting her butt kicked at OrangeTheory.

goodreads.com/author/show/31022409.Kathryn_Kincaid

instagram.com/authorkathrynkincaid

amazon.com/stores/Kathryn-Kincaid/author/B0C2K59RGZ

tiktok.com/@authorkathrynkincaid

Printed in Great Britain
by Amazon